Books are to be returned on or before
the last date below.

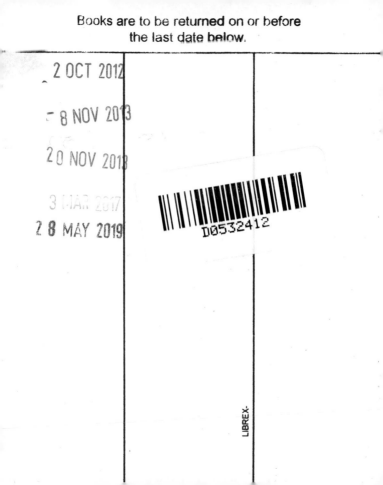

D0532412

LIBREX-

9+

JERRY and the JANNANS

ELLY BREWER

BLOOMSBURY

First published in Great Britain in 2006 by Bloomsbury Publishing Plc
36 Soho Square, London, W1D 3QY

A CIP catalogue record of this book is available from the British Library

ISBN 0 7475 8213 0
ISBN-13 9780747582137

All papers used by Bloomsbury Publishing are natural,
recyclable products made from wood grown in well-managed
forests. The manufacturing processes conform to the
environmental regulations of the country of origin.

Typeset by Hewer Text UK Ltd, Edinburgh
Printed in Great Britain by Clays Ltd, St Ives plc

1 3 5 7 9 10 8 6 4 2

www.bloomsbury.com

For Jerry
(worth every bloomin' penny . . .)

CHAPTER ONE

Jerry surfaced from his morning bus-ride snooze, to find three pairs of eyes peering down at him. Personal space, guys! And what were they staring at anyway? Don't say he'd been snoring. (Andy was always banging on about how he snored like bath water going down a plughole, but that was just older brother wind-up.) Jerry rearranged his features from sleep-crumpled, into what he hoped was a giving-it-some-attitude, so-you'd-better-back-off, kind of face.

Hang on, they were staring *down* at him. Surely he hadn't been in such a deep sleep that he'd slid to the floor? Nope. He could feel the familiar, scratchy fabric of the Number 183 seat under his hands. Or could he? Jerry scrambled upright as the realisation whammed home. Not only were three pairs of eyes peering down at him, but they were three pairs of yellow eyes, set in three large, dappled green, scale-covered faces.

*

As the alien made a sudden move, Rashila shot a protective arm around Chad.

'Don't worry, Wife,' Harchi smiled. 'Kaye assured me, this species isn't dangerous.'

'Really?' Rashila's ears flipped back, but she tried to keep the irritation from her voice as she told Chad: 'You must still be *very* careful, until we know more about your father's latest . . .' (through gritted teeth) '. . . most generous, gift.'

'Yes, Mother,' Chad replied, sidestepping her restraining arm to make his way to the kitchen area, where he started rifling through the chiller unit.

Checking he was out of earshot, Rashila growled at Harchi: 'What mania possessed you, to buy such a huge animal?'

Harchi shrugged. 'I thought it would be fun for Chad,' adding proudly, 'he's the only one of its kind on the whole of Pastinare.'

'And what *is* its kind, Harchi?'

Oops. 'I, er . . . Don't you think it's an interesting colour?' Harchi studied the pink, scrawny creature, pretending not to notice Rashila glaring at him, disapproval written all over her scales. 'It's supposed to be *very* intelligent.'

There was a lifetime's marital irritation in Rashila's tut. 'You'll be telling me it talks next. Kaye must have seen you coming.'

Chad padded back with a few zambon leaves. 'I want to try giving it something to eat.'

2

Harchi beamed his approval. 'Handle it gently, son,' he warned, waving a claw at the creature's scale-free exterior. 'It has unprotected skin.'

Rashila snorted, all pretence at composure gone. 'Expensive, large and fragile! Another well researched purchase from Harchi Jannan.' She stomped off to her quarters, the normal curve of her tail a rigid line of contempt.

'She'll soon get used to it, Harchi-pa,' said Chad, wafting the zambon in front of the alien's face, 'and I think it's the best present you've ever bought me!'

*

Jerry stared up at the creatures, who were waving bumpy orange leaves at him, and repeated 'It's only a dream, it's only a dream,' even as his brain fought to disagree. He strained to hear the comforting rumble of the bus engine over the snorts and grunts the creatures were making. Nothing. Nor a scrap of sound from his mates, bickering about who fancied who, or blagging Speccy Bates for his maths, so the rest of them could copy it. Not looking good.

Trying to keep calm, Jerry ran back through his morning, grasping for clues as to what might be going on. He'd had the duvet yanked off him by Andy; grabbed a shower while Woolfie thumped on the door, 'cos he'd beaten her to it; yelled goodbye at Mum as he legged it for the bus, then fallen asleep on it as usual, expecting his best mate AJ to supply the daily wake-up kick in time for Jerry to stumble off to school.

Same old, same old. Except Jerry hadn't felt a kick yet. And this *so* wasn't school. Pinch. Pinch. Pinch. Pinch. Pinch. Ow! He definitely wasn't asleep. But what other explanation was there? Jerry decided to stick with the dream theory. Because dreams did that, didn't they? Bent reality every which way. The sooner he went with the flow, the quicker he'd wake up. Yeah, that felt better. Jerry squared up to his over-active imagination . . . bring it on!

*

'I think it wants the zambon!' exclaimed Chad, as the creature held its arm up. 'Look at its funny hands!'

'Five digits!' Harchi's snout wrinkled in distaste. 'Too wriggly.'

'And how does it cut food, without claws?' asked Chad. 'Give it the leaf and let's see.'

Just then, Gale called Chad for his scrub. As he turned to shout he'd be there soon, Harchi noted with satisfaction how the alien made an irritated noise when the leaf was snatched away as he'd been about to take it. He'd show Rashila – he knew it was intelligent!

*

Were these creatures dumb, or what? Handing him something, then snatching it away again. That was one of Woolfie's speciality acts. Hey! Maybe that's why it was happening now – because it was on his mind from last night? (Which would make this a dream, right?) She'd wound him up something chronic, pretending she was passing him the remote so he could watch MTV, when he should have known she'd never give up that toe-curling chick flick and . . .

All thoughts of Jerry's younger sister vanished, as a metal replica of the lizard-looking creatures swooshed into view and hovered in front of him, its matt silver casing catching the light. While it beeped and whirred at the shorter lizard, row after row of coloured lights lit up on its chest. The creature rasped and grunted back, before walking away, followed by the larger one. Then the robot started whirring and beeping at Jerry.

'Sorry, Tin Chops, can't help you – I don't parlez robot.'

The robot bent to claw at a cluster of tiny knobs on its lower section, which made its sounds change. It reminded Jerry of his daily bathroom battle with the radio, after Mum had tuned in to her Golden Oldies snorefest and he had to get it back to his indie one.

The robot suddenly straightened up and faced Jerry, its eye-lights winking on and off. 'Greetings and welcome to the dwelling of Rashila, Harchi and Chad Jannan,' it said in a sing-song voice, which pulsed from its oval mouth speaker. 'I am Chad Jannan's Fossic, Gale Phase 12deluxe2.'

Fossic? Must be their word for robot. Jerry gave a small bow. (Should he have bowed to a robot? Who cared. He was enjoying himself.) 'Greetings. I am Jerry Patterson. Class 3B, Year 9. And this is turning into one cool dream.'

'Negative on the dream, JerryPatterson Classthreebee Yearnine,' beeped Gale.

Jerry laughed. 'Yeah, right. So where am I then . . . (giving it his best Star Trek Voice-Over voice) . . . on a planet in the Delta Quadrant, light years from my solar system?'

Gale whirred like mad. 'Unable to process the data, so will respond to what I am able to translate. Where? On the planet Pastinare, inhabited by Pastinaceans.'

'What?' gasped Jerry.

'You are on the planet Pastinare, inhab—'

'I meant *why*? *Why* am I here?'

'You should avoid the use of imprecise language, it causes confusion.'

'And meanwhile, back at the "why"?'

'You have been purchased to be Chad Jannan's livestock companion.'

'WHAT?'

'Do you mean "why"?'

'I mean . . . are you seriously telling me,' Jerry's voice dripped with disbelief, 'that I've been brought here, to be somebody's pet?'

'Affirmative.'

CHAPTER TWO

The wallow room was exactly how Chad liked it. Hot enough so the mud was at perfect meltiness, oozing over his body as he sank back into it. Steamy enough so the ceiling released cooling, pinpoint drips of condensation.

'I've been thinking, son.'

Chad was on instant red alert at the excitement in his father's voice, which reached him through the steam from where he sat on his favourite boulder, cleaning his tail tip with his teeth, from the sound of it. Chad hoped Rashila-ma didn't come in and catch him at it. She was in enough of a temper already.

'I'm listening, Harchi-pa.' Chad tried not to sound too encouraging.

Gale hovered along the walkway with the cleansing broom and Chad braced himself against a boulder while she started scrubbing his front from the neck down. There was a gloopy splosh as Harchi slid into the mud and waded over.

7

'If Gale just managed to talk to JerryPatterson with her Universal Translator, why don't we try hooking it up to the Infoscope and see if we can talk to him too?'

Chad sat up and grabbed Harchi's arm so fast, Gale was forced into a complicated hover manoeuvre to avoid being tipped off the walkway into the mud.

'That's a fantastic idea!' said Chad. Harchi's chest puffed with pride. 'D'you think Rashila-ma will have time, before she goes to work?'

Harchi's chest lost its puff and his smile went off to find it. 'I . . . I wasn't going to bother your mother with this, son,' he faltered. 'I thought we'd surprise her with it later.' He sounded so hopeful.

'If you undertake this task, Harchi Jannan, based on your previous history . . .' Gale scrubbed as she whirred a calculation through her probability chip, '. . . there is a ninety-five ding seven fantarg chance of failure. Turn,' she commanded Chad.

Chad flopped on to his front, twisting his head to watch his father, while Gale applied the broom to his shoulders.

'Ninety-five ding seven?' Harchi was thoroughly dejected.

As Gale scrubbed Chad's back, a wave of guilt washed over him along with the mud. What kind of son was he, if he couldn't show a little faith in the father who'd just given him the most amazing pet on the whole of Pastinare?

'Which means there's still a three ding seventeen fantarg

chance of success,' said Chad, forcing some confidence into his voice. 'You go for it, Harchi-pa!' He breathed a sigh of relief, as Harchi's snort of pleasure reached him through the steam.

*

Jerry only managed to shake himself out of his shock when his brain could no longer ignore the fact that his bladder was two drips beyond full to busting. Getting up off the floor, he saw that the loft-sized living area, and the kitchen which opened off it, were distressingly empty of loo-providing lizard creatures. Live, or metallic.

Hearing noises coming from an archway on the far side of the room, Jerry walked towards it, then stopped. What if he wasn't allowed through there? Wasn't allowed! If only Andy was there, to rabbit-punch some sense back into him. These guys could dream on, if they thought he was going to buy in to their pet caper!

Marching across the living area, Jerry had to admit, this was one classy gaff. Woolfie would be mad for it. Her idea of a good time was scarfing a Mars bar, while she drooled over swanky celebrity houses in *Hello!* Still, who wouldn't drool at swank if they lived at the Patterson's? Wasn't Mum's fault – three teenagers on the go, that's got to be expensive, right? And it's not like she was raking in a fortune, working on the fish counter at Tesco. Most of their furniture came from the charity shop, was old-fashioned and slightly battered, and had the permanent whiff of rain-soaked old ladies.

The thought of rain reminded Jerry of his quest and he hurried through the archway, then found himself in a short corridor. Up ahead, wisps of steam escaped from a door and he could hear the creatures' grunting and snorting, mingled with sloshy noises. Bathroom-type sounds. So there had to be a loo.

Jerry couldn't see a door handle and was trying to work out how to get in, when there was a roaring behind him and the steady 'thwack, thwack, thwack' of lizard feet hitting the floor as they headed his way. Jerry dashed along the corridor, searching for somewhere to hide as the creature roared and rasped what sounded like a terrible warning from the other side of the archway.

Could it smell him? Was it going to punish him for being there? Did he want to stand around asking dumb questions, or get the hell out? Looking wildly about him, Jerry spotted another doorway and ran over to it, but again, he couldn't find a handle. The creature was closing in on him. Slamming both hands flat on the door, Jerry shoved sideways. Nothing doing. Now it was only a few steps away, still roaring.

Jerry broke into a terrified sweat, both from not being able to open the door and the agony of his protesting bladder. He swiped at his forehead to stop sweat dripping into his eyes, and with a whisper of sound a gap opened along the top of the door, gaping wider as it slid into a recess in the floor. Jerry fell into the room with a squawk of relief as the door swished back up behind him.

*

Harchi lay on his front in the mud, humming happily as Gale scrubbed his back. Chad was enjoying the jets of warm air pumping over his body from the rock wall as the drying pad slowly revolved. Their companionable peace was shattered as the door swished sideways and Rashila stormed in.

'Didn't you hear me?' she snarled at Harchi, who rolled over and saw that she was so angry, her ears were flat against her head. 'It's nine orange, three ochre – you're going to be late! You should have reminded him,' Rashila snapped at Gale, who was hovering past to hand Chad his shorts and tunic as he stepped off the drying pad.

'If I had to remind Harchi Jannan every time there was something he should have done,' beeped Gale, 'I'd have no time for your son. Besides, they've been so busy discussing Jer—'

'Nine orange, three ochre!' Harchi scrambled on to the walkway, clearing mud from his body, with the backs of both claws. 'I had no idea!'

Chad took his father's cue and headed for the door, hobbling into his shorts and trying to cram his tunic on at the same time.

'Stop!' barked Rashila, eyes narrowing. 'You're up to something, aren't you?'

11

'How could we be up to anything?' asked Harchi innocently. 'There isn't time.' He made a tiny gesture with one claw, to indicate that Chad should leave and take Gale with him. 'You jump in the shower first, Wife, I'd hate to make you late.'

With a growl, Rashila stood on the shower pad, asking herself, as she often did, why she'd had the misfortune to be Bonded to such an infuriating partner. But that question was quickly replaced by another, as the jets came on and she puzzled over what had happened to the filtration system to turn the water yellow.

*

Jerry walked back down the corridor, relieved that the roaring had stopped – and that he'd managed to find the loo in time. The last thing he needed right now was to start acting like he wasn't house-trained. Weird loo, though. Just a large, clear, rectangular tank, with a coil of pipes in the centre, which somehow kept the water swirling and fizzing with tiny bubbles. No flush either.

Jerry's stomach rumbled. He hadn't eaten anything yet today. If it was still today. It had to be – he felt I've-just-missed-breakfast hungry, not I'm-starving-'cos-I-haven't-eaten-for-days. His watch said 08:17, but he couldn't see a clock anywhere, to check it against. There was nothing on the living area walls, except a long, thin, vertical panel, roughly two-thirds orange at the top, blending into ochre at the bottom.

Gale was in the kitchen area with the shortest lizard, and Jerry noticed a matching panel on her front, so he started wondering whether the panels had something to do with the way they told the time around here. Then he stopped thinking about colour-coded clocks the second he saw Gale start taking boxes and dishes out of cupboards.

Jerry went across to muscle in on the breakfast action, deciding that as soon as he'd eaten, he'd sort out how to get home.

*

The water was still yellow as Rashila stepped off the shower pad. 'I'll tell Gale to look into it,' she told Harchi as they swapped places and he began washing the mud from his scales. She watched him briefly, before speaking. 'I've been thinking, Husband.'

This time, it was Harchi's turn to be on red alert. That casual tone. Her use of the all-persuasive 'Husband'. He stepped back off the shower pad and shook the water from his ears so he didn't miss anything.

'That pet's nearly as big as Chad, and it's almost certainly not fully grown. It's going to get under our feet all the time and it'll cost a fortune to feed. Not to mention the vet's bills – you know they always bump up the fee for exotic animals.'

'But . . .'

Rashila held up a claw and Harchi knew better than to

carry on speaking. 'If you do it straight away,' she continued, 'it won't be so painful for Chad.'

'Do what straight away, Wife?' queried Harchi, though his hearts sank, knowing what her answer would be.

'I want you to take JerryPatterson back to the shop.'

CHAPTER THREE

As Director of the Bureau of Fossic Affairs, Morton took her responsibilities very seriously. So seriously, that her life revolved around the BFA, occupying her every waking thought and many of her sleeping ones.

Yet in spite of Morton's passion for her work, at this time every year, the weight of her responsibilities hung over her like a loose wallow-room boulder, threatening to crush her. For she was agonising over new ideas for the annual Fossic Upgrades.

Working her claw into a tangle of hair which she'd twiddled into a knot earlier, Morton mulled over what a handicap it was being so brilliant at her job since it made it that much harder to do. With the improvements she'd devised last year, Morton had taken the Phase 12 range up to a deluxe2, creating the Bureau's most sophisticated Fossic ever.

It was outrageous of the Better Homes, Better Planet Ministry Committee to expect someone of her stature to improve on near perfection, on demand!

Morton toyed with announcing there'd be no further Upgrades, until she judged it necessary. But the future of the planet depended on its Podders being reared and educated to the highest possible standard by the Fossics under her control. It was her civic duty to come up with new ways to build on their existing skills.

Not only that, but failure to announce Upgrades at the traditional time would cause planet-wide panic, with rumours that the Ministry no longer had the interests of its citizens at hearts. And there'd be economic chaos from the loss of revenue. No, if improving on perfection was required, there wasn't a Pastinacean alive better qualified to do so, than the Director of the Bureau of Fossic Affairs herself.

Morton glanced across the lab to where her assistant was dismantling a Fossic arm, as part of their research on Jolty Elbow Syndrome in the Phase 9s. Ordinarily, she'd have suggested a brainstorming session to help loosen up her thoughts, but Morton could tell from Rashila's flipped ears that she was in a temper, and Morton couldn't be bothered to listen to her icy politeness as she tried to hide it.

On the other claw, it might be amusing to winkle out the details of whatever Halfwit Harchi had done this time to send his wife into yet another fury. Then recognising that for the delaying tactic which it was, Morton forced herself back to work.

*

16

Jerry fidgeted in an armchair, watching Gale beep at Chad, as he sat at the dining-room table. She had to be teaching him something, because he wasn't saying much, just giving the odd snort, or series of grunts, every so often.

He switched his gaze back to Harchi, who was kneeling on the floor beside a huge screen, which he'd wrenched off the wall and placed face down, so he could fiddle with the brightly coloured tangle of wires behind it. It looked like an explosion in a mattress factory.

Before handing her Universal Translator chip over to Harchi, Gale explained that he was wiring it into what Jerry had thought was a TV (but must be their computer), so they'd all be able to understand each other.

The only thing Jerry wanted them to understand was that they had to send him home. And once the computer was back online, he was going to see if there was any way to message Mum, to say he was all right. Jerry checked his watch. It still said 08:17. He rummaged in his pocket to check it against his mobile, but the display had melted.

It must still be morning because they'd not long had breakfast (breakfast – were they having a laugh?), which meant he had a school day's worth of time to work something out before Mum started going off on one. If it was still the same morning.

Jerry's stomach complained. If they tried giving him that breakfast muck for lunch, they'd have a fight on their hands. It had been off-the-top-diving-board gross. Not the big orange leaf thing, the zambon. Jerry had quite liked its minty, slightly bananary taste. But that dry stuff! It looked and stank like rabbit poo. He'd nearly chucked up when Gale stuck it in a dish then poured green slime over it to 'de-solidify it'. He didn't care how many nutrients she said were in it, he'd binned the whole lot, when no one was looking.

Without warning Jerry was suddenly overcome with exhaustion, probably intergalactic jet lag, and slumped back in the chair for a doze, smiling as he felt the cushions remould. He'd been totally thrown by it when he'd first sat down – it was like being sucked into a giant dollop of stiffly beaten egg white – but now he liked the way the filling shifted every time he did. Mum would adore a chair like this after being on her feet all day at Tesco.

He'd probably be able to buy her one once he'd made shedloads of dosh flogging his story to the tabloids. Play his cards right, he might even get on the chat-show circuit. 'Sorry, Mr Barkow, haven't done that essay on Hitler; I was abducted by aliens. Didn't you see me on the telly?' Sweet.

*

Harchi smiled fondly at the latest assault on his credit card, asleep in the chair. He'd have to train him not to sit there – Rashila would shed her tail tip if JerryPatterson left marks. When she came home and heard their pet talk . . . Had he unclipped that chequered illmington coil from the pink ebrington rod or the brown one? Brown; it matched the family hair clump . . . he knew she'd be grateful he'd disobeyed her and kept the pet. Not disobeyed, that sounded like he was some young Podder who had to be told what to do. Gone against her wishes, maybe.

Glancing at the clock, Harchi was staggered to see it was five red over one purple. When had it got that late? He'd looped through to the Weather Enhancement Unit first thing and left a message for his boss that he'd be late, but he was going to have a hard job explaining away two and a half bandwidths of lateness. Gornish was such a stickler for maximum attendance.

Harchi worked faster, then faster still, turning the tangle of circuitry into a neat tapestry. And his frantic desire to get to work meant that a few, well some . . . all right most of his reconnection choices may have been based on favourite colour combinations, rather than hard electronical fact.

At last every brightly coloured coil was clipped to a prettily matching rod, and Harchi was rather impressed by how much he'd improved the actual look of the thing. Shoving the Infoscope back into its housing, he turned to find Gale and Chad watching him expectantly.

'Ready to chat to your new pet?' Harchi asked Chad, claw poised over the 'on' button. (Was there ever a father of which a son could be so proud?)

'Ready, Harchi-pa!'

Gale beeped angrily as Chad left Lesson Session without asking permission and hurried over to his father.

19

Jerry was jolted awake by a blast of static, which was quickly replaced by a cheery, gruff voice calling: 'JerryPatterson?' Harchi stood, arms wide, face split by what Jerry desperately hoped (given the quantity and evident sharpness of teeth on display) was a smile. 'Welcome to our Pastinacean world!'

'Thank you, Harchi,' said Jerry, then burst out laughing as Harchi and Chad started jumping up and down, yelling: 'It works! It works! It works!'

Jerry was walking across to shake hands, when the Infoscope started buzzing, growing in volume, until it was louder than the booming bass beat from a vast set of speakers at a thrash metal gig. As the buzz burst into the firecracker snaps of a thousand short circuits, Harchi and Jerry dived behind the nearest piece of furniture, while Gale hurtled across the room and threw herself over Chad.

Everyone hit the deck seconds before the explosion ripped through the wall. Then there was silence. It hung in the air, along with the shattered remains of the Infoscope, which dangled from its wires revealing the charred remains of Harchi's beautifully colour-coordinated, electronical handiwork.

*

Rashila was keying in her Jolty Elbow notes, when a call looped through. She hadn't even got to the end of saying her first name before she had replaced it with roaring her husband's. Morton thought there were few phrases guaranteed to cause greater irritation than: 'There's nothing to worry about', particularly when accompanied by singed hair tufts and an uncertain smile on a face scorched with grime.

Under normal circumstances, Morton would have made her displeasure clear at Rashila receiving personal calls. But Harchi's battered appearance, and Rashila roaring in front of her boss, made it clear that circumstances were far from normal.

The Jannans were arguing about Harchi not being at work and having failed to return something to a shop, which had somehow damaged their Infoscope. That meant Harchi must have looped through on his hand-held, but why was he keeping his face so close to the screen? He had to be hiding something.

Unlocking a secret compartment in her desk, Morton scrolled through the Fossic I-Cam listings hidden there, then tapped the code she'd been looking for into her control panel. As she hid the listings again, the image on her screen changed and Gale's eye-cameras provided a widescreen view of the wreckage Harchi was wisely concealing from his furious wife.

Chad was helping Gale pick fragments of shattered Infoscope and circuitry off the floor. Their mobile churner hovered in the middle of the room and as Chad stood up and went to throw the debris away in it, Morton was gripped by the sight of the strangest creature she'd ever seen who'd been kneeling beside him, blind side to the I-Cam.

21

It was a scraggy, pointy-faced alien, with long, stringy hair on a ridgeless head, wearing some kind of loose-fitting tunic and baggy shorts that reached right to the floor! It must be an incredibly fragile species, because it had barely any bulk and no claws, tail or protective skin-covering.

As it crossed the room to the churner, Morton watched the alien communicate with Chad with nods, gestures and smiles. It was obviously a creature whose intelligence went far beyond mere animal instinct.

So that's why Rashila was growling about taking something back – Harchi must have bought it at Kaye's! Morton winced at how much something that exotic would have cost. On the other claw, a fascinating pet for Chad; just a pity it hadn't come in a smaller size.

Morton's thoughts were abruptly interrupted by Rashila roaring, 'I don't care if it can talk . . .' (so that's what Harchi had been doing with the Infoscope) '. . . take it back to the shop NOW!!' Bored since she knew the story, Morton was about to close Gale's I-Cam, when Chad grabbed Harchi's hand-held.

'Please, Mother, *please*! It wasn't his fault Father had an accident.' (Morton was struck by the strength of emotion. Highly unusual in a Pastinacean, even a Podder.) 'Don't make Harchi-pa take him back,' he begged. 'He really can talk; I've heard him! I'll feed him, I'll clean up after him, I'll train him. I'll do anything you say, only *please, please* let me keep him!'

'I'm sorry, son . . .' The last image Rashila saw as Chad cut the loop, was his unbelievably disappointed face.

Morton shut down Gale's I-Cam, her brain in hyperdrive. 'That was a quite extraordinary display!' She sprang to her feet and started pacing around the lab.

'Please accept my sincerest apology, Director,' pleaded Rashila, cursing Harchi as she hurried after her boss, 'not only for taking a personal call, but . . .'

'Not you – Chad! Did you see how passionately he felt about his new pet?'

Rashila sighed. Morton had heard everything. 'I know, but . . .'

'This is the breakthrough I've been looking for,' said Morton, fired up with the brilliance of her thoughts. 'Alterations like this would be so extraordinary we could bypass the 3 and jump straight to a deluxe4. Imagine that!'

Imagine what? How had they gone from Rashila trying to apologise to Fossic Upgrades?

'That pet has generated a huge amount of passion in your son.'

'It's true, but . . .'

Morton cut Rashila off with a click of her claw. 'Don't interrupt my thought process.' Rashila's ears flopped in shame. 'If we could transfer Chad's passion for his pet to his Fossic, think how much more effective his education would be. Now multiply that passion planet-wide!'

23

Rashila was sharp enough to get the magnificence of the concept straight away. Yet sharp as she was, she wasn't prepared for Morton's next barked order, issued as she dropped into her chair, already reaching for her keyboard to make notes.

'Loop back through to Harchi. You're keeping that animal – he's the answer to this year's Fossic Upgrades!'

CHAPTER FOUR

As Jerry helped Gale tidy up, he was grateful Mum couldn't see him. She'd have him nudging a hoover about and giving a quick flick round with a duster faster than Andy and Woolfie could yell 'mummy's boy'.

The truth was, Jerry was so desperate to keep busy, he was even prepared to (whisper it) do housework. He couldn't understand anyone since the Universal Translator blew up, but you didn't have to be Speccy Bates to work out something major-league bad had happened during that phone call just now. Particularly as Harchi and Chad were moping about, droopy-eared and -tailed, refusing to make eye contact with him.

It was tying Jerry's stomach in knots, imagining what was going to happen to him. So he concentrated on collecting clumps of melted wire and chunks of shattered circuitry, hoping it'd stop his thoughts whizzing round like a blender on overdrive. Wasn't working, though.

They had to be gearing up to take him back to the shop.

What would he do, if they tried to put him in a cage? What if the other pets turned on him? Or they sold him to a freak show? Or couldn't sell him and decided to have him put down? Jerry's heart hammered against his ribs. His chest felt tight. He couldn't breathe.

Stumbling into the kitchen to splash water on his face, Jerry was vaguely aware that Harchi had answered the phone. It must be the pet shop, ringing to arrange his collection! He'd have to make a run for it, except he didn't even know where the front door was, so how was he suppo—

Dooof! As Jerry leant over the sink in a stress-panic funk, a powerful force grabbed him from behind and started joggling him up and down. Jerry struggled, flailing his fists and trying to kick himself free, bellowing 'put me down!' until he realised the dreadful pet-penalty of that remark and just stuck with the kicking and punching.

Without warning, Jerry was released. The speed made him almost drop to his knees, but a strong arm stopped him falling. He twisted round to face his attacker, blinking water from his eyes and saw a beaming Harchi, dancing about while he held Jerry up. Then Chad's face swam into view, grinning and patting him on the back.

He hadn't been attacked – he'd been on the receiving end of his first Pastinacean hug. Woah – these guys were strong and . . . hang on! Grinning, pointy-eared, perky-tailed Pastinaceans must mean . . . they were keeping him! He wasn't going to be put down! Jerry started bouncing about with Harchi and Chad, laughing like a maniac and leaping as high as he could to punch air.

*

The superior auditory chip in the Phase 12deluxe2, meant Gale heard the arrival alert above the vocal disturbance. Although even a basic Phase 4 would have known to activate the entry portal at that point since it was eleven red over seven purple. Time for Chad's daily Social Session with Gilpin Carney.

The portal swished sideways and Gilpin entered smiling a greeting at Gale, followed by her Fossic, Naish, whose automatic room-scan picked up an unidentifiable alien engaged in an unprocessable physical and vocal activity. Naish shot ahead of Gilpin, to protect her Podder.

'You should have notified me there was an alien in your dwelling,' beeped Naish, swivelling her head back round to face Gale. 'I would have prepared a threat assessment instead of exposing Gilpin to risk.'

'You have failed to take all the available data into account, Naish,' Gale replied.

'Impossible!' Naish's circuits buzzed with indignation.

'Indisputable,' countered Gale. 'Observe: Chad is with the alien. From this data, you should have deduced that I had already carried out a threat assessment and concluded there was none.'

Naish gave a beep of annoyance as she permitted her Podder to pass.

'Harchi!' Gilpin's ears and tail reached for the ceiling in surprise as she gave the strange creature the once-over. 'What have you bought him now?' she asked, peaking Chad's hair tuft affectionately.

'He's from Kaye's,' said Chad. 'Isn't he amazing?'

'In a strange kind of way,' agreed Gilpin, wrinkling her snout. 'What is it?'

'Harchi-pa?'

'It's . . . um . . . he's . . . a . . . Ridgeless Pink,' Harchi announced, wishing he'd thought of that when Rashila had asked.

'Do they come in other colours then?' asked Gilpin, peering at the alien's skin. Without scales, it looked like someone had peeled it.

'We don't know,' Chad told her proudly. 'He's the only one on the whole of Pastinare!'

'Really?' snorted Gilpin, making Chad wish he hadn't been quite so boasty. 'I wouldn't want to clean out the litter tray for something that size! And all that floppy hair's going to take a lot of looking after.'

Gilpin reached out to feel it, then snatched her hand back as the animal jerked its head away and made an angry noise. 'Does it bite?'

'He. And no!' said Chad, patting his pet on the shoulder. 'He's probably nervous, that's all.'

'He's usually very friendly,' said Harchi. 'Aren't you, Jerry-Patterson?' He beamed at the alien, to make him smile back.

Gilpin frowned her disapproval. 'Why d'you give him such a daft name?'

'We didn't,' said Chad. 'He told Gale that's what he's called.'

'Honestly, Chad!' Gilpin barked a laugh. 'I didn't hatch yesterday!'

*

Chad and Harchi were grunting at him and the burnt-out Infoscope hole, so Jerry guessed they were explaining to the girl-lizard what had happened. He reckoned she was a girl because she was less stocky than Chad, wore a patterned top and her shorts matched her lemon-yellow hair tuft. Besides, only a girl would try to mess with his hair. She was lucky he hadn't played pet and bitten her.

She was rasping at her Fossic who hovered over with Gale. They were identical – how could she tell them apart? Although babies all looked the same to Jerry, but mums seemed to know which was which. Must be the same with Fossics.

Noise levels jacked up as everyone started grunting, snorting, whirring and beeping at each other. Then the Fossic began fiddling with the controls on its lower section. Great! It must have a Universal Translator too. This time there were no bursts of static or ear-blasting screeches, just a robot voice slightly lower than Gale's.

'Greetings, JerryPatterson, I am Naish Phase 12deluxe2 and this . . .' the Fossic pointed a long, metallic claw at the

29

girl-lizard '. . . is Gilpin Carney, Chad Jannan's Bonded Partner.'

'Hey,' said Jerry with a nod, still wary after Gilpin's Offence Against Hair. So she and Chad were an item? At least, Jerry presumed, that's what 'Bonded Partner' meant.

When she heard him speak, Gilpin cracked a huge grin and Jerry wondered if they paid Pastinacean dentists danger money to poke about amongst the unbelievably sharp teeth everyone had here. She was grunting again.

'Gilpin asked if you know how to say anything else,' beeped Naish.

'No,' stated Jerry flatly. Did they think he'd balance a ball on his nose if they threw him a fish? Gilpin gave Chad a look of such triumphant smugness when Naish translated what must have been obvious, that Jerry had to wipe the smug right off her scaly face. Wouldn't hurt to get his message across to as wide an audience as possible, either.

'Tell Gilpin I'm hungry and I want to go home.'

CHAPTER FIVE

Rashila was adapting a replacement Infoscope so it would send a continuous stream of images back to the lab from the hidden cameras Morton had ordered her to install in the Jannan dwelling.

As a scientist, Rashila agreed that Jerry and Chad's behaviour wouldn't be natural if they knew they were being watched. As a wife she also agreed Harchi was enough of a liability without telling him confidential Bureau information, then demanding he keep it to himself. That didn't stop Rashila being angry with Morton for making her keep secrets from her family – and forcing them into a high-risk project with an unknown alien.

She had considered refusing to keep JerryPatterson, except Rashila had worked her claws blunt to get this job and she wasn't going to talk herself out of it now. Particularly at the start of their most important Upgrade Project ever. She knew the bulk of the praise would go to Morton – it always did – but as Rashila's family was directly involved, surely some reflected glory would spill over on to her this time?

'How are you getting on?'

Rashila hated it when Morton crept up on her. 'Nearly finished,' she said, snapping the last ebrington into its groove.

Morton nodded approvingly at Rashila's outstanding handiwork. 'The workshop looped through to say they've finished with Theydon. Why don't you chute back with him now and he can carry the Infoscope?'

A Pastinacean of Rashila's status, seen in public with a Phase 4? She'd rather have her scales brushed backwards with a stranger's wallow-room broom. But Morton had never allowed her to leave early, so Rashila buried her distaste under a (forced) grateful smile. It may be worth enduring the inconveniences of the JerryPatterson project if her boss was going to start treating her decently.

*

Harchi was in an agony of indecision. Should he face Gornish's wrath by going into work so late that it was almost time to come home again? Or stay put and suffer a verbal lashing from Rashila, who was due back any time now?

He decided to get the Rashila rant over with – it was unavoidable anyway, and it would only stoke her fury if he left her to ferment. Harchi checked the living area. All the debris had been cleared away and apart from a small . . .

OK, slightly larger than small . . . hole in the wall and one or two . . . all right, quite a few . . . scorch marks, the room was practically back to normal.

Chad and Gale were immersed in their afternoon Lesson Session. And JerryPatterson was . . . Harchi groaned; he was asleep on the furniture *again*! He had to get him off that chair before Rashila came back. He hoped Kaye hadn't conned him into paying a small fortune for a pet that slept all the time. If only he'd thought to buy a petbed last night, he could have put it next to Sneb's and . . .

Waves of tension cramped Harchi's tail. Sneb! He hadn't seen Rashila's best beloved snebbit since the explosion. Had there been any snebbit fur amongst the wreckage? Harchi didn't think so. What if he just hadn't noticed? Did he have time to get to Kaye's and buy another one? Would Rashila notice the difference if he did? And how would he explain the new one if the old one turned up?

Refusing to gloom until he'd exhausted all the possibilities, Harchi hurried to the kitchen to get some chibberts. If there was a breath of life left in him, Sneb would appear when he heard the snacks rattling in the tin.

'Sneb?' Harchi called in a high voice, trying to mimic Rashila as he shook the tin. 'Here Sneb, Snebby, Snebbity, Sneb the snebbit.'

Jerry was woken by the sound of Mum shaking Barclay's cat-biscuit box so she'd come downstairs and be locked in the kitchen for the night. Then he opened his eyes and realised where he was, but was confused when he heard the 'burroop' purr chirrup Barclay made when she was pleased about something.

A Day-Glo pink tangle of knitting hurtled past heading for the kitchen at high speed, and Jerry was about to go and check it out when a door swished and Rashila marched in, trailed by a Fossic struggling with a huge screen. If it was a Fossic. This one looked like a scrap-heap version some bored kids had thrown together on a rainy Sunday.

Hearing loud grunts and snarls, Jerry looked away from the Fossic and was horrified to find Rashila charging towards him, claws snapping, teeth bared. He wrenched himself out of the chair, clambering, then falling over the back of it in his race to bolt across the room and hide behind Harchi.

'You're scaring JerryPatterson!' Harchi told his wife, emboldened to speak out by having been chosen as the animal's protector.

'Good. Maybe that'll teach him to keep off my furniture!' growled Rashila.

'I'll train him not to do it again,' said Harchi, reaching behind him to hold on to the pet – the poor thing was trembling. 'And if he's left any marks I'll clean them off.'

Harchi saw Chad heading over, and forced Rashila to maintain eye contact while he nudged pet towards Podder, who led him away. 'Why don't I mix you some sour tea while you show *Theydon* where to put the new Infoscope?'

34

The reminder that there was a non-family member in the dwelling brought Rashila to her senses. She'd hate Theydon telling his Podder they'd been fighting over a pet. Clacket Layne would spread it round the building in a claw-click.

'Theydon!' snapped Rashila, going to inspect the damaged wall. 'Come and put that down over here.'

Harchi's mission complete, he strolled into the kitchen to mix some sour tea.

*

Since Rashila left, Morton had been hunched over her desk, constructing a ground-breaking piece of equipment for the Upgrade Project. With a snortle of satisfaction, she arched her back, then stretched her legs and flexed her toe-claws one by one, as she admired the finished item, which sat beside her still-warm solder-stick, surrounded by snippets of wire and curls of metal.

Even after all this time, Morton could still surprise herself with her own magnificence. Who else would have thought of making a mobile translation unit for JerryPatterson so he didn't need a Fossic to translate? And even if they'd stumbled across the idea, no one even came close to having the skill to make it happen.

Glancing at her screen, Morton saw through Gale's I-Cam that she was closing the portal behind Theydon, which meant Rashila must have wired the new Infoscope in. She wouldn't be able to install the cameras until every-one was asleep, and she'd have to come up with a reason for powering Gale down while she did it. Morton could have provided a reason, but it was essential her assistant felt part of this Project. Allowing her to supply small ideas like this was one way of drawing her in.

Of course, if Morton really wanted to get the most from Rashila, the best way would be to play on her monstrous vanity. What if she honoured the Jannans with a visit? Rashila would have to work her scales off to repay the massive debt of obligation. Or was it too big a gesture?

Who was Morton fooling? She was desperate to study JerryPatterson up close. And test her mobile translation unit. She clawed in the number and looped through to the Jannan's.

*

Hunger drove Jerry to leave the sanctuary of Chad's wardrobe. His watch said it was only 08:19, but he'd been with the Jannans for the best part of a day now and his stomach was definitely telling him it was half past supper time.

All he'd had to eat so far were a few zambon leaves. And if he hadn't been so hungry he'd have told Gilpin where to shove the ones she'd given him, which she'd only let him have after making him say 'please' and 'thank you' as she handed him tiny sections, bit by bit.

Jerry had the impression there'd even been a fuss about him having those, judging by the beeping and whirring from Gale when Chad came back from the kitchen with them. According to Naish, the word 'lunch' didn't translate and

36

Pastinaceans, like pets, only ate twice a day. Not this pet, Tin Chops. Although Jerry wasn't going to stick around long enough to need to fight that battle.

Walking into the living area, Jerry was surprised to find it zipping with action. Gale was whizzing around the kitchen; Harchi was painting over scorch marks; Chad was polishing the table and Rashila must be checking for exploded Infoscope fragments because she was fiddling with a tall metal bin-ish machine, like the one he'd thrown his breakfast away in.

Keeping well clear of Rashila, Jerry headed over to Gale and looked hopeful. She ignored him. He felt a pang of guilt for all the times he'd blanked Barclay, as she'd buffaloed for cat biscuits whenever he was in the kitchen.

Gale had a football-sized, lime-green fruit speared on one claw. Jerry gulped as a blade pinged out from the tip of her other claw, then watched, fascinated, as she began to carve an elaborate shape, working faster and faster, until the cutting edge was almost a blur.

Jerry leant on the counter to get a better look. 'That's amazing, Gale!'

Without pausing from her carving, Gale barged Jerry away from the counter. 'Step away from the food area, JerryPatterson! You are a risk to hygiene.'

Jerry staggered back, clutching his side. 'All right, no need to get violent!'

The blade on Gale's claw slid in again as she stopped slicing and scooping. With a beep of what Jerry took to be satisfaction, she placed a perfectly carved little fruity Fossic in the centre of a large plate covered with bumpy, blue leaves.

Jerry had to admit it was a neat party trick. 'What's going on, Gale? Everyone seems a bit frantic.'

'We are preparing for a visit from esteemed Director Morton.'

'Trying to impress Harchi's boss, are we?' asked Jerry, trying to sneak a piece of leftover fruit from the worktop, while Gale's back was turned.

Gale swivelled and jabbed Jerry's hand away, just as he was about to take the fruit.

'Rashila's. It is an honour that has never been bestowed on anyone who has worked for the Bureau of Fossic Affairs before.'

Go Rashila. (What the hell was the Bureau of Fossic Affairs?) Jerry wondered what she'd done to deserve it. Meanwhile, back to the subject in hand – his empty stomach.

'Can I get something to eat, Gale? I'm starving,' said Jerry, pumping up the volume, because Rashila had started pushing the machine around the living area and from the racket it was making, it was either a broken hoover or a bin with a waste-disposal unit.

'Inaccurate!' beeped Gale, raising her voice, to match Jerry's. 'I fed you this morning and Gilpin Carney fed you snacks less than two bandwidths ago. How can you possibly be hungry?'

38

There was a grinding noise followed by a primeval roar from Rashila as the lid of the machine flew off and a fountain of soggy rabbit poo cereal sprayed over the entire living area. Jerry struggled to look innocent, only too painfully aware that Rashila had just provided the answer to Gale's question.

CHAPTER SIX

Morton stood outside the lab, her claw tip in the security groove, listening to the swish of locks sliding into place. As the alarm-activated button glowed green she picked up her briefcase and headed for the chute.

The earlier emotional high at having finished the mobile translation unit (safely stowed in her briefcase) had worn off and Morton had become increasingly irritated as images from her visit started popping into her mind.

Here's Gale, whirring with self-importance at the destination chute, to escort Morton to the Jannan dwelling. There's Rashila at the entry portal, cheek scales twitching with the effort of maintaining that hospitable smile. See Chad, skulking in the background, too shy to come forward but aching to be introduced. And here comes Halfwit Harchi, bumping into furniture in his eagerness to fawn all over her.

Morton groaned as a table covered with food laid itself in her mind. With Rashila's obsession with protocol, Gale was bound to have prepared a banquet. Morton's stomach churned at the thought of having to plough her way through endless delicacies. And Gale would have carved a fruit Fossic in her honour, which she'd have to admire at length before forcing it down, mouthful by sickly sweet mouthful.

The closer Morton got to the chute, the slower she walked. How dare Rashila attempt to force the Director of the Bureau of Fossic Affairs to endure such agony? Didn't she realise it was more practical to test the mobile translation unit on the alien in the lab in case they needed to make any adjustments? Morton flicked her tail round and marched back to her office to demonstrate to her assistant which one of them was in charge.

*

Harchi had swapped Gale's claws for the suction attachments which came with the deluxe2. Then, boosting up to hyperdrive, she'd vacuumed the splattered nibrim pellets from the walls, floor and furniture while Chad jogged behind, catching the mush in a bucket as it plopped from the outlet pipe with which Harchi had replaced Gale's tail.

Rashila had been so traumatised at the thought of Morton arriving when the dwelling was filthy, she wouldn't stop roaring. Ignoring the risk of bruising from her thrashing tail, Harchi had stepped in close, grabbed her by the shoulders and yelled: 'Wife!'

Stunned to hear Harchi shout at her, Rashila had finally

41

shut up. 'Go and take a shower!' he ordered. 'Unless you want to greet a highly respected dignitary covered tail tip to ridges in mashed nibrim?'

'What about the mess?' wailed Rashila, staring wild-eyed around the living area.

'We'll take care of it,' Harchi told her firmly, waving a claw to include Chad and Gale.

Still she'd hesitated, until Gale whirred forward. 'It is the only course of action.' With a sigh, Rashila had hurried off to the wallow room.

The room was eat-off-the-floor perfect by the time she'd emerged from her quarters, freshly scrubbed, in her Greeting the Director outfit. Even Sneb, curled up on a chair (Rashila's 'no pets' rule didn't apply to him) had been given the once-over and was nibrim-free and fluffy.

'You look full-scale fantastic, Rashila-ma!' said Chad, with a snort of admiration.

'Thank you, son,' she smiled, as she took in the spotless room. 'And thank *you*, Husband – I really appreciate you pitching in to help.'

Harchi looked up from re-attaching Gale's tail and caught Rashila's grateful smile. What a magnificent creature his wife was. And what a pity she didn't look at him like that more often.

Harchi was about to tell her she was welcome, when a call looped through on Rashila's hand-held. He was dismayed to see her ears and tail droop as she listened to the caller. The only word uttered was a surprised 'Now?' thinly veiled by anger.

'What's wrong?' asked Harchi, as she cut the loop.

'She's not coming,' Rashila reported bitterly.

'Oh no!' Chad gave a groan of disappointment, while Harchi padded over and gave Rashila a hug, desperately trying to think of something to say to make her feel better.

'Well . . . she said she was going to,' he managed finally, 'so it still counts as an honour, because she's never said that to another employee.'

'What a waste of time and effort,' snarled his wife.

'It's not a waste,' Harchi insisted brightly. 'Morton's going to miss a great banquet, which I'll be enjoying with my favourite son and my beautiful wife! Chad, let's escort your mother to the table.'

Harchi moved to take Rashila's arm, but she pulled away, shaking her head. 'I can't. She wants me back at the lab.'

'Now?' Chad and Harchi spoke in unison, all four ears peaked in surprise.

*

Jerry saw the wardrobe door opening and tensed in case Rashila had come to roar at him, but Harchi's smiling face appeared so he knew it was safe to come out. Taking the proffered claw, Jerry levered himself off the wardrobe floor, blinking in the light. Had the boss been and gone? Or had Harchi come to show him off? Jerry might be starving, but they'd be whistling Dixie (as Mum liked to say) before he'd perform for scraps from their table.

Mum! Hungry as he was, he couldn't eat until he'd asked Gale to help him try to send a message on the Infoscope. Jerry didn't know how long he'd been gone – his watch must have broken, 'cos it still only said 08:19 – but it had to be early evening. Mum'd start panicking if he didn't make contact soon, let alone find a way to get back.

Harchi was waving a short stick at him. So not going to play 'fetch', pal. But instead of throwing it, Harchi gave a soft grunt and, with incredible daintiness for someone with such terrifying teeth, nibbled the stick, smacking his lips with theatrical pleasure. He held it out to Jerry again, so he took it, sniffed it (nothing) and cautiously bit the end off. Harchi laughed (think rock on cheese grater) seeing Jerry's eyes light up, as his mouth filled with flavours that were ten types of fabulous. He grinned at Harchi, who clapped a hand around his shoulder, gesturing that Jerry should eat some more. He didn't need telling twice and crunched off a big chunk this time . . . chocolate, marshmallow, candyfloss, peaches, strawberries, prawns (prawns?) . . . the flavours kept on coming.

Walking into the living area with Harchi, lost in sweet-stick heaven, Jerry felt something drop over his head from behind, then tighten around his neck. Choking and spluttering, Jerry dropped the stick as he scrabbled desperately with both hands to loosen the noose.

A chorus of loud grunts and snarls kicked off as Chad and

Harchi bellowed at Rashila who appeared from behind Jerry, pushing a button at her wrist. As the noose loosened Jerry started gasping for breath. A flash of white-hot fury burned through him, as he realised he'd been put on a lead! And Rashila held the other end.

'Get this off me!' he yelled at her, trying to wrench the lead over his head. Then he turned on Harchi. 'You tricked me! How could you?'

Harchi issued some grunts and Gale hovered into vision to translate. 'Harchi Jannan apologises. It was for your own safety. Rashila has to take you out and they were worried you might get lost.'

Harchi picked up the stick and handed it to Jerry, looking so guilty, Jerry didn't have the heart to stay mad at him. Rashila was holding the lead, it was obvious she'd forced him into it. Hold up – take him out where? Harchi and Chad were both smiling and Chad patted his arm, so Jerry guessed Rashila wasn't hauling him back to the shop.

'Where's she taking me?' Jerry asked Gale.

'To meet esteemed Director Morton, who will fit you with a mobile translation unit.'

Jerry saw the food on the table hadn't been touched. So, had the boss changed her mind?

'Have they got Infoscopes where she works?' asked Jerry. No way was he leaving the flat, unless it involved trying to contact Mum.

'Affirmative.'

'OK, I'll go. *If* she gets rid of this.' Jerry tugged at the collar and looked at Rashila, who grunted and shook her head.

'She says no,' Gale whirred helpfully.

Stand-off time. 'I refuse to leave here, tied up like an animal.'

Gale relayed this information to Rashila, who snorted twice.

'You are an animal,' Gale provided.

'Not where I come from,' Jerry snapped. 'The sooner she understands that, the better. Tell her, if she takes the lead off, I'll behave. And if she doesn't,' he paused for dramatic effect, 'I will embarrass her in front of her esteemed Director, in ways she couldn't possibly imagine. Even if I drew pictures.'

Harchi and Chad's gasps of amazement as Gale relayed Jerry's message proved she'd delivered it word for word. So Jerry played Eyeball Chicken with Rashila, until she caved and pressed the button to loosen the lead. Yanking the collar off, Jerry tossed it to the floor, then sauntered to the front door – making sure Rashila saw his smirk of triumph first.

*

Morton was using her time productively as she waited for Rashila, by hacking into Kaye's Infoscope to search for information on JerryPatterson. Although Kaye had all sorts of exotic pets listed in his purchase orders, there was nothing about the alien. She widened her search. Pet food, cages, toys, training manuals, exercise aids, beds, collars – the lists went on and on, without a scrap of information about her research subject.

About to give up, Morton noticed an entry in a diary file: 'Biped alien. Sold to Harchi Jannan.' Followed by yesterday's date and a sum of money so outrageous, it confirmed Morton's opinion of both JerryPatterson's rarity and Harchi's stupidity.

The alien was obviously an off-planet import, so the lack of purchase data breached Ministry livestock regulations. This was getting interesting. Even more so when Morton found a 'miscellaneous' file in a sub-directory containing data so astounding, it positively made her tail quiver. It was a partially coded note about a recently purchased molecular scrambler. One with a time-fold overlay pump!

There were only a clawful on Pastinare, used to beam mineral or vegetable matter in from nearby planets for scientific research. Permission for use was granted after filing an application, followed by an 'explanation of need' presentation to the Ministry Committee, who then debated whether to issue a short-term licence. A highly unauthorised piece of equipment for an exotic pet-shop owner to have in his possession.

Kaye had illegally transported JerryPatterson in with the

47

scrambler. That much was clear. (As a scientist, Morton was fascinated by the revelation that scramblers worked on livestock and had to concentrate hard to stop her mind hurtling off down that side track.) Now she knew how the alien had got here, but was no closer to knowing *what* he was.

Morton was slipping out of Kaye's Infoscope, when the impact of her discovery struck her. If the Better Homes, Better Planet Ministry Committee ever discovered that JerryPatterson's arrival had been illegal, it would be a disaster. They'd lose all faith in the research results which would ruin the Upgrade Project – and Morton's reputation along with it.

It was Morton's duty to protect the citizens of Pastinare from the distress caused if they had to watch their favourite icon defend her position. And she had to protect the Ministry Committee from the inevitable backlash they'd suffer from pitching her into that position in the first place. The requirement was obvious. Morton would have to put certain safety measures in place to ensure neither situation arose.

*

Jerry tramped along hallways and round acres of bends with Rashila. And from the wide-eyed double-takes from the creatures they passed, Jerry knew they'd never seen anything like him before. Feast your eyes, guys, this is a one-off appearance!

48

He'd been hoping to get a look at the outside world, but so far all Jerry had seen were hallways with a few front doors dotted along them. Everywhere beautifully decorated and brightly lit. No graffiti. No weaving your way round buggies and bikes. No dodging puddles of unidentified goo leaking from bin bags, like on the estate where AJ lived.

Jerry was puzzling over how he hadn't seen any windows anywhere, when Rashila stopped and rested her claw in a groove in the wall which set a line of tiny lights flashing. With a barely audible 'swoosh', an entire section of wall slid into the ceiling, and Jerry stepped back in surprise when a huge, elongated capsule swung into place. As it slowed to a halt the curved front flipped up and Rashila ushered him in.

Jerry took one of half a dozen seats on offer then flinched as Rashila walked over, snorting and waving her claws about, until he realised she wanted to fasten his seat belt for him. Then she strapped herself in and tapped something into a keypad beside her which made the front flip closed, followed by a whooshing sound and . . .

. . . WHAM! The air flew out of Jerry as violently as if someone had whacked a mallet into his back and he felt his body being pulled apart, like a human elastic band. Stretch. Stretchier. Stretchiest. Dragged, thinner, spreading sideways, transparent breaking point SNAP! Jerry's body blasted into a million tiny elastic pieces twisting spinning tumbling spitting in a gazillion directions never to be joined again then BAM! Swirling lifting hurtling clustering jostling building until finally . . . finally . . . the churning slowed and slowed then stopped and everything clicked back into place again. Human.

CHAPTER SEVEN

Jerry was too scared to open his eyes in case the movement made his body shatter again, but the rock-hard surface was killing his back and he couldn't lie still any more. He slowly squinched up his eyes and let a tiny chink of light in. Not even a hint of elastification. So far, so good. Jerry decided to risk it and opened his eyes properly.

'Rashila! He's coming round,' declared a throaty, female voice and Jerry's horizon was blotted out by a pair of enquiring yellow eyes, which peered so closely into his, he was almost nose to snout with their owner. As the eyes withdrew, Jerry's skin prickled with apprehension when he saw they belonged to a Pastinacean in a white coat.

Had Rashila taken him to a hospital after sweeping up all his bits so they could stick him back together again? What if they'd had a Humpty Dumpty moment? Jerry wiggled his ears, wrinkled his nose and did a quick internal check around the rest of him. Everything seemed to be where it should.

As Rashila came to stand next to White Coat, Jerry could

tell Chad's mother was much younger. The clue was in their scales. Rashila's were a rich, dappled green, with a soft sheen to them and neatly overlapped, whereas White Coat's were faded and ramshackly, as if they'd been flung into place by a cowboy roofer.

White Coat was way scruffier too, in her mad professor's lab coat with its overflowing pockets, burn marks and stains. And her knotty purple hair reminded Jerry of the time some of his superglue had fallen into the thatch on Woolfie's favourite Troll. Yet something about her screamed power. She was giving off a Mrs Morris 'listen up, because I'm Headmistress' vibe. In a blink, Jerry got it – she had to be esteemed Director Morton!

'Feeling well enough to move?' she asked Jerry. Her voice was kind, full of concern.

'Think so,' he replied, swinging his legs round and sitting up.

Woah! Head rush. As his vision settled, Jerry realised they'd had him laid out on a workbench . . . in a lab. Dizziness was wrestled to the ground by panic. Had they been probing him? Sucking out bits of his brain? Or sticking bits in? Yeah, that's it . . . they'd been filling him with implants, to control him and . . .

Jerry spotted an angular metallic object, poking from the knee of his trousers and gave such a huge gasp of fear, the air went down the wrong way and he had a coughing fit. They *had* been experimenting on him!

52

'Are you all right?' asked Morton anxiously, patting him on the back.

Jerry fought to breathe normally. 'What's that?' he croaked, gesturing at his knee.

Morton lifted the fabric and the object rose with it. 'It's your mobile translation unit.' She let the fabric fall and the unit thunked lightly into place above Jerry's right knee. 'Didn't you notice? We've been talking without a Fossic translator?'

Jerry smiled and nodded. Dough-brain. Morton helped Jerry down from the bench and escorted him to a chair at an incredibly cluttered desk. As she went to sit behind it, Jerry's stomach rumbled.

'If your digestive system operates on the same principle as ours,' said Morton, with a twinkle, 'I'd say you were hungry?'

Are aliens green? 'Starving. I haven't eaten all day.'

Morton's smile vanished, her eyes narrowed and her ears flipped as she barked at Rashila, who'd been putting equipment away on the other side of the lab.

Through many years of (unavoidable) research, Jerry had sharpened his skills at determining in any given group who gets to yell at who. And as he watched Rashila come and silently take a verbal pasting for not having fed him properly, Jerry knew that in terms of the pecking order around here, Morton was strutting on the hen-house roof.

*

'Director Morton—'

'Morton will do, JerryPatterson.'

'And just Jerry's good for me. Can I ask you something?'

'Anything you like . . .'

'Thanks. I need to send a—'

'Once you've eaten. I don't want you passing out again.'

'But—'

'Eat, Jerry. Then we'll talk.'

Morton watched Jerry tackle the dish of food Rashila had brought, fascinated by how he managed with those stumpy little teeth and no claws. And he used all ten digits at once without biting himself. He'd obviously been reared to eat as much and as fast as he could before another creature stole his food, so it must be scarce on his planet. How ridiculous of the Jannans, to buy an expensive pet then starve it! No wonder Jerry had collapsed in the chute.

Morton had raced down there, as soon as Rashila looped through, to carry the lifeless creature back to the lab. Initially, she'd blamed herself for not having realised that, having been transported here by molecular scrambler, Jerry's cells wouldn't be strong enough to take a second blast of molecular displacement so soon. How typical of her assistant to try to make Morton take the blame, when it was far more likely the pet's collapse had been caused by her neglect.

They'd laid him out on the workbench, then waited to see what would happen. Morton was just devising the best way to preserve the body so she could dissect it, when Jerry started breathing normally again, although he was still out cold.

It was Rashila who'd come up with the idea for the sonic implant. It was a gadget she'd invented for molecular scrambler licensees to stop their samples crumbling after off-planet import, and worked a bit like atomic glue.

Even though Jerry obviously wouldn't have been molecularly scrambled on to Pastinare (Morton's only response, a clipped 'quite') Rashila felt a sonic implant might still protect him from future chute distress. Her sole reservation being that it had never been tested on livestock. Morton despaired of her assistant as she was forced to point out that here was the perfect opportunity to do so.

Rashila had suggested inserting a microchip tracking device too, but Morton didn't want her assistant getting above herself by having two suggestions accepted. Besides, it was a waste of equipment – pets never went anywhere unaccompanied.

They'd worked fast in case Jerry came round, slotting the implant into the soft, fleshy section at the base of his ear, going in from behind so he wouldn't notice the incision. Morton had considered inserting it into Jerry's tail, but the ear was easier to get at should there be any kind of emergency afterwards.

Morton and Rashila had both been intrigued by Jerry's frontal tail. They'd never heard of a creature with one before, let alone seen one, and couldn't imagine the purpose of such a curious little attachment. It was too small to help with balance. If it was a secondary nose for special-occasion smelling why was it tucked away inside a security undergarment? And if it was a weapon which activated when the body came under attack, surely it would have been on display as a warning to predators?

None of it made sense so Morton went for the only logical conclusion, which Rashila seconded. The frontal tail was a bodily remnant which this species considered an evolutionary embarrassment and therefore kept hidden.

*

Leaning back in his chair Jerry undid the top button of his trousers and exhaled, wishing he hadn't eaten quite so fast. But as Morton refused to talk until he'd finished, he'd had no choice. And he had been two galaxies beyond hungry. Literally, probably. Morton was making some notes on her computer, so Jerry coughed to make her look up.

'Feeling better now?'

'Much. Um, thanks,' said Jerry, eager to get to the point. 'Morton, my mum's going to be really worried about me. Is there any way I can send her a message?'

'Your species is new to me, Jerry,' she told him calmly, 'which means you've come from a far, far distant planet. The chances are, it's outside our messaging range.'

'It can't be!' blurted Jerry, then caught the stern look on Morton's face and pulled back.

'Or I wouldn't be here . . . would I?'

'I can see how, logically, you would arrive at that conclusion.' Jerry knew there was bad news coming when Morton paused before continuing. 'But as I don't know how you got here, I'm afraid I don't know how to send a message back.'

Jerry's throat tightened. 'Then how am I going to get home?'

This time the pause turned into a hideously long silence. The food in Jerry's stomach churned itself into a wall of lead bricks.

'Wait! I know! Harchi bought me in a pet shop, didn't he?' Jerry was almost shouting. Morton nodded. 'I believe so.'

'Let's ask them how I got here. Then you'll know whether we can send Mum a message – and how I get home again.' Jerry couldn't believe he hadn't thought of that before.

'I'll look into it in the morning,' said Morton, with a maddening lack of urgency.

'Morton, *please* – can't you do it now? My mum'll be sick with worry if I'm not back tonight and she hasn't heard from me!'

'I'm sorry, Jerry, the shop won't be open.' She softened the refusal with a smile.

'What if Rashila takes me round there? I could—'

'Jerry.' Morton's voice was firm, but kind. 'Are you intelligent enough to understand that a pet-shop owner's

57

more likely to cooperate with the Director of the Bureau of Fossic Affairs than a recently sold item of stock?'

Jerry nodded and gave a small smile to show willing, completely unprepared for the verbal punch to the guts that was coming.

'Don't get your hopes up,' Morton warned him. 'There would have been a long chain of buying and selling before you reached the shop. The owner may not know how you got here. And even if he does, off-planet imports are immensely complicated. No one's ever tried to reverse the process.'

The wall of lead bricks collapsed, liquefied and flooded Jerry with nausea. He hardly dared breathe in case he choked on the lump in his throat.

CHAPTER EIGHT

The male Jannans were letting their food ferment, having made a serious dent in the feast Gale had prepared for Morton. They'd waited an entire bandwidth for Rashila before Harchi announced they'd start, keen to eat with no one to nag him about claw marks in the table, growl as he took thirds, or stop him lobbing titbits into Chad's mouth. All they'd talked about was JerryPatterson. The tricks they'd teach him. The pet parades they'd enter. The best way to groom him. Now they'd moved on to where he was going to sleep.

'Can we put his bed in my room, Harchi-pa? *Please?*' wheedled Chad.

'It is unhygienic for a pet to share your sleeping quarters, Chad Jannan,' beeped Gale, who was collecting dirty dishes. 'I cannot permit it.'

'I can!' countered Harchi. Who was master of this dwelling, anyway?

Chad snortled back a giggle as his father leapt from the

table, turning to pull a face at Gale's back as he strode off to Chad's quarters.

As Gale clattered about marking her irritation by clearing up as noisily as possible, Harchi and Chad found his hatchling bed rolled up in the top of his wardrobe. It was the perfect size for JerryPatterson.

They were busy jumping along the length of it to get the curl out of the outer coating, when Chad looked up and saw JerryPatterson standing in the archway, staring at them.

'You're back!' Chad went over to pat him on the back.

'Did Morton fit the Mobile Translation Unit? Can you understand us?' asked Harchi, hurrying across to join them.

'Yeah,' said Jerry, showing them the chunk of metal on his floor shorts. 'You're coming through loud and clear.'

'That's incredible!' said Chad, peering to look. 'How kind of Director Morton to go to all that trouble.'

'That's how highly she thinks of your mother, son,' said Harchi, then suddenly noticed the pet's pale face. 'Are you all right, JerryPatterson?' he asked.

'It's just Jerry. And I'm fine, but I'm really tired.'

'It's been a long day for you,' said Chad sympathetically.

'A bit of fun'll perk you up.' Harchi grinned, nodding encouragingly at Chad.

'Oh yes! We've thought up a counting trick to teach you!' said Chad. 'We say a number then show you how many times to stamp—'

'– and it makes it look like you're counting!' interrupted Harchi, desperate to join in. 'So, I say "five" and then you go stamp, stamp, stamp, stamp, stamp.' Harchi stamped enthusiastically to demonstrate.

'And that means five, see?' finished Chad, trying to claim the trick back.

'Go on, Jerry!' urged Harchi. 'You try!'

Their pet was staring blankly at them. Harchi's tail drooped with guilt, in case he'd spoiled the fun by starting with too high a number.

'Sorry guys,' mumbled Jerry, 'I'm not in the mood.'

Harchi looked at Chad and could tell they were both trying to hide their disappointment, neither daring to think they had a pet on their claws who wasn't playful. No. Jerry's voice had been flat and his body looked drained of energy. The poor scrap was obviously exhausted.

Chad rushed into the silence. 'You must be worn out, Jerry. Look, we were just getting your bed ready. As soon as we've hung it, you can step into it.'

'You sleep upright?' Jerry's eyes were like saucers.

'You don't?' chimed Harchi and Chad, equally crockeried.

Harchi's snout wrinkled, he gave a little snort, then threw back his head and roared with laughter. 'No wonder you were so expensive,' he hooted. 'Kaye obviously charged extra for a creature with a sense of humour!'

Jerry was giving them blank eyes again. 'I think he's

61

serious, Harchi-pa,' said Chad, jabbing his father in the arm in case he offended their pet.

Harchi was making a valiant but not entirely successful attempt to stop laughing as Rashila came in, followed by Gale.

'What's all the noise about?' asked Rashila.

'Oh, Wife!' rasped Harchi, dabbing at his eyes. 'Our new pet sleeps with his feet the same height as his head!'

'See, Rashila Jannan,' beeped Gale, waving a claw at the bed, 'it is as I told you. It's unhygienic and should not be allowed.'

'Unhygienic! Excuse me?' fumed Jerry.

'Gale's right, Chad,' said Rashila, then turned to Harchi. 'You'll have to find somewhere else to put him.'

'Hello? I am standing here, you know!' Jerry shouted at her, with a sudden burst of energy.

'I already told Chad he could have Jerry in his quarters, Wife,' said Harchi, trying to sound firm. He hated it when Gale and Rashila ganged up on him.

'Over here?' Jerry waved his arms in the air. 'Anybody see me?'

'Please, Rashila-ma! There's no room in the kitchen, you won't want a petbed in the living area and it's too clammy in the wallow room. At least he's out of the way in here.'

'Out of the way? What am I, a suitcase?' yelled Jerry, but nobody took any notice.

Out of the way. Rashila suddenly remembered she had to

install the hidden cameras tonight. She couldn't risk the pet catching her at it.

'Chad Jannan, I have told you it is unacceptable and—'

'All right, Gale. Chad – Jerry can sleep in here,' said Rashila.

'Thank you, Mother!' said Chad, rushing over to give her a hug, eyes shining.

'You're welcome, son.' Rashila hugged him back with a smile.

'Rashila Jannan,' buzzed Gale. 'I must protest!'

'Then do it in the kitchen, while you mix me a sour tea – I'm exhausted,' said Rashila, leaving the room, trailed by the grumpy Fossic.

Harchi led Jerry over to the bed, which curled slightly at either end. 'Here you are, Jerry. It'll flatten out once you get in. Are you sure you don't want us to hang it for you?'

'Positive. Thanks, Harchi.' Jerry dropped on to his bed, too tired to stay upright a moment longer.

'Would you like me to take your foot coverings off so you can walk up and down on the bed and imprint your smell?' asked Chad.

'I'm good, thanks Chad,' said Jerry as he curled up and faced the wall.

'Let's leave him to settle in; he might be too shy to do it while we're watching,' Harchi whispered to Chad. And the two of them tiptoed out.

*

Without windows, Jerry couldn't tell how late it was but it felt like the middle of the night; dark and cemetery silent, apart from the faint snorty snuffles drifting down from Chad who hung in his bed, fast asleep.

Turning over to get more comfortable Jerry smiled despite his mood as the filling reshaped around him. This egg white stuff rocked and a body-mould-bed hadn't freaked him out as much he'd thought it would, once he knew they weren't going to force him to sleep dangling from the ceiling.

Jerry's ear was still giving him grief. He rubbed the lobe but couldn't shift the tingling. It had started bugging him in the chute as he and Rashila travelled back from the lab. Morton told him Rashila had added a technical adjustment to the Universal Translator, so his body wouldn't feel like it was falling apart on the return journey. And apart from some understandable butterflies, he'd felt fine. Apart from his fizzy ear.

No point mentioning it though. Rashila wasn't the kind of mum you'd run to for a hug if you hurt yourself. (Unlike his who was Sympathy Central.) What would she have done about it, anyway – taken him to a vet? A huge yawn overtook him. Even though physically Jerry was desperate for sleep, he couldn't switch off mentally.

His watch said 08:20, but he must have been here eighteen hours or so. Mum'd be totally freaking out. Jerry never took off without telling her where he was going, however (deliberately) vague his information was sometimes. She'd have endlessly tried his mobile and drawn a blank, same with AJ and the rest of his mates. And if she'd got the police involved, there'd be no clues. On the bus one minute, gone the next.

Jerry knew Mum would be perched on the back of the sofa in the bay window, feet on the ledge, watching the top of the road, willing him to turn the corner from Woodcock Hill into Dovedale Avenue. He added Woolfie to the picture – she'd never sleep if Mum was upset. Then he threw Andy in while he was at it. He'd be threatening to rip Jerry's liver out for scaring Mum, but behind the front he'd be well rattled. And he'd probably have got Grandpa round, on back-up Mum Watch.

They'd all be going over and over the last conversations they'd had with him. Why would he take off like that? Was he being bullied? Was he hurt? Was he being held against his will? Was he milking this big time? No. Jerry knew he wasn't. Morton had made it clear – he could be stuck here forever. That gave him the right to be homesick and stress about his family.

Then again . . . Morton also told him she'd talk to the pet-shop owner, that there might be a way of sending him home she wouldn't know about. And it wasn't like he was under a railway arch, tucked up in a newspaper blanket. With a sigh, Jerry decided there was nothing for it but to try and get some shut-eye and see what turned up in the morning.

*

The bed swayed as Rashila forced an ear out from the seal and listened: the only sound, the soft swish of air from the tail-tube flicking about, as her appendage twitched with anger inside it. Here she was, claw-gnawingly tired, yet she was going to have to start creeping about in the middle of the night installing hidden cameras.

Rashila had calculated it would take a bandwidth and a half to install six cameras: living area (two); kitchen area; Chad's quarters; Harchi's quarters; wallow room. She refused to install one in her own quarters, and Jerry was banned from there anyway. They didn't need one in the plumbing suite either.

As Rashila understood it, the whole point of involving Jerry in the Upgrades was to watch him engage with Chad. She'd told him never to follow Jerry into the plumbing suite where they'd put his super-size litter tray (her snout wrinkled in distaste) because she didn't want Chad exposed to alien germs. Or run the risk of stressing Jerry into forgetting he was dwelling-trained.

Satisfied everyone was asleep, Rashila lowered her bed. Sneb heard her step out and gave a sleepy 'buurrooop' of pleasure from the depths of his designer nest on a shelf halfway up the wall.

Reaching in, Rashila tickled the tangle of coarse fur on his stomach and felt five sets of suckers and claws touch

66

down as he curled round her hand. 'Shshshsh, go back to sleep,' she soothed. But as she took the cameras and toolkit from her briefcase and quietly left the room, Rashila heard Sneb scuttle down the wall after her.

Before she'd gone to bed Rashila had set Gale to offline defrag since she was easier to shut down in that mode, intending to install the hidden cameras and boot Gale up to finish defragging afterwards. Rashila hadn't completely worked out what she'd say in the morning when Gale reported the inevitable time lapse in her log, but had been tugging out the strands of a story about a power cut and auxiliary battery failure.

Gale's docking block was behind the water tank, in the far corner of the plumbing suite. By the time Rashila (followed by Sneb) had crept past Harchi's quarters, across the living area and along the corridor to the plumbing suite, she'd formulated a very different plan.

Hidden cameras by definition had to be kept secret. And they would be . . . from Harchi, Chad and Jerry. Morton hadn't mentioned Gale. Something about this Upgrade Project was making Rashila's scales itch and she had a hunch that having evidence of the camera installations recorded on Gale's hard drive would make her feel less scratchy.

Pausing outside the plumbing suite Rashila decided it wasn't a hunch, it was a theory. And as a scientist she had a duty to put that theory to the test.

*

Morton sat in her quarters sipping a last mug of sour tea before stepping to bed. What a day! She couldn't wait till morning and the start of the JerryPatterson Upgrade Project. She wondered whether Rashila had installed the hidden cameras yet. It was seven green, five indigo. She must have done it by now.

Although sorely tempted to go through the hidden portal dividing her quarters from the lab to check, Morton forbade herself that treat. Once she was in there she'd never step to bed and she owed it to the Upgrades to be properly rested.

Licking the last dregs of tea Morton strolled over to the kitchen area with the mug. It was less a stroll, more an obstacle course really, because the Director's dwelling was as cluttered as her desk and almost as narrow. Though what it lacked in width it made up for in length.

Shortly after she'd been appointed Director of the BFA Morton had programmed some Fossics to work through the night, building a false back wall to the lab then installing a wallow room and plumbing suite up one end of the space they'd created. She used the rest of it as a combined kitchen, living and sleeping area.

Once the Fossics had finished the private chute and hidden exit Morton had wiped their construction memories, edited their time logs and moved in.

Closing the dishwasher Morton decided she was too tired to clean her teeth. It was pointless now anyway; she'd be eating breakfast in less than a bandwidth's time. Walking carefully around the molecular scrambler which she'd propped against the wardrobe, Morton wondered whether Kaye would have much appetite for breakfast. She doubted it. He'd been so surprised to find the Director of the BFA looping through in the middle of the night, his ears had almost doubled in height.

'It's late, so I'll get straight to the point,' Morton had announced, seizing her deliberately created advantage. 'You've been using an unauthorised piece of equipment to source illegal off-planet imports for your shop.'

Kaye opened his mouth to protest.

'Think carefully before denying it,' she warned. 'Do you imagine I would make a call like this unless I was in full possession of the facts?'

Kaye's ears flopped. 'I . . . I . . . was only going to say, it was "import" singular,' he stuttered. 'I've only used the molec . . .' A look from Morton made Kaye verbally skid to a halt. '. . . the equipment . . . once,' he finished, swallowing nervously. 'I got it from—'

Morton held up a claw. 'That is not the purpose of my call.'

Kaye frowned, one ear starting to rise, hoping against all logical hope that the Director's face on his hand-held meant something other than the ruin he'd pictured.

'I have my own reasons for not wishing to take this matter further.' Morton watched his other ear creep up. 'Chute to the lab, with the . . . item in question . . . and I'll explain.'

'Thank you, Director,' gushed Kaye, so relieved that he'd flashed a smile revealing a jewel-dotted tooth. 'I'll be there first thing in the morning.'

As demonstrated by the vulgarity of his tooth, here was a Pastinacean with more money than sense.

'Kaye!' barked Morton, the chill of her tone chasing the smile from his face. 'Surely even someone who's been as foolish as you appreciates that this requires maximum secrecy?'

Kaye nodded. 'Of course, Director. I'll be there in—'

Morton cut the loop. Her task complete, there was nothing more to say. Barely two bars on, Kaye hurried into the lab with the scrambler in a holdall. Morton despised him for having dressed to try to impress her, appalled by the tasteless embroidered tunic that strained over his belly to meet the glittery waistband of his shorts.

'Morton,' he oozed, 'I've always been a huge admirer of your work and—'

'Don't waste your breath, Kaye,' grunted Morton. 'I'm only saving your scales for Rashila Jannan. Or rather, Chad. My assistant tells me her son's really connected with that creature you sold Harchi Jannan.'

'I only sell the friendliest pets—'

A warning growl from Morton was all it took to silence Kaye. 'If anyone discovers it's an illegal import the Ministry Committee would have it put down, which would be devastating for Chad. Almost as devastating as the shame on the Jannan family should Harchi be caught up in an unlicensed scrambler scam.'

'Your concern does you credit, Director,' grovelled Kaye.

'This isn't about me,' Morton snarled. 'This is about the Jannans, who you've put at risk through your greed and stupidity.'

'What do you suggest?' asked Kaye warily.

'You're to leave the scrambler with me. I'll destroy it,' said Morton.

'All right,' Kaye agreed, almost managing to hide the wince. It had obviously cost him a complete fortune.

'Then download this on to your records.' Morton handed him a memory stick. 'It's documents outlining and legitimising the pet's history: how it was discovered in the cargo hold of an inter-planetary trade ship; how the Captain sold it to you, and how you took the appropriate medical precautions for alien pets before selling it to Harchi Jannan.'

'I'll do it as soon as I get back to my dwelling, Director,' Kaye assured her.

'And know this,' Morton barked as he carefully unpacked the scrambler from the holdall, 'I shall not be so soft a second time. If you ever use an unlicensed scrambler, breathe a word of our encounter, or change the story of the alien's arrival in any way—'

'I won't, you have my word on it!'

'—I will inform Chair Bluhm of the Better Homes, Better Planet Ministry Committee. Which given the multiple

71

offences you've committed, will mean your personal and financial ruin.'

'I've learnt my lesson, Morton,' Kaye assured her passionately, as she ushered him out. 'I'll never do anything like this, ever again.' He paused in the open portal and he must have been eaten up by curiosity, to risk the question: 'How did you know?'

'I am the Director of the Bureau of Fossic Affairs,' said Morton, drawing herself up to her full height, so she towered over him. 'I know everything.'

As Morton stepped to bed she smiled at the memory of Kaye humbly nodding as she'd let the portal swish shut behind him. She congratulated herself on having legitimised the Upgrade Project. Almost. It wouldn't be completely secure, until she'd convinced Rashila of a more complex version of Jerry's arrival story which served the Upgrades better. Still, how hard would that be? She was Morton.

*

Jerry was in the middle of a Rachel Davis Dream. And even as he slept part of his brain chalked this up as his bang-on reward for such a hideously angsty day. It had been about six months since he'd formed a deep and unshakeable passion for the golden-haired goddess whose earthly form was class babe, Rachel; and dreams about her were rare.

So far this was Jerry's best one ever. Rachel, realising how much time she's wasted on current squeeze, guitar whiz Bobbie Clifford, has dashed on stage during assembly to publicly dump him and declare 'It's Jerry She Loves!' AJ's shoving Jerry out of his seat to claim his prize, so he legs it up on stage and launches into his 'I Knew We'd Get Here in the End' speech. Even black-hearted Barkow's dabbing a hanky to his eyes, then has to lend it to Mrs Morris 'cos she's laughing and crying all at once.

Everyone starts baying for the happy couple to go smoocher to smoocher. Jerry looks deep into Rachel's eyes and runs his fingers through her strawberry blonde hair, with half a sleepy thought that it feels coarser than he'd thought it would. Almost woolly.

He closes in for that first delicious snog and . . . Jerry's hand snagged on a tangle. Do goddesses tangle? Forget it. He's so close, he can feel Rachel's breath on his face. It smells . . . weird. Stick with the snog. No, it smells *really* weird.

Jerry felt as if he was suffocating, but that had to be excitement, right? Mmmm, now he's finally kissing gorgeous goddess Rachel and her lips feel like . . . knitting?

A livid circle of pain burnt into Jerry's forehead, cheeks and chin. He jerked upright, yelling, but the sound was muffled and all he could see was a thick pink cloud which he started trying to bat off his face.

There was a yowl, followed by suckers popping and pinkness vanishing. Jerry saw the creature shoot across the floor, to be plucked up by Rashila, who shoved him at Gale, who shot out the room with him. What the hell?

73

'What's going on, Mother?' asked Chad sleepily from his bed.

'Nothing, son, go back to sleep,' Rashila reassured him, crossing to Jerry who looked up at her, totally bewildered. 'Do not engage with Sneb, he gets jealous,' she growled.

'Hey! Your psycho wool attacked me in my sleep!' snapped Jerry.

'Nobody is to blame. Animals find their natural order,' was all Rashila said by way of an apology, before hurrying from the room.

Jerry rubbed his throbbing face and flung himself back down again. He'd never get to sleep now. For one thing his face totally caned. For another he'd been cruelly robbed of the ending to his best Rachel Davis Dream ever! Finally, and more worryingly, what had Rashila and Gale been doing in Chad's room in the middle of the night?

CHAPTER NINE

Harchi was determined to be on time for work today. Especially after yesterday, when he'd been so late it was this morning before he was ready to go in. As soon as he'd finished breakfast he was going to shower, without dipping even a claw in the wallow pool.

Although Rashila had gone to work, so there was nothing to stop him finishing his sour tea and zambon while he wallowed.

Heading for the wallow room, mug of tea in one claw, zambon in the other, Harchi saw Jerry stumble sleepily from Chad's quarters and greeted him with a cheery: 'Morning!'

'Hey, Harchi,' said Jerry, yawning and stretching. A gap appeared between his tunic and floor shorts, revealing an ugly, bumpy, knot of flesh in the centre of his stomach. It must be a bad vet's repair from a scrap with another pet over food.

'Has Morton rung for me?' Jerry asked, suddenly wide awake.

Harchi didn't have time to ask why Jerry thought the

Director of the BFA would loop through to a pet or explain how he knew she wouldn't, so he simply shook his head. Seeing his pet's hopeful expression drown in disappointment made Harchi's ears and tail lose all their perk.

'She was going to ask the pet shop how I got here to see how I'd get home again,' he muttered sadly.

'You are home, Jerry,' Harchi gently explained. 'You live with us now.'

Jerry sighed. 'And she was going to see if I can send a message to my mum. She'll have totally lost it about me going missing, Harchi.'

'If Morton said she'd look into it for you, I'm sure she will,' said Harchi, not believing it for a moment, but keen to cheer his pet up. Morton must have said it to calm Jerry down at the lab last night. 'The pet shop won't be open yet, that's probably why you haven't heard.'

'Oh yes! I hadn't thought of that.'

As Jerry smiled up at Harchi, he noticed the telltale circular pattern of sore claw and sucker marks. 'I see you've had a run in with Sneb.'

'He attacked me in the night,' said Jerry, touching the red bits with his funny clutch of fingers. His face looked extremely painful, but there was bound to be more damage on scale-free skin.

'Come into the wallow room and we'll get Gale to have a look at it,' said Harchi.

'Be right there, after I've been to the loo,' said Jerry.

Watching Jerry trudge off to the plumbing suite, Harchi told himself it was only natural for a new pet to miss his mother. He'd forget about her soon enough once he'd settled in. And anyway, he couldn't worry about that now – he had to get to work.

*

Before Rashila had even left for work – and Morton knew because she'd watched her do it – her boss had already moved a spare Infoscope to the far end of the workbench in the lab, out of sight of prying eyes. Then she'd networked it to the Jannans' Infoscope to receive the live feed from the hidden cameras in their dwelling.

Now Morton and Rashila stood watching the screen. The picture was hazy because of the steam in the wallow room, but they could still see Gale swapping her claw for a toothbroom attachment to give Chad's teeth a scrub. Harchi was lying in the wallow pool, chewing zambon washed down with slugs of sour tea. Had he forgotten everything his Fossic had taught him about good manners when he was a Podder?

Rashila would be furious with him for eating in the pool and disgracing her by doing it in front of her boss. Morton could almost hear her assistant straining to stop her ears flipping, though a quick check confirmed she hadn't been able to keep the kink of outrage from her tail.

If she was going to get distracted every time they saw Harchi doing something disgusting, Morton might as well hire another assistant for all the use Rashila was going to be.

'It is a sad fact of life, Rashila, that not everyone can be Bonded to a well-mannered male.' So far, so good: Morton could see she had Rashila's complete attention. 'Rest assured I won't be judging *you* for anything revolting Harchi does on camera during our research period.'

Rashila inclined her head in acknowledgement, but when she spoke it was to change the subject. Morton allowed it, realising she was (naturally) too moved by her boss's kindness to express herself further on that topic.

'Did you tell Jerry you'd talk to Kaye?' Rashila asked.

'You know I did,' replied Morton. She hated it when staff forgot a conversation.

'No,' Rashila insisted, 'I missed your conversation because you'd sent me to the workshop to build him a litter tray.'

Morton ignored her rudeness. It was probably shock – Harchi had just started cleaning his tail tip with his teeth. Plus, Rashila had just presented her with the perfect opportunity to set up Jerry's arrival story.

'I spoke to Kaye last night,' Morton began. As if by silent consent, they both looked away from the screen to continue the conversation. 'Apparently he bought Jerry from an inter-planetary trade ship Captain, who'd found him in with the cargo.'

'So Kaye doesn't know where he's from?' asked Rashila.

Morton shook her head. 'But he's been medically vetted,' she added.

'He'd never sell a pet that wasn't,' Rashila replied. 'But that means Jerry can't send a message to his mother.'

'Did you send a message to your snebbit's mother when you bought it? He's an animal,' rasped Morton, with a dismissive wave of her claw. 'He'll bond with Chad and in a day or so he'll have forgotten all about his family.'

'But he seemed so sad when he was talking to Harchi just now,' said her assistant softly.

Morton felt like roaring Rashila's ridges off for such an unscientific assessment. 'I see Jerry's got under your scales as well as Chad's,' she snapped.

'I was thinking of the Upgrades,' came the swift response. 'If Jerry's unhappy his behaviour with Chad will be different from normal, which will affect our research.'

'Our?' How dare she! Trying to muscle in on Morton's Upgrade idea. 'I've already thought of that,' she retorted. 'We're going to tell Jerry he was transported here by molecular scrambler. One with a time-fold overlay pump.'

Rashila gasped. 'Jerry's never going to believe something as far-fetched as that!'

'You doubt me?' growled Morton.

Rashila shook her head nervously. 'No, Director.'

'A species that still fights over food and uses litter trays won't have developed molecular scrambling or the ability to compress time.' Morton spelt it out for her soft-brained assistant. 'So he won't know whether it's far-fetched or not. The only part Jerry'll be interested in is the time-fold overlay pump.'

'It would stop him worrying about his mother,' agreed Rashila, finally catching on. 'But we'd have to keep the explanation of time compression theory very simple,'

'Keep it as simple as you like,' grunted Morton. 'Just make sure he understands that no one will realise he's missing.'

'Me?' cried Rashila, shocked at being given such a daunting task.

'Of course you,' barked her boss. 'What would Harchi and Chad say if I looped through to your pet?'

Rashila's ears flopped. 'Forgive me, Director, I wasn't thinking.'

'Don't waste my time stating the obvious,' Morton snorted irritably. 'Engage your brain and let's press on.'

Before long they had the rest of the plan in place. Once Harchi had left for work Rashila would message Gale, instructing her to tell Chad of Jerry's stowaway arrival and why they were telling him the molecular scrambler/ time-pump version instead. And they'd copy Naish so she could brief Gilpin, in case Jerry mentioned it to her. Then Rashila would loop through to tell Harchi. Even though he was hopeless with secrets this one should be easier, because he only had to keep it from a pet.

Rashila went back to her desk to put their plan into effect, but Morton was too excited to settle. As she padded off to the workshop to get the Duty Fossic to clean her teeth, Morton felt the scale-tingling glow of satisfaction at a job extremely well done and a ground-breaking Upgrade Project underway.

*

If Jerry reached the wallow room in an even number of paces, Morton would have found a way to send Mum a message. Odd number, she wouldn't. And if it was a number that was a double, say, like eleven or twenty-two (obviously twenty-two was better) then Morton would have found a way to send him home.

If it wasn't odd or a double . . . or not Mum, Andy, Woolfie, AJ or Grandpa's birthday . . . or within three, no four days of someone's birthday that he knew, real or celebrity, including Barclay . . . then he was stuck in Lizard Life for ever.

A few steps away from the wallow room, Jerry was trying to remember how many days there were in June so he'd know how many pigeon steps to go forward to get to the door on the 4th July, which was his birthday, except it wasn't a double figure, except it was if you thought of it as two plus two, which made it even and double, message and home, how did that dumb rhyme go? Thirty days hath September, April . . . THUNK! and NovembOUCH!

Something light but agonisingly painful had landed on Jerry's head. As his hands shot up to whack it away his fingers caught in a hideously familiar tangle of scratchy, woolly fur. Jerry wrestled to disentangle Sneb's vice-like, claw-and-sucker grip from his scalp, his howls of pain mingling with the type of protest yowls familiar in the Patterson household whenever one of them accidentally trod on the cat.

Through a curtain of hair and snebbit fur, Jerry registered the wallow room door swish open and Harchi, Chad and Gale pile out.

'Drop it, Sneb!' shouted Chad.

Jerry's pink pincer helmet briefly stopped trying to gouge into his grey matter but refused to release its grip.

'Get it off!' yelled Jerry.

'Stop them fighting!' wailed Chad.

'Gale, do something!' ordered Harchi. 'Chad's getting upset.'

Gale's arm shot out and she hooked her claw through Sneb's knotty fur, then hoiked him sharply from Jerry's head whereupon the former hissed and hurtled along the wall into the living area, while the latter yelped and dropped to his knees, holding his head in agony.

'Is he badly hurt, Harchi-pa?' Jerry heard Chad ask. 'We won't have to have him put down, will we?'

Jerry quickly staggered to his feet before anyone rang the vet. Next time, they could chop off a leg and he'd keep on dancing if that's how they reacted to him getting injured.

'No Chad, see? He's all right. You are, aren't you, Jerry?' boomed Harchi, slapping him on the back.

82

Woah! Hard claw, man! 'Never better, Harchi,' wheezed Jerry, sucking air back into his lungs, then with a brave smile at Chad: 'Bit of a headache, that's all.'

'Come in here and let Gale get rid of it,' said Chad, tenderly taking Jerry by the arm to steer him into the wallow room.

*

Checking Gale's front, Harchi saw it was eleven orange, three ochre. He still had two bars to get to the Unit. He could do that. No time for Gale to scrub his scales now. He'd shower the mud off. Jump into his suit. Grab his case. And be out the portal in a tail-flick. As soon as he'd made sure Chad was all right. Harchi hated seeing him upset like that. He should have thought to warn him: pets often fought over territory.

Chad was getting dressed near where Jerry sat on a boulder, rubbing his scalp. As his head appeared through his tunic top, he caught Harchi watching him and smiled.

'I'm OK, Harchi-pa. You get going, or you'll be late for work.'

Harchi blew a happy snort at the son who loved him so much he could almost read his mind, then padded through the steam to the shower. Stepping into his shorts, Chad glanced at Jerry who was looking extremely nervous as Gale approached him, her medicinal claw flashing.

'It doesn't hurt,' said Chad, seeing Jerry back away as Gale raised the blue claw above his head.

'Where I come from, that remark is *always* followed by pain!'

'Would it help if I held your hand?' offered Chad, holding his claw out, then dropping it again as he saw Jerry's expression. They obviously didn't hold hands on his planet.

As Gale moved her flashing claw in a circle around Jerry's head, Chad explained she was beaming white cell nanoparticles into his scalp to repair the subcutaneous disruption. He didn't think Jerry understood, but it covered the hand-holding awkwardness.

'I told you it wouldn't hurt,' said Chad, pleased to see Jerry start smiling as the headache obviously disappeared.

'That's totally incredible – I've never seen anything like it!' Jerry told him.

Chad realised Rashila-ma had been right about Jerry's race being primitive. As a Phase 12deluxe2, Gale's medicinal claw was super effective because of its hyperbeam setting, but even lowly Phase 4s (like rickety old Theydon) had medicinal claws. How did Jerry's species heal wounds without them?

Although curious, Chad didn't ask Jerry. Harchi was on the drying pad so he'd be coming past any moment. He'd love a conversation like that and Chad didn't want him sidetracked from leaving for work.

Gale finished Jerry's scalp, then grabbed his jaw in her free claw and tilted his head up so she could treat the snebbit wounds on his face. Chad watched the red scratch and sucker marks disappear as Gale methodically moved her blue flashing claw from left cheek up to left brow, across to right brow, down to right cheek.

Harchi had joined them, chuckling at Jerry's delighted expression as he felt his face heal. 'Feeling better now?' he asked, stepping into a clean pair of shorts.

Jerry couldn't answer because of Gale's jaw clamp, so he gave a tiny nod as she moved her medicinal claw round to the last sore place, on his chin.

Pulling his head through his tunic, Harchi was proud to see he still had one and a half bars to get to work. Harchi Precision Timekeeper Jannan. As he looked back at Gale's front to double-check the time her claw started buzzing, the blue light flicked on and off, the buzz speeded up to a FIZZ! flipped into a SNAP! exploded into a BAM! and a zigzag of white blue light threw a sizzling bridge between Fossic claw and pet chin.

Gale shot backwards taking Jerry's jaw with her as the rest of him paddled air, trying to get free. For the second time that morning, Chad yelled 'Drop it!' and Gale opened her claw, throwing Jerry off balance head first into the wallow pool, promptly followed by Harchi and Chad, who jumped in fully clothed to save their pet from drowning.

As all three surfaced spluttering mud, Harchi wiped his eyes and was relieved to see that Chad and Jerry were fine, although Jerry was rubbing a muddy finger along the inside of his bottom row of teeth.

Clambering out of the pool, Harchi called across to Gale who was on the walkway, unscrewing her medicinal claw which had blue smoke wisping from the tip. 'Gale . . . ?' Harchi started. She swivelled to face him. 'Could you . . .'

'I have already sent the "late" message I had stored in my Draft Outbox file,' she whirred, the disapproval tone set to high on her vocal chip.

Harchi peeled off his muddy suit. Tomorrow, he absolutely *definitely* was going to get to work on time.

*

Rashila sank back in her chair, watching Chad help Jerry from the wallow pool as Harchi went to take another shower. A tension ache started in her tail tip, then pulsed its way up to the base of her spine, at the thought of the extensive research period that lay ahead of her. And she was barely past breakfast on Day One.

CHAPTER TEN

As Jerry had hoped, Gale and Chad forgot about him in the rush to get Harchi off to work and Chad his breakfast. Shucking off his muddy trousers and top Jerry stepped into the shower and closed his eyes as the water cascaded over him, enjoying the echo in the cave-like room and the ooziness as the mud slid down his body – only to be stung from the moment by a vice like grip round his upper arm as Gale yanked him painfully out of the water.

'That shower is not for pets!' she blared at high volume.

'So how am I supposed to get clean?' snapped Jerry, wrenching his arm free.

'With your tongue, like other animals,' whirred the unhelpful response.

Jerry was sure he'd started calmly enough explaining why on all sorts of levels *that* wasn't going to happen. But by the time he was reminding Gale how it was *her* fault he'd been coated in mud and needed a shower in the first place, he must have been giving it some wellie 'cos Chad came running.

Shrewd enough to realise that trying to negotiate whilst wearing nothing but wet pants and attitude was probably a handicap, Jerry decided to lay on some shivering.

'Why's he shaking like that, Gale?' asked Chad anxiously.

'From shame, at being caught somewhere he shouldn't be.'

Wrong! Jerry cranked up the shivering.

'It's getting worse!'

And threw in a monster fake sneeze.

'I think his head's going to explode!' Chad sounded desperate.

'It is unlikely.'

'Jerry! What's wrong?'

'N . . . n . . . nothing, Chad. My sp . . . sp . . . species gets sick, if we're exposed to t-t-t . . . t-t-t-t . . . too much cold, that's all,' Jerry managed to spit out, through chattering teeth.

'Quick, Gale! Let's warm him up in the shower!'

'Negative! Pets do not shower. The same effect would be achieved by re-clothing him.'

'Th-th . . . they're all d-d . . . damp and mu-mu . . . muddy.'

'Jerry's right, we can't use his clothes. I'll get him some of mine!'

'We do not dress pets in Podder clothes.'

Jerry delivered an Oscar-winning batch of shivering,

topped off by a sneeze that all but blew the boulders into the pool.

'He's really ill, Gale! He's going in the shower!'

Jerry allowed Chad to bundle him into the shower, then felt the hot water come on. Result! He wound down the shivering and grinned at his saviour through the water.

'Look, Gale! He's smiling! He must be feeling better! Are you, Jerry?'

'Much better, Chad. Cheers.'

'Your recovery was swift, for a creature in so much distress,' beeped Gale.

'That's how it is with us humans, Gale. Keep us warm, keep us happy.'

'Come Chad, it is time for Lesson Session,' Gale whirred irritably, hovering away.

'Will you be all right on your own?' asked Chad, checking his pet for signs of sickness.

'Oh yeah. You go ahead.'

By the time Jerry emerged from the wallow room, Chad was at the table, listening to Gale blah-di-blah at him. He wanted to shove his muddy clothes in the washing machine, but went to borrow some of Chad's first, in case Morton rang. He wouldn't feel right, talking to someone like her in his underpants.

As he rootled through Chad's wardrobe for something to wear, Jerry realised at least one good thing had come out of his run in with the medicinal claw – his ear had finally stopped tingling.

Jerry found a tunic top that could almost pass for West Ham's colours, so although it fitted him like a dress, he told himself he was wearing it for the Boys – and attached the mobile Translation Unit to the hem, so no one could accuse him of wearing a brooch. He didn't bother with any shorts. Chad was a good couple of tree trunks wider than him; he'd need braces to keep them up. And there'd be a monster draught from the flappy gappy bit these guys had where their tails slotted through.

Wandering out to the kitchen, Jerry shoved his clothes in the washing machine and started looking for soap powder. Next thing he knew old Tin Chops had whooshed in and was giving him grief.

'It is not permissible for you to wear Chad Jannan's clothing. Remove that garment immediately!'

'Soon as I've washed my stuff. If you give me the powder I'll put it in,' Jerry offered, trying to show willing by being helpful.

'Powder? What powder? And where do you intend to place it?'

'In. The. Washing. Machine,' said Jerry, jerking a thumb at where he'd stashed his clothes.

'Oh dear,' came Chad's voice behind him.

Gale beeped angrily as Chad crossed to the machine and carefully removed Jerry's muddy trousers and top.

'Return to your Lesson!' she whirred, snatching the clothes from Chad.

'Give him a break, Gale – he was only trying to help,' said Jerry.

'Do not issue me with instructions concerning my Podder!' beeped Gale, throwing Jerry's clothes on the counter, her lights going crazy she was so agitated.

'Not till you stop bullying him!' Jerry shouted back.

'Get on your bed – you are in disgrace!' said Gale, nudging Jerry away from the kitchen.

'I haven't done anything!'

'You placed your muddy outfit in the Jannan's chiller unit and ruined their food.'

'I didn't know! It looks like a washing machine, with that round door on the front.'

'Stop arguing and let's sort it out,' pleaded Chad.

'I'm sorry Chad, I didn't mean to get mud on your food,' said Jerry. 'I'll wash it off.'

Gale blocked Jerry's path to the fridge. 'No. You have done enough damage today.'

'Have not!'

'You broke my medicinal claw.'

'You gave me an electric shock.'

'*You* gave *me* an electric shock. With your mouth.'

'I've had that bit of wire on my bottom teeth for, like, ten hundred years. I forgot the orthodontist left it there.'

'That word does not translate! You have made it up so I won't . . .'

'That's enough, you two!' ordered Chad, stepping between the warring factions. 'Gale, why don't you put Jerry's clothes in the cleaner while I fix him some breakfast?'

'Yeah, Gale,' sneered Jerry, 'why don't you?'

'Negative. We will return to our Lesson Session.'

'But Gale . . .'

'If you do not comply, Chad Jannan, I shall—'

Gale's threat hung in the air, cut off by a call coming in.

'Quick, Chad – grab it!' cried Jerry. 'It might be Morton.'

'I answer the calls in this dwelling,' beeped Gale, slowly hovering to the Infoscope.

Jerry knew she was only doing it to wind him up. He watched as the screen changed, hoping with everything crossed that it was Morton, then gave a sigh of disappointment as Rashila's face appeared. Great. Now Gale had started snitching on him. It was pointless going over to defend himself; those two had it in for him anyway.

Jerry was opening the fridge, to see if he could find something to eat that hadn't been speckled with mud, when he heard Rashila's voice.

'Summon your pet, Chad – I have some information for him.'

*

'I'm sorry, Chad, but it's a total crock!'

'That's not translating, Jerry, but I can tell from your tone you're unhappy.'

'You bet I'm unhappy! Time-fold overlay pumps? Molecular scramblers? Rashila can't seriously expect me to fall for stuff like that!'

Jerry was pacing up and down Chad's room in a complete lather. Even Gale had backed off and left them to it.

'But Jerry, I heard you say you'd seen molecular scrambling on one of your star treks, so you know it's real!' urged Chad.

'We don't do star treks, Chad. Well, at least we do, but people like me don't.'

'Your species don't send pets into space?'

'I am *not* a pet. And they do, actually. But *Star Trek*'s a TV show I like where they're always beaming people down to unknown planets and . . .'

'What's a TV show?'

Jerry stopped in his tracks and stared at Chad. 'You don't have TV?'

Chad shook his head. 'Is that bad?'

'It's criminal! And way too big a topic to go into now. But trust me, we're coming back to it.' Jerry gave Chad a long look. 'OK, so maybe I was brought here by molecular scrambler. But are you *honestly* telling me there's *really* such a thing as a time-fold overlay pump?'

'Honestly, Jerry. There really and truly is!' said Chad, consoling himself that he was telling the truth even if it wasn't in relation to his pet's arrival, then realising it hadn't made him feel any better. He'd never told a lie before and though he understood Gale's explanation for why they were doing it, he hated deceiving Jerry.

'D'you get how it works?' asked Jerry. 'I couldn't keep up once your mum started banging on about compression engineering and the space-time continuum.'

'She gets a bit carried away – it's one of her favourite subjects,' Chad told him, grateful Jerry appeared to be calming down. 'I'm a bit vague on the detail, Gale's only just started teaching me time-compression theory.'

'Vague is good, Chad. It's the only way I'm going to get it.'

'Um . . . let's see, how can I put this simply . . . oh, I know! An overlay pump keeps folding time in on itself over space, until it's so squashed up it's almost at a single point where it more or less stands still.' Chad looked up from concentrating to see Jerry frowning and shaking his head.

'Are you saying that while I'm here, time's stood still at home?'

'Nearly, yes. So, your mother won't be worrying about you, because she won't know you're missing.'

Jerry checked his watch. 08:21. It would explain the snail

time. 'But that's crazy, Chad, 'cos if I'm here for a week, I'll be a whole week older, so when I get home, where does that week go? It's not like everything's frozen while I'm here, is it?'

'I'm sorry, Jerry, I just don't know enough about it. Shall I ask Gale to explain?'

'What's the point, I wouldn't understand,' sighed Jerry. 'But it's impossible no one will realise I'm missing for the rest of my life! I have to find a way home, Chad, I just have to!'

'But Jerry, Rashila-ma told you – nobody's ever scrambled livestock off-planet before!'

'How many more times?' shouted Jerry. 'I'm not livestock! I'm human!'

'I didn't mean to insult you,' said Chad, 'but however you describe yourself, the reality's still the same.'

Jerry slumped on to his bed.

'I'm sorry you're sad, Jerry. But I promise, I'll always look after you. Always keep you well fed, safe and warm. And I know you'll come to like it here once you get used to it.'

There was no answer. Jerry wouldn't even look at him, so Chad left the room with a boulder-ish feeling in his stomach. He'd thought it would be fun, owning such an exotic pet, but it was going to be a lot harder than he'd anticipated. Not like helping Rashila-ma with Sneb, whose circular demands were so basic; eat, litter tray, play, sleep, eat. Although, in many respects Jerry was similar. It was his ability to talk that was making everything so complicated, and of course was what made him unique.

*

'Gale?'

'Chad?'

They were on their way to Gilpin Carney's dwelling for today's Social Session. At least they had been. Chad had stopped walking and even though Gale hadn't had him in her viewfinder when he'd spoken, her aural chip detected his vocal agitation. Swivelling to face him, the peaked state of her Podder's ears and tail confirmed that he was troubled.

'What happens if Jerry's memory comes back, he remembers stowing away on the interplanetary spaceship, realises I've lied to him and doesn't want to be my pet any more?'

'Firstly, Jerry is just a pet and though unusual, he does not deserve the power over your emotions that you have granted him.'

'But I feel sorry for him, Gale.'

'Pity is no excuse for indulging an animal, Chad. If you do not train him to know who is master, he will make your life a misery.'

'But Gale . . .'

'Are you happy, Chad?'

'No,' he admitted, shaking his head sadly.

'Which proves my point. Secondly, to answer your question: Jerry Patterson's inability to recall any aspect of

96

his journey here indicates that repeated exposure to inter-planetary hyperdrive has probably traumatised him to such an extent that it has wiped his memory. Since you and Rashila Jannan have just supplied him with an alternative, it would be exceptionally rare for him to retrieve the original.'

'Thank you, Gale.'

'You are welcome, Chad.'

They were almost at the Carney's entry portal, when her Podder stopped again.

'Gale?' Not anxiety this time, but confusion.

'Chad?'

'You've always taught me it's wrong to lie. I understand we've lied to Jerry to help him settle in, but it's still a lie, isn't it? So how can it suddenly be right?'

There was a whirr, a beep and more whirring. 'Insuffi-cient data to respond. An error message states: this question is beyond a hard-drive capability and should be redirected to a creature with a fully functional brain.'

While Chad sounded the arrival alert and they waited for Naish to activate the entry portal, Gale's outer casing may have been idling but her internal system was on red alert. She was a Phase 12deluxe2 state-of-the-art Fossic. And yet she'd just given her Podder an error message. A first. And unacceptable.

Rashila Jannan installing hidden cameras was another unacceptable first. Regardless of the reason she had given:

that it was to stop someone stealing the pet, and she didn't wish to alarm Chad or Harchi Jannan by informing them.

As Naish appeared at the portal Gale followed Chad into the dwelling, beeping a greeting at her fellow Fossic while opening an Unacceptable Firsts file for all the data she was collecting. And logging a prompt to monitor this situation closely.

These unacceptable firsts were all linked to JerryPatterson. In the day and a half that he'd been with the Jannans, he had also caused a number of outbursts of emotion in Chad that fell outside the acceptable norm. A Fossic's prime directive was to protect and educate her Podder. If this pet continued to have a harmful effect on Chad Jannan, Gale would be compelled to take action.

*

'Anything happening?'

Rashila turned from the screen, where Jerry lay gazing at the ceiling, and shook her head at Morton, who was at her desk on the other side of the lab. 'No. He's still on his bed.'

'Go and make a start on your notes. I doubt he'll do anything now till Chad gets back.'

Rashila stood and, taking a deep breath, approached her boss's desk. 'I'm concerned about Chad.'

'How so?' asked Morton, tilting her ears slightly, to warn that she deemed it extremely early in the research process to be voicing concerns.

'He's not his normal, easy-going self and . . .' Rashila

paused, noting the ear tilt, '. . . well, I just wanted to mention the behavioural changes, that's all.' she finished.

'This is an experimental process,' Morton reminded her assistant in a clipped tone. 'If there weren't behavioural changes, it wouldn't be worth doing.'

'But Chad's been exhibiting strong emotions which could be damaging for him.'

'This project isn't just about Chad,' said Morton. 'It's to enrich the future . . .' she raised her voice and stabbed the air with her claw, '. . . of every single Podder on this planet! And surely you know I'd never do anything to put your son at risk?'

'Yes, Director.'

As Rashila went back to her desk, a chill ran over her ridges. Morton had never taken the trouble to reassure her about anything before.

*

Jerry decided to look in one last cupboard, and if that didn't produce a washing machine he'd go and see if this was the kind of posh gaff with a laundry service in the basement.

West Ham colours or not, wandering around in a tunic-dress was doing nothing to improve his temper. And Jerry was going stir-crazy. Serve them right if they came home and found he'd gone missing.

He wasn't going to run away – where would he go, anyway? But if he just went out for a while it might stop him endlessly going over what Rashila and Chad had said about him being stuck here for ever. 'NO WAY THAT'S GOING TO HAPPEN!' shouted Jerry at the ceiling, knowing he'd never, *ever*, give up on getting home.

Jerry was staring into a cupboard full of boxes and tins. He picked the biggest one, in case it was where the sweet sticks were kept. Rashila must have passed on Morton's instruction about giving him lunch, 'cos Chad had left a dish of food by his bed which Jerry scoffed the second they'd gone out, but he still had space for a sweet stick or two.

The lid was stiff so Jerry had to tug to get it off, which rattled the contents. The tin was full of little balls of grit. Didn't look very appetising, but then neither did sweet sticks, and they were bliss on rollerblades. Jerry was just giving a gritball a very cautious lick, when he felt something woolly rub against his ankle. The Pink Peril! Jerry spat the lick out as he realised he'd been sampling snebbit snacks.

Jerry kicked his foot out to get rid of the evil creature, but Sneb scuttled straight back and started moofling round him, rearing up on its three back legs (three!) and rubbing against Jerry's calf. What kind of freak was this? Its mouth was in the centre of its belly and each of its five legs had a round, floppy sucker on the end. Gross.

'Would you like a biscuit?' asked Jerry sweetly, in the voice Mum used on Barclay, crouching to show Sneb the tin.

The tangle of knotty fur was quivering with excitement

and squeaky-purring as Jerry let it come close, closer, closest, right up to the open tin, then CLANG! slammed the lid back on, just as Sneb was about to tuck in.

'Think twice before you savage me next time, Psychofur!'

The purr lowered into a yowl. Jerry wanted to leg it, but his muddy clothes were on the other side of Sneb. And the yowl was getting growlier. Jerry flung a handful of gritballs into the living area, and as Sneb dashed after them he grabbed his washing and bolted. As the door swished shut behind Jerry the only sound in the dwelling was Sneb, scuttling and crunching as he scouted for snacks.

CHAPTER ELEVEN

It took Rashila a while to realise Jerry was missing. She'd been working at her desk while Morton was in the workshop, supervising a repair on a Phase 9standard3 with a hover mechanism fault. The Duty Fossics were more than capable of carrying out the work, but the Fossic belonged to Bluhm and Morton felt obliged to show respect to the Chair of the Ministry Committee. Although she'd complained bitterly about it.

It wasn't until she returned and grumpily demanded an update that Rashila went to check the screen and discovered Jerry had left Chad's quarters. Clicking from area to area she'd been unable to locate him, so they'd assumed he was in the plumbing suite.

As a few bars passed and he'd still failed to appear, Rashila began to fret that either Jerry had fallen into the water tank and drowned or worse, he'd left the dwelling. If only Morton had let her insert that tracking device in Jerry's other ear when she'd done the sonic implant, they'd know where he was now.

'I don't know why you didn't install a tracking device when you did the sonic implant,' rasped Morton over Rashila's shoulder. 'How could you be so careless with such a valuable animal? He's obviously run away – send Gale out to find him.'

'She's still at Gilpin's. If I message her, how will she explain to the others that we know Jerry's missing?' Rashila refused to say 'run away' until she had proof that's what had happened.

'It's your pet, you work it out,' Morton growled, storming back to her desk. 'Only do it fast before he ruins my Upgrade Project and your employment history.'

*

As Jerry tried to find his way to the basement along the maze-like hallways, lone adults steered well clear of him, and Fossics moved to protect their Podders when they saw he was unaccompanied. He gave it some major lip-stretching action on the smile front, to show he was friendly, but the reaction was always the same. Plague City.

Rounding yet another bend and having lost all sense of direction, Jerry found himself in a stubby chunk of hallway. There was a door at the end with a sign above it in spaghetti-tangle writing, which Jerry hoped was Pastinacean for either 'basement' or 'fire exit'.

Dropping his muddy clothes, Jerry waved his hands about trying to find the 'swish' point. That's when he noticed his blood pumping faster at the thought that this door might lead to the street. Jerry hadn't caught a glimpse of his surroundings or had a breath of fresh air for two days – and he definitely, urgently, *instantly* needed to do both.

A blanket of claustrophobia suddenly smothered him. Jerry had to get out. NOW! He waved, knocked, thumped and jabbed at the door, faster and faster as his panic increased but it refused to budge: he was hyperventilating; an orange starry haze burst inside his head as he crumpled against the wall straining to fill his burning lungs and . . . and . . . was that wishful thinking or could he really hear, barely audible above the sound of his ravaged breathing, a soft . . . a whispery . . . swishshshshsh?

Opening his eyes Jerry saw his trainer had nudged the bottom of the door which was now sliding into the wall to the right. He grabbed his clothes and staggered gratefully through the gap where a wonderful warmth flowed over him. Jerry dropped his clothes again and bent over, hands on knees, gulping air; the gulps gradually subsiding as the panic vanished and his lungs went back to work.

Straightening up Jerry saw he wasn't on a street. Or in the basement. He was on the roof, looking at a panoramic view that took his new-found breath away. He quickly covered the ground to the far side to get a better look, hanging on to a metal safety rail so he could lean over the perimeter wall to take in his surroundings, his mouth hanging open in a soundless, extended gasp.

He'd never seen anything like the sight which spread out

in front of him. It could have been lifted straight from the cover of one of Speccy Bates's sci-fi books (which Jerry and AJ would sometimes 'relocate' if they needed to persuade Speccy to be more generous with his maths).

Jerry was on the tallest building around; one of only a handful with a flat roof. The others were all topped off with domes and although similar in tubular shape, stood at various heights and angles. None of them had windows. All of them were the colour of old flower pots with the same rough-textured finish.

Jerry couldn't see anything that passed for transport, but then realised there weren't any roads. Just flower-pot textured buildings dotted about on flower-pot coloured ground, as far as the eye could see, as if a race of giant men, women and children had poked their fingers and thumbs up through a monster piece of clay.

When he finally looked up above the buildings, Jerry was astonished to see a deep purple sun in a pale lavender sky, threaded with ribbons of pink. Then he gawped as he turned his head to the left and saw *two* more suns! Both purple, though slightly paler, and streaked with crimson. No wonder it was warm.

A raspy noise behind him made Jerry break out in a cold sweat. Thinking he was about to be attacked he spun round, then relaxed as he saw a Chad-sized Pastinacean in a pea-green outfit that matched her hair clump, sitting with her back to the far wall under a bank of dials and levers. She made the noise again and Jerry recognised it as the rock-on-cheese-grater laugh.

'You laughing at me?' asked Jerry.

'Doesn't everyone?' She wandered over, waving a claw at his legs, arms and face.

'You look funny without scales, your ears are weird and so's your hair.'

'At least it's not green.'

'At least it's not stringy. Do you know your name?'

'So, you're finished with the insults?'

'For now. Do you? Know your name?'

'Yup. How 'bout you?'

'I'm Clacket Layne. That's Clacket and Layne. Never just call me Clacket. Theydon saw you when he helped Rashila Jannan install their new Infoscope, so I know you're JerryPatterson. In case you're only pretending to know your name.'

'Thanks for the reminder, Clacket Layne.' She was a complete flakehead but wasn't coming across as dangerous. 'And just call me Jerry – Patterson's the family name.'

'Layne's the family name,' Clacket Layne grabbed her tail and started scratching the tip. 'But I use both because it takes longer to say so you have to think about me longer while you say it.' She gestured with her tail tip, from Jerry's neck to knees. 'Did Gilpin Carney dress you like that?'

The one thing she could have laughed at and hadn't. Go figure. 'No. I borrowed it off Chad. I fell in their mud pool.'

'Wallow pool.'

'Whatever.' Jerry pointed at his muddy clothes. 'I'm trying to find a washing machine.'

More tail tip scratching. 'On the roof? Why didn't you look in the kitchen? That's where we keep them, in the kitchen. That's where they are.'

Did she think he was an utter twonk? 'I've looked in the kitchen.'

'Keep your eyes open next time.' Clacket Layne changed claws and started scratching the other side of her tail tip.

'Do you have to do that?' It was making Jerry feel itchy.

'Yes. It helps me forget I'm not Bonded.' Furious scratching.

'Right,' said Jerry, feeling some kind of response was called for.

'I hate talking about it, but if you're going to nag . . .' And she was off. 'I used to be Bonded but his family moved away: his name was Carlton Ogden – Carlton and Clacket go well together don't they, but they'll never get a chance now, come and live with me?'

'What? Er, sorry – I can't.'

'I shouldn't have asked; you belong to Chad Jannan.' She sighed heavily.

'I don't belong to anyone!' snapped Jerry.

'Hurrah! So you can live with me.' Clacket Layne dropped her tail. 'See? I'm so pleased, I've stopped scratching.'

'Clacket Layne, I can't live with you – the Jannans invited me first.'

'They didn't invite you, they bought you 'cos they're rich,' Clacket Layne corrected primly. 'When they get bored with you, which won't take long, you can live with me. And I won't sell you, even though we're poor and could trade Theydon in for a better model with the money and I might get cleverer and find another Bonded partner. I'd never do that. Oh no.'

Before Jerry could respond Clacket Layne was heading for the door. 'See you around, Jerry, not Patterson.'

'Wait!' Jerry called. 'I'll come with you.'

'You won't,' said Clacket Layne, activating the door with her foot. 'If you're with me, someone will notice and tell Theydon I went out without him.'

'Really?' Jerry couldn't believe she wasn't old enough to go out on her own. 'OK, but can you tell me how I get back to the Jannans'?'

'Yes.' Clacket Layne paused in the doorway, her snout wrinkling with concentration as she thought for a long moment. 'Take the same route you used to get here, only backwards.' With a flash of pea-green, she was gone.

Jerry wondered whether you could strangle a Pastinacean

with its own tail. What a dipstick! Pausing briefly to stamp the view into his memory, Jerry grabbed his clothes then set off on what he was certain was going to be a very lengthy search for his temporary home.

*

'Update!' Morton barked, startling Rashila who hadn't heard her walk over, so intent had she been on the live feed as if willing it to offer her more than an empty, pet-free dwelling.

'Gale's left Chad with Naish and gone to scan the market area. She told them . . .'

Morton held up a claw. 'Don't burden me with detail.'

'Of course, Director. I'm sorry.' Rashila wondered whether she'd get anything right today. 'Gale will message as soon as she has information.'

'You'd better chute home in case she can't find Jerry so you can be with Chad when he returns from his Social Session.'

'Are you sure? There's so much to do here,' said Rashila, preferring to stay put and let Gale handle that particular situation. But Morton gave her such a vicious stare Rashila went to her desk and started packing her briefcase.

'I shall expect you to work twice as hard tomorrow,' said Morton, 'to repay my generosity at letting you leave early two days running.'

'I always try to work twice as hard, Director,' Rashila replied, shutting down her Infoscope.

Morton sighed with relief as her assistant finally left the lab. At least now if anything bad had happened to Jerry, she'd be free to experiment with the molecular scrambler to try and source a suitable replacement.

*

Ever since he was old enough to understand he was Bonded to Rashila, Harchi had longed for the day his wife would meet him from the chute after work. But in all the years they'd been Fully Bonded it had never happened. Not once. Not even when he'd asked.

When Chad was a toddling Podder, Gale would sometimes walk him to the chute to meet Harchi. He used to love the way Chad would trip over the tail he hadn't quite mastered yet in his rush for a hug. Then as Chad grew older and Gale increased the complexity of his timetable, he no longer had the time to meet his father.

The pinch of disappointment each afternoon was so familiar now Harchi barely noticed it. But he never gave up hope. And today as the chute docked, Harchi's patience was finally rewarded when he stepped into the hallway and saw his pet rounding the bend towards him.

'Harchi!' cried Jerry, his stretchy skin changing shape to accommodate a big smile.

Harchi was so thrilled that the sight of him had given Jerry such pleasure, he almost dropped his briefcase and scooped him up in a hug. Then anxious about non-scaled alien scoopability, Harchi contented himself with an equally chirpy rejoinder of 'Jerry!'

'Are you going home?' asked Jerry, falling into step beside him.

'Yes,' said Harchi, his tail lowering slightly as he realised Jerry's trip to the chute was obviously unplanned. Ungrateful old scaler! Planned or not, there was no denying how pleased Jerry had been to see him. What if he trained his pet to meet him every day?

Harchi had a sudden thought: 'Who let you out on your own?'

'Chad and Gale went to Gilpin's.' Jerry showed his muddy clothes. 'And I was looking for a washing machine.'

Harchi's ears flopped. He'd never train Jerry to meet him if he hadn't the intelligence to find a clothes cleaner in a kitchen. 'I see.'

'I ended up on the roof – it's a blinding view!'

Disappointment turned to alarm. 'You didn't touch my weather gauges, did you?'

'I didn't touch a thing Harchi, I swear. Are you a Weather Man, then?'

Harchi didn't know what a Weather Man was, but Jerry was expressing an interest where no one ever had before so he wasn't about to put him off by asking questions. 'I'm a Senior Technician at the Weather Enhancement Unit,' he said, by way of an answer.

*

'Senior Technician!' Jerry whistled, impressed. 'What d'you do?'

'Oh, nothing much,' said Harchi. 'Basically, it's my job to make sure the weather's always warm and sunny.'

Harchi glanced down to savour the last flicker of interest in his small companion's eyes, before the familiar bored glaze set in. And his chest puffed with pride as he saw Jerry staring up at him, eyes wide with wonder.

'Woah!' Jerry's voice hummed with awe. 'You know how to change the *weather*?'

Harchi's chest was so inflated, he could hardly manage the nod.

'If you knew how to do that where I come from, they'd treat you like a god!'

'Sorry Jerry, "agodd" isn't translating.' Harchi guessed it was something good, but he badly wanted to hear it out loud.

'Harchi, my friend . . .' Jerry leant across and took Harchi's case, '. . . a god is like someone, no, well, it's not really a person actually, although sometimes it is, but I mean, um, a god is someone – or -thing – who everyone worships and fights over and, er, oh, I've got it! . . . a god is the most important being in the whole wide world!'

'No!' Kaye may have charged a scandalous amount for this pet, but Harchi knew at that moment he'd been worth it.

Jerry was nodding. 'Oh yeah. Nobody knows how to change the weather.'

'How curious!'

'One minute it's sunny, next it's raining, then it's windy, hailstones, snowing, thunder, lightning, fog, sometimes all at once and . . .'

Harchi couldn't follow the untranslatable torrent of words, but it didn't matter. He owned a pet who was interested in weather! No, better yet – Harchi owned a pet who was interested in weather *and* admired him. Was there a luckier creature on the whole of Pastinare? Harchi beamed down at Jerry who chattered away beside him, pausing only to turn and grin up at him as he felt Harchi's hand rest lightly on his shoulder.

*

Rashila was mixing some sour tea when she heard the entry portal activate. Hurrying out of the kitchen expecting to find Gale – at best with Jerry, at worst with bad news – Rashila was surprised to see Naish hover in with Chad and Gilpin.

'What's wrong, Rashila-ma? Why aren't you at work?' asked Chad anxiously.

'I'm fine, son,' said Rashila, giving him a hug while she tried to think what to say next. It wasn't meant to happen like this, Gale was supposed to be here. 'I came home early, that's all.'

'I conclude from your presence, Rashila Jannan,' whirred

Naish, 'and Gale leaving Social Session early to perform a confidential errand for you, that this is a family matter. Once I have been thanked for escorting Chad home after his Fossic failed to appear at the appropriate time, Gilpin and I will leave.'

'Thank you for bringing Chad home, Naish,' said Rashila.

'So where's your famous pet then, Chad?' asked Gilpin, looking around.

The moment Rashila had been dreading.

'He'll be here somewhere. Jerry? Jerry! Here, boy!' called Chad, peering into his quarters.

'Perhaps he's not bright enough to come when you call him?' taunted Gilpin.

''Course he is,' said Chad. 'He's probably using his litter tray.'

'Is he, Rashila?' asked Gilpin.

Rashila couldn't bring herself to answer.

'Has something happened to Jerry?' Chad grabbed Rashila's arm, fear creeping into his voice. 'Is that why you're home?'

Rashila was about to explain when the entry portal activated and Gale hovered in. At last, help was at hand!

'I was unable to locate JerryPatterson,' she announced.

*

Jerry's memories of his father were so vague, he could barely remember his face without a photo. Nor did he waste much

114

time trying. Apart from the odd scrawled postcard or naff birthday card without so much as a pound coin taped into it, there'd been no father figure in Jerry's life for years. And he refused to miss what he'd never had.

Now, strolling along the hallways with Harchi as they bunnied on about the weather, Jerry let a sliver of a thought prick his mind; about what a blast it would have been growing up with a laid-back dad like Harchi. Or any dad at all. Slam! Clunk! Lock! So not going there.

Jerry tuned back into the conversation. They'd been through drizzle and downpours and moved on to thunderstorms. Harchi had been so bug-eyed with wonder at a species who'd put up with the inconvenience of not knowing when or where it was going to rain, that Jerry decided to save hail, fog and snow for another time.

Ordinarily Jerry couldn't care less about the weather. You looked out of the window and there it was. But once Harchi said he knew how to change it? Man! Jerry was into that big time – and the way Harchi was so totally blown away by everything he said.

A couple of bends back Jerry had returned Harchi's case to him, the better to provide a full-on demonstration, complete with leaps, gestures and sound effects of thunder and lightning. Harchi was just getting his head around the concept of wellie boots, when they both cracked up laughing as they realised they'd walked past their front door.

As they retraced their steps, Jerry began a (somewhat patchy) explanation of lightning conductors, while Harchi activated the swish point. The pair of them sailed into the flat deep in conversation, which shallowed, then trickled and dried as they saw Rashila, Chad, Gilpin, Gale and Naish lined up, staring at them.

With the speed of calculation required of such situations, Jerry checked for allies, noting the first stare as hostile, second as relief with a worry top, third didn't care and the last two, metallic. Not good odds for a rescue.

Rashila kicked off the interrogation with Gale providing back-up grief, while Chad chipped in with some, 'I'm so pleased you're home/safe/are you all right?'

The only way to recover was to attack. Jerry was about to wave his muddy clothes around and throw a how-dare-you-make-me-wear-a-tunic-dress hissy fit, when Harchi stepped in front of him, holding up a claw for silence. The others were so surprised they obeyed.

'Jerry came to meet me at the chute,' stated Harchi, looking at Rashila as if daring her to challenge him on this unspoken topic.

'Perhaps you'd be good enough to inform Gale next time, Husband,' replied Rashila carefully, 'to save us all a lot of worry.'

'Of course, Wife,' said Harchi. 'I'm sorry to have caused alarm.'

The sliver of Jerry's previous father-thought turned into a

116

wedge. Harchi had stepped into the firing line for him. What a guy!

'Yes sorry, everyone,' said Jerry, appearing from behind his living shield.

Rashila watched Harchi hand the muddy clothes to Gale and tell her to clean them, thinking that Chad wasn't the only one whose behaviour was being effected by the new pet.

*

Morton observed the reunion with mixed feelings. On the one claw at least, now Jerry was back the research could carry on uninterrupted. On the other, she couldn't stifle a pang of regret as she thought of the molecular scrambler hidden at the back of her wardrobe.

CHAPTER TWELVE

Chad took the bundle of sweet sticks from the cupboard and broke one off for Jerry, who was about to grab it when Gilpin snatched it away.

'Chad! He'll think you're rewarding him for going out on his own.'

'I'm rewarding him for coming back, Gilpin,' he told her patiently.

'Like he's going to understand the difference?' she snapped.

'Like he understands you now,' said Jerry loudly.

'He understands,' said Chad, breaking off another stick and holding it out to Jerry as he asked in a mummy voice: 'What do we say?'

'Don't treat me like a moron?' supplied Jerry helpfully, seizing the stick and munching it with a grimace at Gilpin.

She tutted. 'He'll be impossible to train if you keep spoiling him like that.'

Jerry felt a stab of anger as he saw Chad's ears flop.

'Actually Gilpin, Chad's a brilliant trainer he's already taught me a trick.'

'Let's see it then,' challenged Gilpin and Jerry tried not to smile as Chad went peak-eared in panic.

'Sure. Chad, give me a number between one and five.'

Light dawned, ears relaxed. Go Chad! 'Um . . . five?'

'Five it is!' Jerry turned to Gilpin. 'Madam, before your very eyes I will demonstrate that I know how to count to five.'

'Chad! You've taught him to count? I am *so* impressed!' gushed Gilpin.

'Well, it was nothing really, I . . .'

Jerry lifted his foot like a prancing horse and slammed it down. 'One!'

'Shshshsh,' Gilpin ordered Chad. 'He's started!'

Stamp. 'Two!'

'Harchi, look at this – Chad's taught Jerry a trick,' Gilpin called into the living area.

Stamp. 'Three!'

'Well done, Chad,' said Harchi, rushing into the kitchen.

'Don't distract Jerry, he's counting,' Gilpin told Harchi importantly.

Stamp. 'Four!'

'Rashila! Come and see Jerry count!' shouted Harchi, eager for her to join in.

'No,' came the barked refusal. Everyone pretended they hadn't heard.

Jerry paused, listening to the imaginary drum roll for his big finish.

'Oh,' came Harchi's groan, 'is he stuck? How many's he doing?'

'Five,' whispered Chad.

'Don't help him!' hissed Gilpin.

Gale hovered in with Jerry's dirty clothes, shoved them into what he'd taken for a microwave, clawed some buttons on a keypad, then hovered out again.

'Why's she put my clothes in the microwave?' cried Jerry, running over to the machine.

'It's all right.' Chad ran to reassure his pet. 'It's a clothes cleaner. What's a microwave?'

'I knew he couldn't count,' Gilpin confided to Harchi quietly.

'He was probably nervous with everyone watching,' said Harchi, disappointed their pet had messed up the trick in front of a non-family member. Still, he hadn't done badly, considering. Maybe the chute meet was a possibility, after all?

Harchi and Gilpin went over to join Chad and Jerry in time to catch the end of his explanation about microwaves and cookers.

'You set fire to your food?' Chad gasped as three sets of ears and tails raced for the ceiling.

The guinea-pig diet Jerry had been subjected to suddenly made sense. He launched into the difference between cooking and chucking your grub on a bonfire and was heading for a detour on barbeques, when a pinger sounded on the cleaner and Gale hovered in and removed Jerry's mud-free, immaculately folded, trousers and polo shirt. His brain was so fried at the impossibility he could barely mumble 'thank you' as she handed him his clothes.

'I . . . I think I'll go and change,' said Jerry, wandering off to the plumbing suite in a daze, escorted by humiliation as he heard Harchi, Chad and Gilpin mark his departure with surround-sound, rock-on-cheese-grater laughter.

*

Jerry stayed in the plumbing suite until he figured enough time had passed for everyone to have stopped laughing. It wasn't that he minded people laughing at him – when *he* was the one actively encouraging it. But unprovoked 'isn't the dumb alien funny' laughter made him want to smash something expensive. (And he'd be easing up on his Speccy Bates material in future, which up till now had been Jerry's banker for getting AJ and his mates going if he was pitching for a quick laugh.)

Even if the others hadn't stopped smirking Jerry was determined to front it out, because he needed to talk to Rashila about getting him home. He was just praying she'd calmed down over him going walkabout.

Wandering into the living area, Jerry saw the Jannans chatting at the table as they ate dinner. Thanks for waiting, people. Gale hovered over with a dish of brightly coloured roots and leaves. As he went to take it from her she bent to

121

place it on the floor by the counter separating the kitchen from the living area and hovered away.

'You just kissed your tip goodbye,' called Jerry, picking up the dish. Going over to the table, he sat next to Chad and started listening for a gap in the conversation so he could leap in and talk to Rashila.

'Get down!' snarled Rashila, so fiercely, the first root froze on its way to Jerry's mouth.

'But I . . .' was all he managed, before she barked at Chad.

'Remove your pet, immediately!'

'Oh, *please*, Mother, he wants to be with us! Can't he . . . ?'

'We do not feed animals at the table,' growled Rashila. Jerry saw Harchi shake his head at Chad.

'Sorry, Jerry,' said Chad, standing up and putting a claw on Jerry's arm.

'Forget it,' said Jerry, shaking Chad's claw off. 'I can take a hint.'

'Did something happen at work today, Wife?' Jerry heard Harchi ask as he headed for Chad's room. 'You never did say why you'd come home early.'

'I don't always have to work late, you know,' she grunted.

'Of course not, and what a pleasure it was to see you, wasn't it Chad?'

'Definitely! Are you going to do it more often, Rashila-ma?' asked Chad.

122

'We'll see.' Jerry knew an adult 'no' when he heard one . . . 'Now eat your leaves before they wilt.' . . . and I'm changing the subject, so consider the topic off-limits.

Jerry went to sit on the floor in the far corner between the wall and the side of Chad's desk so he could see if anyone came in, and thought about what Rashila had said. As a black-belt blagger, Jerry could spot an amateur blag forty metres down an unlit mine-shaft, wearing blinkers. It was obviously very unusual for Rashila to get home early, so why didn't she have a good reason for it?

He suddenly realised she'd never said anything about him wearing Chad's top either which, given the way Gale had reacted to it, he'd expected her to go off on one about. So Rashila had started behaving out of character around the time Jerry had gone out. Coincidence? I don't think so, Your Honour. But how had she known he wasn't here?

Jerry mulled it over, while he worked his way through yet another mystery dish of crunchy roots and leaves. He was having dinner but, at 08:23, his watch still made it yesterday morning.

What was Mum doing? Having a bacon sarnie as the house was quiet now they'd all gone to school, or sitting white-faced by the phone 'cos Jerry had been missing for two days? Could this time-fold pump thing be the real deal? It was so fantastically impossible, it might be true. He desperately wanted it to be. Anything else was too painful.

123

'Hello!' Chad broke into Jerry's thoughts, heading over with a mug. 'I mixed some sour tea for you to try.'

'Thanks.' Jerry smiled as he took the mug, then waved it over the plate in his lap. 'It'll help wash down the rest of the allotment.' . . . ottment.

Jerry was startled to hear his own voice whispering back at him, like a time-delay repeat on a dodgy phone line. He shook his head to clear it.

'Are you OK?' Chad was staring at him.

'Think so. I heard a weird noise in my head.' . . . oise in my head.

As Jerry stopped talking his tongue touched his bottom teeth and his head jerked back at the heat pulsing off the orthodontist's wire.

'What's wrong?' Chad grabbed the mug Jerry shoved back at him as he scrambled up, mouth open, tongue held rigidly clear of his teeth, sending the half-eaten dish of roots and leaves tumbling to the floor. 'Are you ill?'

Jerry forced out a 'No!' and Chad flinched, so Jerry knew he'd shouted. But in his head . . . the gift of silence. He risked a quick touch of the wire with his tongue. Normal mouth temperature. Jerry let his tongue rest there longer. Houston, we are good to go.

'Sorry, Chad.' He grinned sheepishly. 'Couldn't get that noise out of my head, but it's gone.' Jerry took the mug back. 'I'll try that tea now.'

Chad stooped to put the spilt food back in the dish.

'Don't worry, I'll do that in a minute,' Jerry told him, embarrassed Chad was clearing up after him.

'That's OK, you enjoy your tea,' Chad insisted, carrying on with his task.

Jerry hadn't realised how much he fancied a cuppa until Chad mentioned tea. He'd clocked the fact that it was sour, but he was a passionate hot-and-sour souper and couldn't get enough of those 'warhead' sweets that made your eyes squinch up when you sucked them.

Lifting the mug to his lips Jerry chucked back a huge slug, eagerly anticipating the flow of warmth awash with interesting flavours. The arctic cold oral slap delivered as the washing-up liquid with an ear-wax twist mugged his taste buds, was so monumentally vile that Jerry sprayed the entire mouthful in a foamy blue arc over Chad as he crouched on the floor, gathering the scattered supper.

*

Morton was trying to analyse Jerry's appeal to Chad. She'd started a list with the aim, when she had enough data, of using the key elements to form the basis of the sensational Fossic personality programme she was going to write.

Struggling to find an un-knotted piece of hair to twirl as she tried to decide whether 'novelty value' was a valid addition, Morton's claw poised mid-tangle at the sound of the Jannans' arrival alert coming from the live feed.

Strange. It wasn't Adult Social Session night so it couldn't be Gilpin Carney's parents. And when Morton had been watching earlier no one had said anything to suggest the anticipation of untimetabled visitors.

By the time Morton had hurried across the lab to see who it was, the Jannans were grouped in the living area, a trio of surprised ears and tails. Which became a quartet when Morton saw the visitors.

Theydon, heavily prompted by Clacket Layne, was formally presenting Gale with what Morton could only guess was a fruit carving, since the dripping, knobbly green lump on the plate failed to provide even a hint of a clue as to what it was supposed to be.

Morton decided that next time Theydon came in for repair she'd brief the workshop to disable his hover mechanism and tell the Lanes it was irreparable. They'd scrape up the money for a replacement somehow. Any Fossic who'd permit an unBonded female to visit the dwelling of a Bonded male uninvited, was fit only for scrap.

Theydon was still blundering on. '. . . accept this unworthy creation in honour of—'

'—your new pet JerryPatterson,' finished Clacket Layne impatiently.

Whichever angle Morton bent her head she couldn't see how that chunk of butchered fruit represented the alien. And judging by the silence from the Jannans, they felt the same way. Gale was about to usher the visitors out when Chad walked over and took the plate from her.

'Thank you, Theydon. Thank you, Clacket Layne,' he

126

said, smiling at them. 'What an interesting representation. How kind of you to have gone to so much trouble.'

Morton adored moments like these when her brilliance was reflected back at her. What a truly outstanding programming job she'd done on the Phase 12s for Gale to have taught Chad to be so polite.

'You are welcome, Chad Jannan,' Theydon stated gruffly, his vocal chip showing his age. 'Clacket Layne, we should be goin—'

'Sooooo pleased you like it, Chad!' the pushy Podder burst in. 'It was my idea. Not that I've ever seen your pet, but Theydon got a good look at him yesterday. His legs fell off on the way up here so I ate them to be tidy but it doesn't make any difference does it – not Theydon's legs, though they fall off sometimes – Jerry's. Where is he by the way?'

Chad was about to answer, when his pet appeared through the archway to the plumbing suite. Morton already had 'friendly' on the list, but decided to underline it after she saw the way Jerry smiled and went straight over to Clacket Layne. He obviously wasn't hostile to strangers.

'Hi, Cl—'

'Isn't he an ugly little thing?' trilled Clacket Layne, grabbing Jerry's jaw in her claw, turning his head this way and that to get a better look at him.

'Don't be too rough!' warned Harchi, seeing the alarm on Chad's face.

'Sorry, Harchi,' she said, releasing Jerry who stared at her

127

in surprise, rubbing his jaw. 'I'm Clacket Layne,' she told him. 'That's Clacket *and* Layne, never just Clacket.' She raised her voice. 'I. Understand. You. Can. Speak?'

Jerry gave it a beat before answering. 'Yes. I. Can. Whacko.'

Morton had the fleeting impression they'd already met, except that was impossible. Yet she knew to call him Jerry, not JerryPatterson. She was probably just being lazy as usual. If Clacket Layne had met Jerry before, she'd never talk to him as if he barely had the intelligence of a snebbit.

Theydon was trying to stop the never-ending stream of prattle Clacket Layne was inflicting on Chad and Jerry, and get her to leave. Rashila expressed her irritation by marching into her quarters and Harchi wandered off to the Infoscope, but she refused to take the hint.

Finally, Gale snatched the plate from Chad and shot into the kitchen where she flicked the fruit lump into the bin. Then she returned the unwashed plate to Theydon, where he'd gone to hover against the archway wall, as a pointed reminder the visit was over.

'Clacket Layne . . .' he rasped, pointlessly. Morton smiled as Gale barged between the unBonded Podder and Chad with such determination, he and Jerry were forced to take a few steps backwards.

'Clacket Layne,' beeped Gale, in a voice which brooked no argument, 'this visit is terminated. Return to your dwelling.'

'On my way,' she replied sweetly, before bending around Gale's left side to grin at Chad: 'Good to see you. Don't be a stranger!' Then switched sides to wave at Jerry: 'Enjoy the fruit, alien. And let me know when they're bored with you.'

Clacket Layne strolled over to Theydon, whacked him on the arm with her claw, said 'Let's go then, if you're in such a hurry,' and carried on to the portal. A clang of metal made her turn round to find Theydon's claw rocking to a stop on the floor.

Chad and Jerry hurried to help Theydon, while Clacket Layne laughed her ridges off at him for not screwing his claw back in properly after he'd finished carving.

Jerry picked up the offending limb and held it out to Chad. 'You'd better do the honours!' Gale snatched it and thrust it at Theydon, beeping: 'Even a Phase4 knows how to screw its own claw in.'

'How come his is on the floor, then?' asked Jerry.

Morton peered closer at the screen as the pet's face suddenly contorted and he started hitting himself on the ear and flapping his tongue about. Clacket Layne stopped laughing to stare wide-eyed at Jerry, until Gale barged her to the portal trailed by Theydon, struggling to re-screw his claw in and hover at the same time.

'Is it the noises again?' Chad was asking Jerry, anxiously. Morton couldn't think what he meant. Jerry nodded and let Chad lead him to the nearest chair and sit him down.

Harchi glanced across from the Infoscope. 'Chad, you know your mother doesn't—'

'He's not well, Harchi-pa.'

Jerry sat staring into space, his mouth open, repeatedly touching the inside of his bottom front teeth with the tip of his tongue.

'What's the matter with him?' Harchi asked Chad, rushing over.

'I don't know. It happened earlier too. He said he heard noises in his head.'

Morton's hearts sank. Don't say her research subject was mentally unstable? A picture of the molecular scrambler flashed into her mind, giving her enough comfort to refocus on what was going on.

'Should I loop through to the vet?'

'I don't know! What d'you think?'

'Chad Jannan,' Gale beeped fiercely, shooting over from the portal and hovering to a halt beside him. 'Remove your pet from the furniture immediately!'

'Leave him alone, Gale! He's ill,' roared Chad, who hadn't noticed Rashila reappear from her quarters.

Morton sat up, ear tips high with surprise. A Podder raising his voice to his Fossic? Extraordinary! What was it about this creature that generated such protective instincts in his owner so fast?

Chad jumped when he heard Rashila snap her claws behind him.

'You dare roar at Gale?' she growled, ears flat, tail swishing as she came to face him.

'I wasn't roaring . . . I was . . . explaining,' said Chad trying to keep his voice steady. 'Jerry doesn't feel well.'

'Better now, thanks,' said Jerry and raced off, not that anyone noticed.

'And he'll go straight back to the shop if he makes you forget the manners Gale taught you!' barked Rashila in Chad's face.

'I'm sorry, Mother, honestly,' said Chad, backing away. 'I didn't mean to!'

'Yet you insult her further by apologising to me?' Rashila rasped at Chad, who turned to his Fossic, ears and tail flopped in shame.

'I'm sorry, Gale,' he murmured in a low voice. 'I was worried about Jerry.'

'You were wrong. You have apologised. Subject closed,' Gale whirred, then whisked Chad off to the wallow room, presumably to get ready for bed. Harchi opened his mouth to speak to Rashila, who growled at him then stormed off to her quarters. He sighed heavily as he lumbered back to his Infoscope.

Morton felt like skipping back to hers. But she kept it to a sprightly walk, joyfully analysing the Jannans' collective misery as she went, deciding how best to dissect it so it would serve her Upgrade Project in the most effective way.

*

131

Chad found his mother in her quarters sitting on her chair, foot braced against the desk, painting her toe-claws with long sweeps of the brush. She'd already done the middle and outer ones blue and had just started doing the other two silver.

'I love that smell!' said Chad, sniffing the air.

Rashila lifted her snout and sniffed. 'Always reminds me of freshly dug perrin roots,' she smiled. 'Are you stepping to bed now?'

'Yes.'

'I'd scratch your ridges, only my claws are still wet,' said Rashila, waving at him.

'You can owe me one,' said Chad, but he made no move to leave.

'What's up, Chaddy?' asked Rashila, putting the claw-polish brush back in the tub.

'It's Jerry, Rashila-ma,' said Chad, turning to check the archway to make sure no one was listening. 'I'm worried the voices in his head might be his memory coming back, then he'll know I've lied to him.'

'I had the same thought, so I ran an Infoscope check. There's very few cases of hyperdrive trauma listed, but none of them ever regained the memory.' Rashila smiled to see the relief flood Chad's face.

'Can I ask you something else?'

'Of course, son.'

'I already asked Gale, but she said I had to ask someone with a fully functional brain.'

'Really? If she couldn't answer it, I'm not sure I'll be able to. Go on.'

'If it's wrong to lie, how come it's all right to lie to Jerry?'

'Because he's an animal, Chad, and it's for his own good.'

'So it's all right to lie to animals?'

'Well, you're unlikely to find another one who'd be able to understand you were lying, as Jerry might. But, yes.'

'He keeps asking about the time-fold overlay pump – and using a scrambler to go home. And I hate lying to him, even though you say it's all right.'

'Chaddy, he'll never settle in here unless he believes in it.'

'So what should I say next time he asks?'

'That it's too dangerous to risk—'

'He doesn't care.'

'—and we'd have no way of knowing whether he got there. The Committee would never grant a scrambler licence for an experiment where the scientist couldn't assess the results.'

Chad was nodding, but he didn't look much happier.

'None of those are lies, son.'

'They're all built on one though, aren't they, Mother?' he said sadly.

'It's a lie for kindness and it's much better for all of us if Jerry's happy here. You can see that, can't you?'

Chad nodded and left his mother to finish her claws. As he padded next door to his quarters he hoped Jerry would be asleep, and gave a sigh of relief as he tiptoed through the archway and saw him curled up in bed. Lowering his own bed to step into it, Chad jumped as Jerry's voice floated through the darkness.

'I'm sorry if I got you into trouble before. I didn't mean to.'

'I know. It's been a big day for you.' Chad crouched down beside him. 'Any more voices?' he asked, trying to sound unconcerned.

'All quiet,' Jerry grinned, tapping the side of his head.

'Good,' said Chad, standing up again. 'Let's hope it stays that way. Good night.'

'Chad?' said Jerry and Chad's hearts beat faster, fearing what was coming. 'Your mum – she knows all about molecular scramblers, right?'

'She's a leading expert in the field.'

'Great!' Chad could have clawed himself for saying that. 'So will you talk to her for me tomorrow, about getting home?'

'Jerry, it's not that simple—'

'Please, Chad! I don't want to be rude, I mean, it's nice here and everything, but I've got to get back to my family. You can understand that, can't you?'

'I can understand it, Jerry. That doesn't mean she can make it happen.'

'She has to! There must be a way to—'

'No, Jerry! Enough. I can't talk about this any more,' said

Chad firmly, closing the bed seal and activating the hoist to lift it off the ground. 'Good night.'

'G'night.'

Jerry turned over and checked his watch in the dim light. It still said 08:23. He'd give it a rest for now. And he felt sorry for Chad in a way. It must be like being given a giant talking puppy, who'd only yap on about how much it wanted to go back to the litter.

CHAPTER THIRTEEN

Harchi was mixing sour tea while he chomped nibrim pellets, imagining how impressed his boss was going to be when he saw Harchi's new idea in action. Was it his idea? Or was it Jerry's? As a weather technician, Harchi was no stranger to the concept of rain. He had it on a running repeat with sunny-breaks blend over the Plantations. And a three bar in seven setting over the North Quadrant Mountains to keep water supplies high.

Even so, there was no denying it was Jerry who'd alerted him to the possibility of having different types of rain. But who was it with the imagination and technical ability to apply such information? Senior Technician Harchi Jannan, that's who.

Amazing to think a spur of the moment pet purchase had bumped Harchi into seeing the potential in the title: Weather *Enhancement* Unit. He could almost hear the gasp of amazement as he told his boss, 'If the weather's always the same, that's normal, not enhancement. Adding value to the

weather by entertaining our fellow Pastinaceans with it –
that's enhancement, Gornish,' he'd say.

Harchi took a mug of sour tea in to Rashila and watched
his wife as she hung there sleeping, enjoying the luxury of
looking at her, without seeing anger in her eyes. Sensing a
presence, Rashila stirred then hurtled awake at the shock of
finding her husband dressed for work while she was still in
bed.

'It's all right, you're not late,' Harchi calmed Rashila as
she quickly lowered her bed and stepped out of it.

'Is everything . . . ?'

'Nothing's wrong.' He handed her the mug of sour tea.
'I'm going in early to work on a project, that's all.'

Harchi decided he'd go in early for the rest of his life if
that was the depth of feeling it stirred up in Rashila, who
reached up to scratch his ridges and gave him the warmth of
smile she usually reserved for Chad.

'Work hard, Husband.'

His hearts were too full to manage more than a nod.

*

Jerry must have overslept. His watch showed 08:25, which
he presumed was still time-fold overlay time especially as
there was no sign of Harchi or Rashila, and Chad and Gale
were already hard at work at the dining-room table. A pity.
Jerry was keen to carry on last night's going home conversation with Chad.

'Morning!' he called across to them, knowing it would annoy Gale.

'Morning, Jerry,' Chad replied, ignoring Gale's beep of annoyance to point at a dish on the floor near the kitchen. 'Gale's put your breakfast out.'

'Thanks, Gale,' said Jerry just to keep the interruption going, mumbling: 'And may you rust in hell for leaving it on the floor,' as he bent to pick up the dish.

'Hell does not translate. Fossics do not rust. And the Phase 12deluxe2 has the most sophisticated auditory chip on the market,' Gale whirred angrily. 'You will cease disrupting this Lesson Session.'

'You got it!' said Jerry cheerfully, heading back to Chad's room.

'Now!' beeped Gale.

Jerry waited till she'd started whirring at Chad again before poking his head back out of the archway to call, 'Catch you later, Chad!'

Jerry crunched his way through the regulation roots and leaves, trying to decide what to do. He switched on Chad's Infoscope, to see if he could find out anything about getting home, then felt like a total plank, when the screen flooded with spaghetti-tangle images. Duh! Pastinacean computer? Gonna be operating in Pastinacean, bonehead.

In the absence of any other form of entertainment, Jerry decided to do some laundry. Not even Andy wore the same pair of pants three days running. Slipping his pants and socks off, Jerry put his trousers back on and went to the kitchen. There was something full-blown manky about going commando in school trousers, but he didn't exactly have a choice.

Jerry put his socks and pants into the clothes cleaner, then stared at the keypad. It was covered in pictures and none of them made sense, so he jabbed a selection, in a rough attempt at copying the pattern he'd seen Gale use yesterday, then pressed the one on the bottom right, hoping it was 'start'. Result! The machine thrummed into life and by the time Jerry had snaffled a sweet stick from the cupboard, it had pinged to a finish.

Jerry's 'Holy cow!' as he opened the door was delivered with enough surprise for Gale and Chad to suspend their Lesson Session to come and see what had happened. Chad started snorting with laughter at the look on Jerry's face, as an avalanche of pants and socks poured from the clothes cleaner on to the mountain already covering his feet.

'You should ask me if you want clothes cleaned,' beeped Gale, barging in front of Jerry to claw the remaining socks and pants from the machine, before firmly closing the door.

'Then you'd have told me off for disturbing you,' snapped Jerry, hating the way Gale shoved him around. He turned to Chad, who'd stopped laughing when he heard Gale's tone. 'How did it do that?'

'First it carries out an intramolecular analysis,' Chad

began, delighted Jerry was taking an interest, 'to determine whether the fabric's monomeric or polymeric, then—'

'He is a pet: detailed explanations are pointless,' Gale interrupted. 'You set the machine to duplicate,' she informed Jerry, before ushering Chad back to the table.

'But are they clean?' Jerry called after them, horrified by the idea of being swamped with three-day old socks and pants.

'They have come from the clothes cleaner,' came Gale's reply, in a voice which left him in no doubt that for a talking pet, he was spectacularly dumb.

*

Harchi had never had so much fun at work. By the time he got to the Unit, he'd already ditched the idea of verbally presenting Jannan's Random Rain Scheme to Gornish. Why sell it short by describing it, when you could show it in all its glorious action? And he'd been hunched over his keyboard ever since, working out exactly what form that glorious action should take.

As Harchi planned the pilot an interesting pattern emerged, caused by the way he'd allocated varying weights of rain over different areas. (It reminded him of something, but he couldn't think what.) The higher the drops per fantarg of air setting, the darker the shadow – given extra depth because of the lines Harchi had drawn going the other way, to indicate frequency of rainfall.

All this was developed with the fun/surprise theme very

much in mind, and constant checks with the notes he'd made of the names and descriptions Jerry had given him. So downpours were heavier than showers, which lasted longer than drizzle, which occurred with greater frequency. Harchi's claws itched to key in some thunder and lightning, but he knew he should wait until Gornish shared his vision.

Harchi rotated his shoulders, to ease the stiffness in his neck. It was hard work being creative, but the aches and pains were worth it. Jannan's Random Rain Scheme. It would look good on a plinth if they ever built a statue to him. Nothing fancy, no more than life size. Erected in front of the Unit.

Pastinaceans would flock from every Quadrant to gaze up at his gilded self staring at the sky – arm out, palm up, waiting for the first drops. 'That's Harchi Jannan,' they'd whisper to their awestruck Podder, 'who gave us the pleasure of Random Rain.' But he was getting ahead of himself.

*

Jerry sat on his bed, balling socks into pairs, daydreaming of lugging the clothes cleaner home and earning a dosh mountain for Mum by flogging it to someone like Dyson. He was on stage at Speech Day, accepting a Guest Speaker's bouquet from Rachel Davis, and rubbing Barkow's nose in it for saying Jerry'd never amount to anything, when a sock ball he'd chucked on top of the pile rolled off again and carried on through the archway into the living area.

With a loud 'buurroop', Sneb jumped off the chair he'd been curled up in and dived on to the sock ball. Then he rolled back into the bedroom with it, biting and holding on with his front suckers, while biffing it with his three back paws, like Barclay did with her favourite catnip mouse.

Jerry grabbed another sock ball and threw it past Sneb. In a flash, he'd released the first to pounce and roll with the second. Jerry threw another. Same thing happened. When Jerry threw the fourth Sneb pounced, rolled, then flipped himself over again and with a 'buurrooop' flicked the ball at Jerry with his back legs.

Jerry knelt and chopped into its path with his hand, sending it tumbling back to Sneb, who purred, rolled and flicked. Jerry jumped up, laughing as he kicked it back. Sneb returned it, copying Jerry's footwork. The knitting was up for a game of footie!

*

Rashila was surprised at the twinge of ear-drooping jealousy she experienced, as she watched Sneb. He was chirruping with joy as he charged over the living area walls and across the ceiling, to drop on to the roundel of rolled-up foot coverings Jerry was kicking about for him before sending it back, then scrambling up the walls again. Sneb had never done anything like that with her. But then it had never occurred to her that it was an activity her pet might enjoy.

'What's wrong?'

'Nothing,' said Rashila, forcing her ears back up again, 'except a touch of anxiety about Jerry and Sneb disturbing Chad's Lesson Session.'

Morton stared at the screen, where Gale and Jerry were having a heated discussion. It was fascinating watching a pet take on a top-of-the-range Fossic.

'This is the fourth time I have told you to stop disturbing the Lesson Session!' beeped Gale angrily at Jerry.

'And after the third I told you I wouldn't make a noise, and I haven't,' he retorted.

'You are still physically active in our field of vision which is a distraction,' she insisted.

'So face to the left, we'll play down the right – everyone's happy,' stated Jerry.

'Negative.'

'You know, you should be thanking me, Gale.'

'Expand?'

'Pets need a lot of exercise and I'm exercising myself, which saves you the job. You can thank me later.' As if on cue, Sneb jumped on to Jerry's shoulder, a foot-covering roundel between his front suckers. 'Sneb says you can thank him later, too,' he added, tickling the creature's fur, who raised up on his hind legs to rub against the side of Jerry's head.

Morton smiled as the argument continued. 'Jerry's a skilled negotiator,' she said to her assistant, who clearly wasn't impressed.

'If it's a skill to have an answer for everything,' grunted Rashila, forgetting to hide her feelings, distracted as she was by Sneb's display of affection towards his enemy.

Morton felt her tail flick and realised what was annoying her. It wasn't Rashila's rudeness, which she intended to have a stern word about once the Upgrades were over. It was that Jerry was bonding with Sneb when he should be bonding with Chad.

'Message Gale and tell her to cancel today's Lesson Sessions; we need to see Chad in action with Jerry,' Morton ordered.

'But Director, he'll fall behind with his work!' exclaimed Rashila.

'Is that more important than us falling behind with ours?' barked Morton. 'There'll be time enough for Chad to get back to normal once the Project's complete.'

'Yes, Director,' sighed Rashila, worrying whether her family would ever be able to find their way back to normality.

CHAPTER FOURTEEN

Jerry lay on his bed, Sneb asleep in the crook of his knees. He was watching Chad who was perched on the edge of his desk, ears at half mast, absent mindedly scratching his tail tip. Not exactly the jumping-for-joy behaviour you'd expect from someone who'd just been given the day off school.

Chad suddenly realised Jerry was staring at him and dropped his tail as if he'd been caught doing something disgusting. Forcing himself to play the happy host, he smiled and stooped to roll a sock ball across the floor towards Jerry, nodding encouragingly.

'Sorry, Chad, I'm all done with the ball thing for now,' said Jerry, sitting up carefully so he didn't disturb Sneb. 'We could do something else, though.'

'What would you like to do?' asked Chad nervously, reminding Jerry of the type of kid Mum would arrange for him to go home with after school when he was little if she was on lates and Grandpa was busy. The Speccy Bates type. 'Nice boys,' she called them, desperate for him to pal up with one instead of grubbing around with the holey-jum-pered knee-scrapers he preferred.

'Let's look on the Infoscope and read up about molecular scramblers,' said Jerry.

'We won't be able to,' Chad replied.

'How d'you know?' asked Jerry suspiciously.

'It's such a sensitive subject, the Committee deny access to most people.'

'What about your mother?'

'She compiled the data that's available to those with access.'

'Brilliant! So will you talk to her for me when she gets home?'

'There's no point, Jerry. She's already told you there's nothing she can do.'

'But if I came here by molecular scrambler, I don't see why you can't use one to send me home again!'

'Because it's really complicated and I wish you'd stop talking about a subject neither of us knows anything about!' cried Chad.

'All right, all right! I'm sorry – I'll stop banging on about it,' said Jerry, realising he wasn't going to get anywhere with this for now. 'So . . . cancel my Infoscope idea – which makes it your turn to suggest something.' Chad's ears went from half mast to full droop. Now what? 'Look, we don't have to do anything if you don't want to,' Jerry told him.

146

'I would like to Jerry, really I would,' Chad rushed to assure him, 'but I've never had any untimetabled time before, so I'm not sure what to do with it.'

'What?' Jerry jumped up, scaring Sneb who hissed, then went back to sleep. Chad Had Never Had Untimetabled Time Before? Jerry's entire life revolved around untimetabled time. Revolved and depended on it. 'You can't be serious? What d'you do at weekends?'

Chad's brow-scales furrowed into a frown. 'Sorry Jerry, that's not translating.'

These guys didn't have weekends? What kind of nightmare world was this?

'What's wrong, Jerry? Is that bad?'

'Is it *bad*?' Jerry couldn't keep still, he was so agitated. 'It's ten galaxies beyond bad, pal! Weekends are as vital to life as breathing.'

'No!' gasped Chad, with washing-line ears.

'Oh yeah,' swaggered Jerry, all weekend-possession smugness swapped for a wince as Chad grabbed his arm.

'Teach me about weekends, Jerry,' he demanded urgently. 'I want to learn.'

'It's not a complicated concept, but it's an important one,' said Jerry, gently removing Chad's pincer grip and backing him up to sit on his desk again. He was about to start his lecture, when he realised with a jolt that if Chad didn't know what a weekend was, he wouldn't understand 'week' either.

147

Holding his left hand up, palm out, fingers to the ceiling, Jerry tapped his thumb and each finger in turn with the forefinger of his right hand.

'Yesterday, today, tomorrow, the day after and the day after that?'

Chad nodded, concentrating hard.

'One timetabled set of those, is called a week. Now, there's some untimetabled time in there too, but I don't want to confuse you at this stage. So, five timetabled ones equal a week. Then you get the next two off, completely untimetabled – and that's a weekend.'

'What happens with the three left over?'

'There aren't three left over. You just start another set of five.'

'But Jerry, if you get two off out of five, there must be another three left somewhere. Or d'you go on to a third hand?' Chad took Jerry's hands in his and counted digits, including his own. 'No, that doesn't work either, you'd still have three left.'

'Forget the finger-counting, Chad.' Jerry snatched his hand back. 'It's the theory of five days working and two days off that interests us here.'

'I see.' There was a pause. 'It's complicated, isn't it?'

'Complicated? To someone who can explain time-compression theory! How?'

'Setting aside the unresolved leftovers for now, which I'm still not happy about,' said Chad, warming to his theme, 'there's also the question of how you match up all the untimetabled time. I mean, what if mine doesn't tie in with Gilpin's? How would Gale and Naish schedule our Social Sessions?'

'Ah, but that's the clever bit, Chad. Everyone has the same week and weekend. And not just Podders – adults too. So everyone's working to the same schedule.'

Chad's tail hoiked so high in surprise, Jerry could have flown a flag from it.

*

'No wonder this species hasn't evolved beyond litter trays and fighting over food if they stop work for two days out of every seven,' snorted Morton, who'd drawn up a chair beside Rashila. She knew she should be getting on with other work, but there was something strangely gripping about watching Chad and Jerry's relationship develop before her very eyes.

'If he's telling the truth,' said Rashila.

'Use your brain,' rasped Morton. 'The idea's so ludicrous it has to be true.'

'I must do something to stop Jerry upsetting Chad with constant demands to go home.'

'Explaining the consequences more clearly would have been a start.'

'I made myself very clear, Morton. I'm sure he understood.'

'Proved by the fact he wants to risk his life returning to a hideously primitive planet.'

'I think it's a desire to return to his family rather than the planet that's driving him.'

'Spare me the amateur psychology, Rashila,' said Morton, going to answer a call that was looping through on her desk. 'You're a scientist, remember?'

Rashila carried on watching the screen, ear tips burning as she tried to control her anger. She heard Morton growl as she cut the loop, followed by a barked: 'Does she think I have nothing better to do with my time?'

'Bluhm?' asked Rashila, familiar with her boss's standard response to any call from the Chair of the Ministry Committee.

'Who else?' snapped Morton, angrily flicking her tail as she came and sat down again.

'We're rushed off our feet here, bang in the middle of Upgrades, and she loops through to say she wants to bring Conway in *again*.'

'Another glitch on his hover mechanism?'

'No – jolty elbow, apparently.' The 'apparently' was coated with sarcasm to show what Morton thought of owners who provided their own diagnoses.

'He's a Phase 9 – it was only a matter of time,' said Rashila.

'I booked him in for the morning.' Morton started watching the screen, but hadn't finished grumbling. 'And why does she keep coming in with him? You'd think she'd get a Ministry Fossic to do it.'

Rashila shrugged. 'Maybe it's her way of keeping in touch with the Bureau?'

Morton's head whipped round to face her assistant. 'D'you think Conway's an excuse, so she can spy on us?'

'Why would she want to spy on us?' asked Rashila, startled by the depth of feeling caused by her innocent remark.

'I've no idea,' bristled Morton, regretting she'd voiced the question aloud. 'Bluhm's a powerful creature; being devious is part of her make-up.'

*

Harchi knew some bosses didn't look kindly on employees sleeping at work but, as he'd frequently been forced to point out, the word 'sleep' gave the wrong impression. It was actually a Creative Thought Break. And as anyone creative would tell you, the key thing about creative thought is it flows more freely with your eyes shut.

Today, as Harchi awoke and peered at his Infoscope, he knew it had been time well spent. Before he'd begun to explore the depths of his CTB in detail, Harchi had still been struggling to recognise the picture hinted at by his Random Rain Scheme pilot plan. Now, with his head on one side and the benefit of sleep-blurred vision, he saw that with a few minor adjustments the weather patterns in front of him would look just like Rashila!

Swinging his feet off the desk, Harchi attacked his keyboard with enthusiasm. He swapped the downpour he'd programmed over the Dwellings Centre with the drizzle he'd allocated to the Marketplace and boosted the shower density over the Ministry buildings.

Studying the screen from various angles, Harchi felt that although he'd brought Rashila into sharper focus, something was missing. Some unidentifiable something that would turn his accidental pilot tribute into an instantly recognisable dedication to his wife.

A slow smile rippled Harchi's scales as he realised what it was. He clawed in a clutch of lightning flashes for Rashila's ridges and a medium thunderclap for her hair clump. It was a departure from his plan not to programme thunder and lightning until Gornish had approved, but the temptation was unignoreable. Harchi studied his work and saw that he'd managed to pinpoint Rashila's character as well as her looks. It was inspired. He'd really have earned that statue by the time the Scheme was running planet-wide.

Once that had happened, Harchi was going to set up Jannan Random Rain Scheme outlets in every Quadrant, where Pastinaceans would pay him (generously) to programme bursts of weather to represent their loved ones. But he was getting ahead of himself. First Harchi had to demonstrate the joy that was his masterpiece to Gornish.

*

There was nothing on Gale's hard drive that told her how to process untimetabled time. And she knew, because she'd scanned all her data banks searching for it. This had used up

152

a substantial chunk of the time she was researching how to fill, causing her to run a calculation through her probability chip to determine the likelihood of that scan having been a deliberate part of her programme.

From the three ding eleven fantarg score, Gale concluded it wasn't; then assessed it couldn't have been or she'd have had it logged on her data banks; although if she had, it would have negated the original purpose of its discovery. Gale terminated further processing along that line, as her sensors relayed the information that she'd dented the front of the chiller unit by repeatedly hovering into it.

Moving into the living area, Gale amplified her auditory chip to see if she could input further data by listening to the conversation between Chad and his pet that had been important enough to cancel Lesson Sessions.

Gale's circuits sparked as she realised JerryPatterson was instructing her Podder on the importance of having vast and regular bands of untimetabled time. It was as unthinkable as it was dangerous.

Gale would have terminated their conversation with extreme prejudice, except the instruction to allow it had come direct from Rashila Jannan. Gale assessed the only way she could continue to obey that instruction would be to occupy both her hard drive and outer casing. Then she realised with a beep if she did that until Gilpin and Naish arrived for Social Session, she would also have processed the untimetabled time.

Opening the internal storage unit in her lower section, Gale removed the extendable suction attachment and dust bag, running her timetable module as she did so to reallocate Chad's missed Lesson Sessions. A task which would be suitably lengthy, since it necessitated shunting all his remaining Lesson Sessions forward until he matured.

As the programme hummed through her hard drive, Gale dislodged her tail and clicked the dust bag attachment into its housing. Then she unscrewed her claw and replaced it with the suction attachment which she extended to its full length.

Cycling up to full power, Gale bent at the waist to connect attachment with floor, then hovered off at speed around the living area. As she re-timetabled Chad's education and sucked dust, the microscopic evidence of her industry hurtled up her arm and along some internal tubing to shoot from her rear into the air filled bag, bobbing from her tail hole like an angry white cloud.

*

Jerry sat in the plumbing suite, staring at the list he'd written in his homework diary.

NO: Music, TV, Films, Theatre, Radio, Sport, Books.

How could a race of aliens, who were so advanced they could fold time and control the weather, be missing out on all that entertainment? He'd had a hint of it yesterday when Chad told him they didn't have TV, but Jerry hadn't dreamt for a second he'd really meant it; just that they hadn't found a word that translated properly. The full horror was only revealed as he and Chad tried to get to grips with weekends – an idea that had totally knocked Chad sideways.

'So what do you do to use up all that free time?' he'd asked.

'I don't think you've quite grasped the principle, Chad,' Jerry told him, borrowing one of Barkow's favourite phrases, but dropping the sarcasm. 'It's not about "using it up", it's about *making it last*!'

'Sorry, Jerry. I don't mean to be stupid, only this is a really difficult concept for me.'

'I know, Chad. And I can see you're trying to work with me here.'

'So, please could you give me some examples of how you make a weekend last?'

'Certainly,' said Jerry and rattled off a typical weekend. Saturday: sleep till mid-morning; breakfast in front of the telly; Camden Lock or Harrow with AJ and some of their mates: maybe grab a pizza before catching a gig with Andy and his pals or see a movie; late-night chats with Mum; bed. Sunday: more of the same, sometimes with a blow-out grubfest at Grandpa's; bit of footie in the park; tea; telly; (tiny) bit of late-night homework crammed in to keep Barkow at bay.

Jerry began to realise what he was up against when barely

155

anything made it through the universal translator. And each enthusiastic – and increasingly manic – explanation Jerry gave of favourite TV shows, great movies and gigs he'd seen, or books he'd read, drew a total scale-faced blank.

It wasn't only Jerry's social activities that caused confusion either. The word 'mates' had been a major ear-peaker too. When Jerry talked about hanging out with his mates it must have translated as 'Bonded Partners'. Chad was pole-axed to think Jerry had a number of them, demanding to know how his parents and Fossic finally picked one and what happened to those they rejected.

When Jerry explained they were friends, not potential wives; that he'd be choosing his own when the time came, and there was no such thing as a Fossic where he came from, Chad looked thoroughly bewildered.

Jerry knew that look. Guilt had etched it into his memory. It was the one Woolfie had given him when she was a little kid as Jerry tried to get her to understand that Barbie had joined a strict religious group, which is why she'd shaved off all her hair.

There'd been a long pause after that, while Chad and Jerry tried hard to see through the fog of the other one's life. Jerry's mental trip home had made the memories unbearably painful, and he'd been pulled under by such a massive wave of homesickness that he'd rushed off to the plumbing suite to recover.

It wasn't just the desperate longing to see his family and

friends again that had done Jerry's head in, although that was bad enough. But living without them on an entertainment-free planet for the rest of his life? There'd be no point living at all.

'. . . and they beam these televisuals all over the planet, which everyone watches in untimetabled time!' gasped Chad, pacing the living area, unable to sit still and talk about such eccentric behaviour. 'Sometimes Jerry even goes out in a pack to a special building where he *pays* to watch them!'

Gilpin shook her head in wonder. It was a double-wonder mix. The first, at the untimetabled time Chad had been talking about for the last bar and a half (although repetition had slashed the value of novelty) swirled through with the second, of when he'd stop rasping on about his precious pet.

'Yes, you said.' Gilpin faked a yawn. 'Extraordinary. Now, let's—'

'And life without Fossics? I mean, how do they learn anything?'

'By instinct, Chad!' barked Gilpin. 'That's how lesser beings learn. Or have you forgotten your father bought Jerry *in a pet shop?*'

'Yes, but—'

'No but! He's a pet,' Gilpin growled. 'An unusual one. But a pet, all the same. And the sooner you start treating him like one, the better.'

'Jerry's not like other pets, Gilpin,' said Chad, too fired-up to have noticed the growl. 'You haven't spent as much time with him as I have.'

'Judging by the effect he's had on you, I'd say that's a good thing,' she snorted.

'Don't be like that,' Chad pleaded. 'I really want you to appreciate him too, because, well, I don't know the lifespan of his species, but there's every chance Jerry'll live long enough to come with us when we move into our own dwelling.'

Gilpin's ears snapped back against her head. Chad could have clawed himself for not having phrased that last statement as a question. 'After discussing it with you first, obviously.'

'Chad Jannan,' she snarled, jumping to her feet, 'how disappointing to discover you're going to be the type of husband who makes up his mind then pretends to discuss it with his wife afterwards.'

'I'm sorry, Gilpin!' cried Chad, but his apology failed to put a curve in the straight-lined fury of her tail, which pointed accusingly back at him as she stormed off to the kitchen.

*

Harchi had been staring at Rashila's likeness on his screen for so long he almost expected her to speak. If he didn't see Gornish soon, Harchi wouldn't get to demonstrate his weather pilot until tomorrow and he wasn't sure he could bear to wait that long after all the anticipation.

He'd looped through to Gornish's office several band-widths back to invite him to the demonstration, but vision had been off which meant he was probably in a meeting. A voicemail invitation wouldn't set the right tone for such an important event, so Harchi had cut the loop then passed the next few bars by admiring his handiwork and trying Gornish again.

He looped through to a colleague to see if she knew whether Gornish would mind being interrupted if Harchi popped up to his office. Vision off, voicemail on. He tried another one. The same. Harchi looped through to everyone at his level and discovered they all seemed to be in a meeting to which he hadn't been invited. Probably some departmental matter which Gornish didn't consider important enough to merit interrupting the work of one of his most respected Senior Technicians.

Harchi finally tracked down a Trainee Technician on the Quality of Plantation Rain team, who told him Gornish had called his senior staff together to investigate an unidentified energy surge logged over the Metropolis three nights ago. As Harchi had thought: not a weighty enough matter to disturb his work.

Harchi started spinning in his chair to help him decide whether to go home and see Jerry, or stay put in case Gornish emerged from his meeting. He'd just got the spin to the speed where his tail stuck out flat, when a thought struck him. Two thoughts, actually. The first: he was feeling queasy, his usual signal to slow down. The second: with all his colleagues occupied, what better time to pilot his pilot? Harchi Ideas Factory Jannan. They should add that to his plinth.

*

Jerry walked away from the plumbing suite, intending to grab himself a couple of sweet sticks before trying to blag Chad into taking him sightseeing. As he walked down the hallway towards the archway to the living area, Sneb dropped on to his shoulder with a 'buurrooop' of pleasure.

'Hey, furbucket! Grab you some chibberts while we're in the tuck cupboard, shall we?' said Jerry, reaching up to scratch Sneb's back.

Jerry abandoned that plan when he saw Gale and Naish in the kitchen. Naish was holding the fridge door up in the air, while Gale clanged away at the inside of it with the back of her claw. Go figure. No way would he get away with snaffling snacks with a double tin-chop sentry, so Jerry ambled into Chad's room instead. He came to such an abrupt halt at the sight that greeted him, that Sneb dug his claws in to avoid being thrown from his ride, which made Jerry grab his shoulder and yelp in pain.

'Down, Sneb!' shouted Chad, thinking Jerry was under attack again.

'It's OK, Chad, it was my fault – I nearly threw him off,' said Jerry, reaching up to tickle Sneb until he relaxed and draped himself across Jerry's shoulders like a woolly collar.

'Oh look, the pets are bonding,' said Gilpin, with an edge to her voice.

'Hi, Gilpin.' She nodded, without looking at him. Jerry wondered who'd rattled her cage? She and Chad must have had a row about something.

'What are you playing, Chad? It looks amazing!'

'It's called Jarbo,' said Chad, laughing at Jerry's bug eyes.

Who wouldn't make bug eyes at a floating board game? Jerry couldn't stop staring at the three circular boards which hung in a stack, totally unsupported in the middle of the room. The middle board, floating half a board out from the other two, had a few oval tags drifting along its outer edge. Some maroon, some dark green. There was one of each colour skim-hovering over the top left of the highest board, and a maroon one slightly off centre-right.

'Come on, Chad – it's your turn,' said Gilpin.

'D'you want to join in, Jerry?' asked Chad. 'We've only just started.'

'He can't join in with a game for two players!'

'He could help me out.'

'Perhaps you'd rather play Jerry instead?'

162

Ouch. 'That's OK, thanks. I'll watch,' said Jerry, going to perch on the desk.

Chad plucked a green tag from the air and, tapping it against his teeth, walked around the game, thinking. And thinking. Then thinking some more. Jerry could have married Rachel Davis and raised a family in the time it took Chad to come to a decision. At long, very long, last he reached up to the top tier and held his tag near the other two.

'How's that?' he asked Gilpin.

'Be better if it went in the blue sector,' she replied.

'Here?' Chad moved it to the right.

'Perfect!' Gilpin thanked him with a smile, in a good mood again – which she should have been, given the time she'd had to recover. Chad stepped back to let Gilpin get to the floating tags. She took a maroon one and started walking around, studying the boards.

'What's the idea . . .' asked Jerry, then noticed Gilpin shoot him a dirty look, '. . . of the game?' he finished in a whisper.

'You have to move all your petangs . . .' Chad whispered back, gesturing at the tags, '. . . across and down all three tiers in order, then off again at the right claw side, in such a way that it's always to the other player's advantage.'

'Where's the fun in that?' Jerry was so surprised, the volume on his whisper turned up to a shout.

'The fun is in taking part,' said Chad, with a nervous glance in Gilpin's direction.

Dullsville Arizona! Even the green bowls Grandpa was addicted to, that was played at the speed of a slug on sellotape, had winners and losers. (And if Grandpa was on their team, usually losers.)

'So how d'you decide the winner?' asked Jerry.

'Winner? There's no winner, Jerry!' huffed Chad, embarrassed by his pet's ignorance.

'The appeal of a game like Jarbo, as with all Pastinacean games,' Gilpin took over, to explain to Jerry in a you're-so-primitive-you-still-use-a-litter-tray voice, 'is the pleasure of devising the best way to help your opponent.'

'Gilpin's mother plays at National level,' Chad announced, proud by association.

'Wow.' Jerry tried to scramble his impressed face, but from Gilpin's miffed expression, he realised too many elements had slept through the alarm.

'Teach us one of your games, then, if you think Jarbo's so boring,' she challenged.

'I never said it was boring.'

'Jerry's probably bored at the thought of watching us play.'

'Which is why I suggested playing one of his games, Chad.'

'Honestly, I'm good with the Jarbo. You guys carry on.'

'Unless he doesn't know any.'

164

'I'm sure Jerry knows lots of great games. Don't you, Jerry?'

'Sure. Whatever.'

'Why don't you want to play one, then?'

'Because.'

'I know!' Chad cut a path through the silence to Jerry. 'Show Gilpin that game with the foot-covering roundels.'

'She wouldn't be interested.'

'What's a foot-covering roundel?'

'See? She is! I knew she would be.'

Chad dodged behind his bed, grabbed a ball from the socky hillock in the corner and rolled it towards Jerry, who automatically stopped it with the side of his foot.

'That's it?' Gilpin snorted a laugh at Chad. 'You throw an item of clothing and he steps on it?'

She was mocking football! Nobody mocked football. Jerry put Sneb on his bed (in case things turned ugly) before delivering a passionate lecture on The Game. He covered everything – rules; technique; player purchase and sales; hairstyles, and the emotional power of a game which could make grown men bawl like babies.

Jerry ended his lecture in the only way possible, with a series of re-enactments, enriched with fever-pitch commentary, of favourite Hammers' goal moments. Sneb pitched in to help, scuttling up to kick sock balls at him, as soon as he saw Jerry hoof the first goal into the back of the imaginary net, between Chad's desk legs.

By the last, crowd-pleasing penalty, as Jerry slid across the floor on his knees, head back, straight arms fisted at the sky, he was breathless: he'd been glorious – and he'd done his Boys proud. Jerry looked up at his dumbstruck audience and grinned: 'Anyone fancy a kickabout?'

*

'Morton, I think they're going to play the foot-covering roundel game!' Rashila was having difficulty keeping her voice calm.

'So?' said the Director wearily. 'It's a good bonding opportunity.'

'It's a game that has winners and losers. Who knows what the impact will be?'

Morton rose from her desk and padded quietly across the lab. 'In case you'd forgotten . . .' her snout almost touched the tip of her assistant's ear, as she crept up behind her and hissed . . . 'that's why we're doing this – to observe Jerry's impact on Chad's behaviour.'

Morton could tell Rashila was summoning the nerve to speak, so she flicked a dismissive claw at her. 'Go and write up your notes. The research has obviously reached a stage where it needs a more experienced eye.'

Rashila stood. 'Director, I must register my concern that it may be harmful to my son's well-being for him to experience something as dangerous as a competitive game.'

'Just because a concept is unknown to us, that doesn't necessarily make it dangerous,' Morton told her, taking a sideways step towards the chair. Rashila had no choice but to move, but as Morton flicked her tail into place and sat down, she was aware her assistant hadn't returned to her desk.

'Or don't you trust me to watch out for Chad?' asked Morton, dangerously casual.

They both knew the answer was 'no' but one hadn't the power to say so, and the other was too powerful to care. Rashila dropped her gaze and walked away.

*

'. . . and if an attacker is beyond the last man in defence, he's offside, then there's a . . .'

Gale lowered her auditory chip on the babble of data JerryPatterson was delivering. The information seemed overly complex for a game which appeared to demand no more of its participants than the removal of a roundel from an opposing player, with the requirement to deliver it into a pre-selected area.

Gale scanned the roundel (terminology update: 'ball') JerryPatterson was holding to confirm its outer casing had set properly. Affirmative. It was constructed from a blotch nut which Naish had claw-skewered and spun at high speed while Gale coated it in bonding material until it had sufficient depth to deliver the 'bounce-factor' requested.

Even though Gale had provided a ball, she still had a query logged on her hard drive concerning the game. She'd been re-hanging the chiller unit door, having repaired her accidental hover-dent, when Naish alerted her to the fact that Chad, Gilpin and JerryPatterson were moving furniture in the living area.

On questioning her Podder about the intended outcome of his labours, Gale was informed they were preparing the room for a game called 'football'. Chad, though outwardly cheerful, had a vibration in his voice which told Gale he had reservations, while pet and Bonded Partner were displaying high levels of excitement.

Gale demanded more data, and as Chad explained the game and both Fossics realised it was competitive, they chorused 'no'. Except the chorus became a solo, as a message opened in Gale's Inbox, instructing her to persuade Naish of the game's Bonding merit, and allow it to proceed.

Although Gale had carried out the instruction, the message generated a virus query, since Rashila Jannan would never expose her son to the risk of a competitive game. A scan proclaimed the message virus-free, but composition analysis revealed it had not been composed by Chad's mother.

The only other creature with direct messaging access to Gale's hard drive was esteemed Director Morton. But why would she issue instructions concerning a high-risk activity for Chad? And how had she known he was proposing to play in the first place?

The logical deduction was that the hidden cameras Rashila Jannan had installed two nights ago were linked to the Director's lab. Particularly when Gale included yesterday's message, sending her out to search for the pet during Social Session.

Gale's prime directive was to protect her Podder, but Fossic protocol demanded she obey the Director of the BFA. She had not been programmed to deal with such a conflict.

Standard procedure would be to log a query with her Chief Programmer, except in this case her Chief Programmer was the cause of her query – with the power to wipe Gale's hard drive and dismantle her outer casing.

Gale concluded that it would be acceptable for the game to proceed. She reset her auditory chip to normal, in time to register from JerryPatterson's altered vocal tone that he had finished his monologue.

'So, everyone clear how to play?' he asked.

'We have to get the ball and put it in the goal?' Chad offered.

'You got it.'

Naish tore across the room, crashed into the alien, caught the ball as he dropped it on his way to the floor, then threw it between the nearest set of two chairs positioned either end of the playing space to mark out the goal areas.

'So much preparation for so little action,' whirred Naish, as she hovered to the portal. 'I fail to see the appeal. Come along, Gilpin.'

'Wait!' croaked JerryPatterson, straining to breathe normally, as Chad helped him up. 'There's more to it than that.'

*

Morton felt inclined to agree with Naish. But what was this? A squabble had broken out as Jerry proclaimed himself and Chad captains – as he called the leader of each player group. Gilpin, backed by Naish, was extremely vocal in her objections to both captains being male. Gale was equally vocal against Jerry being a captain. Because he was a pet.

'Look, it's my game, so I get to be captain,' he insisted.

'I don't mind if Gilpin wants to be captain instead of me,' said Chad, enjoying the reward of her smile and grateful that he was edging back into favour.

'No! Both teams have to have boy captains, or the game won't be evenly balanced.'

'Chad Jannan! Were you trying to trick me into being a captain?' shouted Gilpin.

'No!' protested Chad.

'I'm going to be on Jerry's side for that!'

'Oookay,' said Jerry.

'Is that a problem?' barked Gilpin.

'Only that, as captain, it's kind of up to me to pick my team,' Jerry pointed out.

'So, you've got a choice between me and a snebbit. Who's it going to be? Thought so.'

Naish hovered over to join Gilpin by Jerry's side.

'What are you doing, Naish?' asked Jerry, starting to get a headache.

'Joining your team.'

'You have to wait to be chosen,' Jerry told her, 'and it's Chad's turn to choose.'

'I have been chosen, JerryPatterson, as Gilpin Carney's Fossic: a duty I have fulfilled from the instant she hatched, and will continue to fulfill, until she is fully Bonded with Chad Jannan.'

'But that gives us an unfair advantage 'cos Chad has to pick Gale . . .'

'I pick Gale.'

'. . . yes, thank you, Chad. So now our team has an extra player,' said Jerry.

'Form a pet team with the snebbit,' beeped Naish, 'then we'll have three equal teams.'

'No!' blazed Jerry. 'You're only allowed two teams.'

Morton was intrigued to see a small smile suddenly flit across the pet's face and made a mental note to add 'inventive' to her Jerry-appeal list, as she heard his next statement.

'I'm such a plank – I've forgotten *the* most important person. The referee! You want to cover that, Naish?'

'I shall be referee, JerryPatterson,' Gale whirred loudly, hovering away from Chad, 'since it's the most senior role and this is my Podder's dwelling.'

'Great! So, Naish – why don't you join Chad's team?'

'Negative. Being in opposition to my Podder goes against my Prime Directive.'

'Give me strength!!' yelled Jerry, tearing at his hair.

'Please, Gale, let Naish be referee, it doesn't mean you're not senior,' begged Chad.

'Chad's right,' added Gilpin, 'we know you're boss of this dwelling, but if you don't let Naish referee, we'll never get to play.'

'Very well,' beeped Gale, going back to join Chad.

Morton heaved a sigh of relief as Jerry and Chad finally stood facing each other in the centre of the room. At a nod from Jerry, Naish placed the ball on the ground between him and Chad, then hovered backwards and emitted a shrill noise.

Both captains dashed to kick the ball, but as Chad's feet were substantially larger than Jerry's he got to it first. Then Sneb hurtled up, nipped between Chad's legs and biffed the ball back to Jerry, who sent it travelling at speed towards Gilpin, who started running and kicking it at the same time egged on by Jerry, who was bellowing at her to head for the goal, but then Gale shot across and . . .

Morton glanced up, startled by the sound of a long, low, rumble over the Bureau.

'What was that?' asked Rashila, equally startled.

'I don't know.'

They both listened. The rumble had gone. Looking back at the screen, Morton growled to find the picture and sound breaking up.

'There's interference on the live feed,' rasped Morton, boiling up to a fury. She'd almost clawed her ridges off in boredom during the build-up. And just when the game looked set to deliver the promise of Jerry's hard sell, she was prevented from watching. Morton struck the monitor with the back of her claw. The picture briefly flickered into life and there was a crackle of sound, then both hid behind a curtain of static.

CHAPTER SIXTEEN

Harchi couldn't decide which he loved more, thunder or lightning. His rain-free, reduced power, pilot pilot had been a definite success. A tingle of anticipatory delight tripped over his scales, at the thought of how much fun (and praise) there'd be tomorrow, as he demonstrated his pilot, with both new discoveries running at full strength.

He was punching in one last, tiny, scratch of celebratory lightning before rushing home to tell Jerry about his triumph, when a call looped through. Harchi was on such a weather roll – please let it be Gornish, *please*!

'Harchi Jannan, Weather Enhance . . .' He'd been expensively trained to smile at callers, but Morton burnt the smile off his face, with the heat of her scowl. '. . . ment Unit.'

'Gornish is unavailable,' barked Morton, 'and so's everyone else, which is why I've ended up with you.'

Harchi remembered his training: half a smile is better than none. He managed half a half, and boosted it with some fawning. 'How may I help, esteemed Director?'

'There've been rumbling noises over the Bureau and interference on our equipment,' she grouched. 'Is there a malfunction with the weather?'

'I know Gornish is currently investigating an unidentified energy surge,' said Harchi, sneaking a claw tip on to his keyboard to delete the celebratory lightning. 'Would you like me to look into it for you?'

'What I'd like,' Morton snarled, 'is the weather returned to Ministry Approved Standards *immediately*.'

'We'll do our best. On behalf of the Unit, please accept our . . .' The screen changed as Morton cut the loop. Oops.

*

Chad lay in the wallow pool, his head on a boulder, swamped by mud and emotion.

'Shall I brush your front?' asked Gale, hovering up the walkway with the broom.

'No thanks, Gale,' he mumbled miserably. 'I'd just like to lie here.'

'I'll go and get you some walsh-pods,' she whirred, putting the broom away.

Chad was touched. When he was a hatchling, if ever he fell and bruised his scales, or caught his tail in a portal, Gale would bring him a clawful of cracked walsh-pods to lick out in the pool, to chase the tears away.

Sometimes, Chad pictured a future where he wasn't Bonded to Gilpin, and carried on living with Gale. It wasn't that he didn't like Gilpin, but it could be very

175

stressful spending time with her. Though after the disastrous competitive game, spending time with Gilpin probably wasn't something he'd need to worry about. Thick though the mud was, Chad still rippled its surface with the force of his sigh.

At first Chad had thought it was fun, running about and shouting. A feeling that quickly faded, as Jerry and Gilpin pounded goal after goal past him and Gale. It wasn't the frequency – although he'd have preferred the final score to have been less crushingly brutal than fifteen to one – but the way Jerry and Gilpin behaved after each goal, which had been so distressing.

Jerry was a pet, he didn't know any better; it was hardly surprising he'd perform swaggery displays of triumph. But Gilpin? Initially, she'd been as surprised by Jerry's behaviour as Chad, but before long, she was joining in! With increased enthusiasm, as their prowess became evident. He'd felt so isolated.

When it was finally, mercifully, over, no one knew what to say. The traditional Pastinacean response of 'Thank you for helping me succeed and making my game so enjoyable,' whilst accurate for half the players, seemed somehow inappropriate.

Gilpin finally broke the silence. And what she'd said had been as painful as a jab in the eye from a flicked tail tip.

'Naish, I've had a fantastic time playing this game

176

with Chad, so why do I feel disappointed when I look at him?'

'I believe it is because you have seen him defeated,' supplied her Fossic.

'I think you must be right,' said Gilpin thoughtfully, 'because my opinion of Chad was high before we began, then sank lower with every goal we scored against him.'

Chad turned to Gale, completely overwhelmed. 'Gilpin says I've disappointed her and in a curious way, I feel I have. I am also experiencing a deep sense of shame.'

'I believe that is an after-effect of being a loser,' Gale had answered him. 'You should be aware,' she continued, addressing both Podders, 'that, factually, nothing has happened here which changes either of you.'

Naish peered into Gilpin's eyes. 'Negative. Corneal scans indicate Gilpin Carney has excess adrenalin in her system. I am removing her from this environment to recover.'

Gilpin had snortled a winner's goodbye to Jerry, who was catching his breath against the far wall near the Infoscope. And although she'd ruffled Chad's hair clump, Gilpin's exchange with Naish as they'd left had made his humiliation complete.

'Naish, do winners always feel superior to losers?'

'I have no data on file, but a probability chip calculation gives a seventy-nine ding fifteen fantarg likelihood of the answer being affirmative.'

177

'And do you suppose winners should only associate with winners?'

'Insufficient data for an immediate assessment,' Naish replied. 'But I will continue to collate information.'

Chad had been about to run and hide in his room, when he noticed Jerry staring into space, mouth open, touching the inside of his teeth with his tongue again.

'Not more voices?' Chad asked, hurrying over.

Jerry had nodded, then exclaimed: 'Harchi! I said I'd meet him at the chute! Is it time?'

Chad checked the clock. 'He's probably already docked, you might as well wait here.'

'No! I promised!' shouted Jerry and dashed out, before Chad could start training him to ask permission first.

Chad looked up as the portal swished, and smiled for the first time in several bars as Gale hovered towards him through the steam with a dish of walsh-pods. If Gilpin was so disappointed in him that she broke their Bond, he'd still have Jerry. And he'd always have Gale.

*

Gilpin Carney wasn't the only one with excess adrenalin in her system; Morton's brain was in hyperdrive. If competitive play was that stimulating with the opposing sides so ill-matched, it must be incredible when they were more evenly balanced.

'I knew competitive play would be bad for Chad!' Rashila was at her shoulder. Again.

'He'll be fine.' Morton gestured at the screen. 'Gale's there. And I heard you make a personal call to check Harchi was on his way home.'

'Look at him, eating walsh-pods in the wallow pool! Gale only lets him do that when he's really upset,' fussed Rashila.

'Perhaps you'd feel calmer if you kept your comments scientific, instead of over-protectively maternal?' gnashed Morton, irritated at the interruption to her thought process.

'Apologies, Director,' said Rashila, stiffly. 'As a scientist, I note that Chad was not the only one affected. Gilpin became extremely aggressive.'

'She became extremely focused,' Morton corrected. 'So focused, that I'm thinking of applying the principle educationally and perhaps assigning one Fossic to a group of Podders.'

Rashila's tail raced her ears to the ceiling. 'Director! How would they ever learn anything in a situation like that?'

'By being competitive, to see who's cleverest,' Morton announced, as if it was obvious.

'What are you going to do? Herd them into buildings and force them to stay until they've achieved the required level of education?' sniped Rashila, too shocked to be polite.

Morton's ears flipped flat. If she didn't need Chad Jannan to finish the Upgrades, she'd have fired his mother in a claw-click.

*

179

Someone was meeting Harchi at the chute. Deliberately. He was so excited, his tail hurt. Drumming his toe-claws through the eternity it took to dock, the 'hello Jerry-pet' froze on Harchi's lips as the portal opened on to an empty hallway. Well, empty of pets. A couple of elderly Pastinaceans who'd been waiting for the chute were watching him, clearly puzzled as to why he hadn't stepped off.

'Sorry, thinking about work,' Harchi mumbled, by way of explanation as they swapped places. He pretended to walk away until he heard the chute leave, then went back, put his case down and waited. Of course Jerry wasn't here yet! Pets can't tell the time; he was bound to be late. Harchi refused to start walking and meet Jerry halfway, it simply wouldn't count as being met from the chute.

*

Why did every twonking hallway look the same? Would it have killed them to paint some in different colours, so Jerry might have half a clue where he was? He raced round another bend, hoping against all hope it might be the one that led to the dead end by the chute. Nope.

Jerry had been so caught up in the game (fifteen–one . . . result, or what!) that he'd completely forgotten his promise to meet Harchi. The totally freaky thing was, he wouldn't have remembered at all if he hadn't lent against the wall to catch his breath and had that whole echo thing kick off again.

Weird, weirder, weirdest. Jerry had heard Rashila's

voice echoing back this time and although he couldn't quite catch what she was saying, he definitely heard what sounded like '. . . archi.' Which made him feel so guilty, he'd just taken off, presuming he'd remember the way from yesterday. Fat chance.

Jerry's chest hurt and the stitch in his side stabbed to be unpicked, but he kept on running. Why? Why was he putting himself through this much agony, over something as lame as meeting some bloke from the tube? Except it wasn't lame. And it wasn't 'some bloke'. It was Harchi. He'd had such a good time walking back with him yesterday, Jerry wasn't going to pass up the chance of doing it again today.

*

Harchi finally had to scale up to it . . . Jerry wasn't coming. Setting off for home, Harchi couldn't shift the droop from his ears and tail, so headed for the roof instead until his extremities had perked up a little. It seemed unkind, returning to the dwelling in such a disappointed state and rubbing his pet's snout in his failure.

Leaning against the safety rail, Harchi tried to recapture his earlier feeling of weather joy by picturing how different the view would look tomorrow, while he piloted Jannan's Random Rain Scheme for Gornish. He heard the portal open but didn't bother looking. He wasn't in the mood for Clacket Layne as she covered him in madness, trying to pretend Theydon knew she was up here. A strangled 'Harchi!' made him spin round.

181

'Jerry!'

Harchi's grin of pleasure creased into anxiety as he saw the state of his pet, doubled over, every breath a painful, lung-wringing wheeze. And his face had turned an alarming shade of scarlet and was leaking water, which had made his hair stick to his head. Harchi could have clawed himself for doubting Jerry. He hadn't met him because he'd been ill!

Harchi hoped the vet's bills wouldn't be too expensive or Rashila would be on his tail again. But never mind that now. Here was a pet who wanted to be with Harchi so much he'd crawled off his sick bed to find him. Ignoring Jerry's snoutingly sour smell, Harchi squatted down, held him close and reassured him again and again that he was going to be all right.

*

Even though this was only Jerry's third day on Pastinare (or ninth minute, if the 08:26 of his watch was to be believed) it was still long enough for him to experience a sense of déjà vu as he and Harchi poled in through the front door and found a rather solemn welcoming committee awaiting them. A committee of one this time. In the grip of a major league downer.

Chad stared miserably up at them, from his blanket-covered base in an armchair, murmured 'Hello,' then looked away again and started picking at his tail tip.

'Chaddy, what's wrong? Are you ill?' cried Harchi, terrified that his son had caught something from his pet. He raced over to feel Chad's snout and see if he was running a temperature.

Harchi's terror was made worse by the sudden recollection of Rashila's phone call earlier, when he'd assured her he was going straight home after work, after she'd suggested Chad and his pet needed supervising. Oops. Well, only half an oops – he had been supervising the pet.

'I'm not ill, Harchi-pa, just sad.'

'What happened, son?' asked Harchi, pulling another chair up close, to sit and hold Chad's claw.

'Chad! You're not beating yourself up about the football, are you?' asked Jerry.

'I'm a loser,' Chad told Harchi.

'Doesn't mean you have to start acting like one,' Jerry told him, hacked off at having lost his place in Harchi's spotlight. The guilt didn't help, either. Except why should he feel guilty? It was Chad who'd kicked off the whole 'let's play a Jerry-game' doo-dah.

'Now I've disappointed you too,' sighed Chad, making Jerry wish Andy was there to dole out one of his back-of-the-head slaps.

'What are you two talking about? Losers? Footballs?' asked Harchi, completely baffled by their exchange.

'Me and Gilpin played a game against Chad and Gale,' Jerry filled him in. 'My team won. No biggie.'

'Your team *won?*' growled Harchi, scrambling on to the arm of Chad's chair and throwing his arms around him, startling Jerry with the passion of his response. 'Gale! What were you thinking?' he roared at the Fossic, who was preparing the evening meal. 'Letting Chad play a competitive game!'

Gale shot out of the kitchen and whirred to a stop, a scale's width from Harchi's face.

'Refer your roaring to Rashila Jannan!' she beeped. 'It was on her instruction the game took place.'

'I'm . . . just going to go and clean up,' murmured Jerry, edging away from the combat zone.

This competitive game stuff was obviously a way bigger deal than Jerry had realised. In which case, why had Rashila allowed it? As he took his clothes off and got in the shower, Jerry wondered whether he could get this football fiasco to work for him.

Maybe Rashila would be so eager to get shot of him for leading Chad astray, he'd be able to tip her over into sending him home? Except she had such a short fuse; he'd have to play it very carefully. He wanted to end up back on Earth, not in a pet-shop window with a price tag round his neck.

*

Rashila had already left the lab, but Morton didn't feel like looping through to her hand-held to warn her that, probably for the first time in his life, Harchi was in a rage. It would serve her surly assistant right for refusing to issue the

184

football instruction and forcing Morton to do it instead. Besides, Rashila's reactions would be more natural, if she didn't know in advance.

Anyway, it looked as if Harchi was calming down. He'd just started a game of Jarbo with Chad. Wisely, Jerry was keeping out of the way in the wallow room. He may be primitive, but at least he kept himself groomed.

As Morton watched Jerry in the shower, her ears peaked in surprise as a stream of water suddenly shot from his frontal tail. So the appendage wasn't a bodily remnant after all, but a waste-water hose attached to two storage tanks!

Fascinating though the discovery was, Morton wouldn't be sharing it with her assistant. Rashila was hostile enough to the pet without making it worse by telling her he wasn't properly dwelling-trained.

*

Harchi waited until Rashila had gone to her quarters to change so they'd have some privacy. He'd never confronted his wife about anything before, and though his tail tip was quivering, he was so outraged by the risk she'd taken he had to know why she'd done it.

'Rashila?'

She straightened up from placing her work suit in the folder. 'Harchi?' Noticing his worried expression, she came to take his claw. 'You're worried about Chad, aren't you? I think he's perking up a bit.'

185

'Do you? He still seems very flop-eared, to me.'

The folder tinged and Rashila raced over to catch her tunic and shorts as they dropped, precision folded, from the base. Harchi seized the opportunity – somehow it felt less scary confronting Rashila's back.

'How could you let him play a competitive game, without consulting me?'

'I . . . I'm sorry, Husband,' Rashila turned from putting her clothes away and Harchi saw the apology was genuine. 'Chad was so keen to play. Gilpin, too.'

'They're only Podders! Far too young to appreciate the dangers.'

'Morton thought it would be an interesting experience for them.'

'Morton! How did she get involved?'

'I'm under a lot of Upgrade pressure, Harchi,' Rashila suddenly burst out, 'and this conversation isn't helping!'

'I'm just trying to understand why you'd expose our son to such emotional risk!'

'Why did you have to buy him a pet who played competitive games?' wailed Rashila.

'Are you saying this is my fault?'

'You're saying it's mine!' she shouted in a shaky voice.

'I'm sorry, Wife!' said Harchi, distressed to see tears in her eyes. 'I didn't mean to upset you, I'm just worried about Chad.'

'So am I, Harchi. And I'm sorry, too. I should never have let the game proceed.'

'And I should have checked with Kaye whether Jerry played competitive games before I bought him. Only it's not the kind of thing you'd think to ask really, is it?' Harchi's hearts sank, but he felt he had to make the offer: 'D'you want me to take him back to the shop?'

'NO! I mean – no.'

'Are you just saying that 'cos you're worried I won't get a refund? Because I could always trade him in for something smaller on Pet-Bay.' Harchi's tail throbbed with tension in case his wife accepted.

'No. Let's keep him,' said Rashila, whose tail also throbbed with tension – at the thought of what Morton would do, if her research subject suddenly disappeared. 'Chad seems very fond of him. Let's not make him any sadder than he is already.'

Harchi smiled with relief. 'At least one good thing's come out of all this.'

'Really?' said Rashila, failing to come up with a single thing.

'At least it was you who told Gale to let the competitive game go ahead. If she'd decided to allow it on her own, we'd be talking about getting rid of her now instead of Jerry. Imagine the damage that would have done Chad.'

Rashila couldn't imagine it. There wasn't enough room in her head with all the other damage-imaginings already fighting for space in there.

*

187

Jerry sat on Gale's docking block in the plumbing suite, in the final stages of the advanced jaw aerobics required to work his way through tonight's guinea-pig platter. The Jannans had been eating when he'd emerged from the wallow room and no way was he going to risk last night's humiliation by joining them.

Rashila and Harchi were ladling on the forced jollity, so Chad was obviously still on his trip to Mope City, and Jerry didn't want to wind Rashila up by hanging about as a reminder of who'd organised the whip-round for his ticket.

Looking round the room, Jerry wondered whether there were any echo spots. Spurred on by the bum-numbingly hard seat and jaw-ache, he decided to find out; although he wasn't sure what it would prove.

Jerry had heard the first feedback echo yesterday morning after Gale zapped him with her medicinal claw, so he reckoned his mini-brace had somehow been shocked into acting as a receiver. Then, when he'd heard Rashila's voice this afternoon, Jerry thought perhaps the echoes marked the location of hidden cameras in the flat to check the nanny wasn't beating her kid.

That squared up with Rashila knowing Jerry had gone out yesterday afternoon – and why she hadn't said anything about him wearing Chad's tunic. Although the 'checking on the nanny' scenario didn't feel right, because from what Jerry had seen Rashila almost behaved as if Gale was Chad's mother. So maybe the hidden cameras were a security device, like a sophisticated burglar alarm system?

Jerry stopped trying to work it out and concentrated instead on sliding round the room with his back to the wall, la-la-lahing, then listening for echoes as he went. He got right the way round without hearing even a hint of sound. Nor had the orthodontist's wire risen a squinch of a degree above mouth temperature. The plumbing suite was obviously an echo-free zone.

Forgetting it was on snail time, Jerry checked his watch to see how late it was. 08:27. Still, the dust must have settled on the football by now and even if it hadn't, Jerry couldn't leave it another night before talking to Rashila.

Walking into the living area, Jerry wondered if it was later than he'd realised because it was in darkness, although the lights were still on in Harchi and Rashila's rooms.

'Good night, Weatherman!' Jerry called through the archway as he went past.

At the sound of Jerry's voice, Sneb came hurtling out of Rashila's room and did a star-shaped sucker jump on to his front.

'Good night, Weatherpet!' called Harchi, and Jerry heard him chuckling over the sound of Sneb's purrs. So far, so good; Harchi wasn't cross with him.

Jerry scratched Sneb's woolly back as he paused just inside Rashila's archway. She was working at her desk.

'Excuse me, Rashila, could I ask you—'

'This room is off-limits to pets!' she growled, then spotted Sneb and came charging over, wrenching him from Jerry's front so fast, his five paws scrabbled air. 'Alien ones.'

'I'm sorry, but I really need to talk to you about something!' said Jerry, determined to keep going, even when Rashila pointed a claw through the archway and snarled into his face:

'On Your Bed!'

Jerry was seriously rattled by the force of Rashila's anger, but he was terrified of not saying what he'd waited an entire day to say, and being forced to wait another whole day to try to say it again. '*Please!* You're the only one who can help me get home. I need to talk to you about it.'

Rashila lowered her voice to avoid the others hearing, which did nothing to lessen the venomous delivery. 'Haven't you done enough damage to Chad today, without begging for help to desert him?'

'I didn't ask to come here!'

'And I didn't invite you. But we're both stuck with it. Now leave! Or late as it is, I shall ring the pet shop and have them collect you.'

'Thought you didn't want me deserting Chad?'

Rashila's answer was a growl and a stinging lash to the back of Jerry's legs from her tail, which sent him spinning from the room with a tortured yelp.

Chad's room was in darkness as Jerry went in. He stood rubbing his burning calves with one hand, digging his nails into the palm of his other, refusing to give that scaly dictator the satisfaction of crying.

'You all right?' Chad's sleepy voice drifted down from his bed.

'Yeah, just a few sniffles. Must be getting a cold,' Jerry told him, as he undressed.

'I'm not angry with you, Jerry, if that's why you've been hiding in the plumbing suite.'

'Thanks, Chad, you're a pal.'

'You're welcome, Jerry. You're a pet. Do you suppose Rashila-ma and Harchi-pa are right – that Gilpin will still want to see me tomorrow?'

'Sure she will. She'd never throw your future away over one pathetic game of football.'

'Do you really think football's pathetic, Jerry?'

'I didn't mean . . .'

'. . . what?'

Chad was revving up to re-angst, so Jerry took a deep breath and crossed his fingers.

'Nothing. Course football's pathetic.' He kept his fingers crossed until the snuffly rhythm of Chad's breathing told him he'd fallen asleep.

CHAPTER SEVENTEEN

Rashila couldn't sleep. She hung in bed, jabbed awake by guilt. She shouldn't have struck a pet, even though he'd been insolent and caused such alarm over Chad. How had such a primitive creature managed to cause this much disruption? And judging by the way Harchi lost no time training Jerry to follow him round, all the discipline was going to be left to her.

If only he'd escape and find another cargo hold to stow away in. She'd have to bear the inevitable backlash of Morton's blame and fury, but however long that lasted it had to be shorter than a Jerry-life.

Flicking her tail tube, Rashila set the bed swaying to help make herself drowsy. What finally sent her to sleep was the rhythm of a phrase tumbling round her head in synch with the swing of the bed: 'He's only a pet. He's only a pet. He's only a pet.'

*

Jerry couldn't sleep. He was too stressed after his run-in with Rashila. Where did it leave him if he couldn't talk to her

192

about getting home? Morton was the only other person he could think of who might help, but he hadn't a clue how to get hold of her without Rashila knowing. His brain was too frazzled to come up with ideas, so Jerry decided to get up and echo-check the rest of the flat. It might come in handy to know where the cameras were hidden.

Listening to make sure everyone was asleep, Jerry extracted himself from his bed and slipped his trousers on. Creeping from the room, he half-expected to see Mum, then remembered all too painfully where he was. At home, when Jerry went to the loo in the night, he'd sometimes find her at the top of the stairs, drinking hot chocolate. 'Specially after Dad first bailed. Didn't happen so much these days.

If he was really quiet Jerry had time to study Mum and see how low she was. He used to think he'd kill Dad if he ever saw him again for making her so unhappy. Then Mum'd sense Jerry watching her and quickly splash on a smile as she patted the carpet next to her for him to sit, pyjama-leg to nightie, and share her hot chocolate.

'You all right, Mum?' he'd ask, trying to keep it light.

'Course I'm all right, kid. Got you, haven't I?' she'd always answer.

Jerry swallowed the lump in his throat and got down to business. He already knew there were two echo spots in the living area, but if he had time, he'd check for more later. Just to be thorough. The wallow room was the biggest space, so Jerry decided he'd start in there. Moving as silently as he could, he crossed the living area in the dark and had almost reached the archway when . . . THWONK! . . . something whacked into his back and sent him stumbling forwards.

Jerry was gearing up for a heart attack, with a side-panic over whether these guys knew human CPR; whether they had CPR at all, and if they did, how did you summon it, when he heard a familiar 'buurrooop'. He exhaled as he felt Sneb scrabble on to his shoulder and rub scratchy fur against his head, purring.

'Happy to see you too, pal,' whispered Jerry, scratching Sneb's underside while his heartbeat returned to normal. 'Be happier still if you'd let me know you were coming.'

*

Morton couldn't sleep. She'd mainly thrown the idea of competitive education at Rashila to stop her fretting about her son like a Phase 2 Fossic with faulty wiring. But the more she thought about it, the stronger its appeal, and although she had stepped to bed earlier her brain was buzzing with ideas so she'd stepped out again. No point hanging there bar after bar when she could be sitting at her table with a mug of sour tea, working.

Morton's claws flew over the keyboard as she recorded her thoughts. She'd need to write an immensely sophisticated, multi-layered programme to enable Fossics to educate Podders competitively: with a response for every imaginable level, from loser up to winner. 'Up to' winner – the sort of language pitfall Morton must guard against. A scheme this controversial would have enough voices raised against it, without her supplying them with ammunition.

Her hair clump was a mass of knots before Morton arrived at the perfect pitch. Competitive education worked on the principles of Pastinacean gamesmanship: if Chad hadn't lost, Gilpin couldn't have won! So obvious, she hadn't noticed it staring her in the snout.

The strength of competitive education is the knowledge that you're helping your fellow group member's educational advance. No Podder should be miserable, whatever their distance from the winner's pinnacle (that was good, winner's pinnacle – Morton underlined it twice) since their position has helped others above them.

The lowest achieving Podder (should she use lowest – perhaps 'most distant' would be better?) should be proudest of all, since they have advanced the educational game . . . no, not game, it didn't sound serious enough, 'improvement', that would do for now . . . the educational improvement of every other member in the group. Sensational!

That was the beauty of being an inspirational thinker – she had the self-belief to discard one idea when a dazzlingly better one presented itself. And it was still based on Morton's initial concept: that Jerry Patterson in relation to Chad Jannan, as applied to Fossics, would be the foundation for this year's Upgrades.

This was far better. Usually Morton only devised Upgrades suitable for installation in higher Phase Fossics, whereas an advancement like this would have to be programmed in across the board. Bluhm and the rest of the Ministry Committee were going to be so impressed with the increased revenue it would generate.

A movement on her Infoscope caught Morton's eye. Jerry and the snebbit were in the wallow room. Was he going for a nocturnal gloop? No. He'd crossed to a boulder on the far side, leant his back against it, then called out something which sounded like 'la la lah'. Whatever it was, it didn't translate.

Morton watched, totally mystified, as Jerry slid over all the boulders, pausing as he went to call out. Even the snebbit appeared puzzled, suckering along boulders after Jerry, then shooting across the ceiling, down the far wall and back to his co-pet, as if urging him to come and do something which made more sense.

Morton's ears flopped. First Jerry heard voices, now he was behaving bizarrely. It was a hideous thought but she had to scale up to it: perhaps it was the after-effects of that second blast of molecular displacement in the chute, perhaps Jerry had hatched like that; but all the signs were pointing to a rapid mental decline.

Her assistant may be stupid, but she was nobody's fool. If the research continued with an unstable subject, Rashila would notice. And if Morton intended to launch as radical an idea as competitive education her source material had to be flawless. Either she carried on using a mentally unstable source, who showed every indication of becoming progressively worse, or . . . Morton looked across at the wardrobe where she'd hidden the molecular scrambler. It was a very powerful 'or'.

*

Gale couldn't recharge. She wanted to process one last batch of data before hovering on to her docking block. Opening her Unacceptable Firsts file, she input the following:

> Gale and Chad had taken part in a competitive game.
> Gale and Chad had come second.
> Podder subsequently suffered severe loss of status in his Bonded Partner's opinion, which had damaged his emotional well-being.
> Purpose of Process:
>   a) Identify cause of current situation, including assessment of possible Fossic negligence.
>   b) Determine appropriate course of action to repair and protect Podder's emotional state.

As Gale ran the programme her ocular chip took in the docking block. If the identified cause turned out to be Fossic negligence it would be her last re-charge. In the morning, she'd report to the BFA for a HDW&D. Even running the

197

initials through her circuits set off a red alert: Hard Drive Wipe and Dismantlement.

*

Kaye couldn't sleep. At least, he had been asleep until a call looped through. And all thoughts of sleep vanished when he saw the caller was Morton.

*

There was a beep as the results log was generated. Gale scanned the data.

Fossic Negligence:	Negative. Unit complied with BFA instruction.
Cause identified:	JerryPatterson.
Action required:	Apply Prime Directive Rule 11^5\~}AETTB-7731+z.

Gale hovered up and locked on to her docking block. Before running re-charge she programmed a reminder to drop down as she booted up. It read:

Devise and Execute Plan for Disposal of JerryPatterson

CHAPTER EIGHTEEN

Harchi had never slept better in his life. He strode along the hallway to the chute, thinking that there was no cheerier way for a husband to start the day than by receiving a 'grateful wife' smile when he hands her a mug of sour tea as she wakes up.

The prospect of a second smile had been too tempting after yesterday's success, but there was another reason Harchi was up early. He wanted to catch Gornish, to book a slot to demonstrate the Random Rain Scheme pilot. Despite the blip with the BFA's equipment yesterday – which could easily have been caused by the unidentified energy surge – Harchi was still convinced he was on to a winner.

Thanks to Jerry. He really was a fascinating creature. Harchi checked the bottom of the doorframes he passed and grinned as he saw the marks Jerry had made on them yesterday. It was a breach of Citizenship Law to vandalise property, but Jerry said it was for finding his way to the chute. And the marks were removable. He had a special stick with a grey pointy mark-making end, but you could disappear the mark by rubbing it with a little pink column on the other end!

Harchi corrected himself – it wasn't a mark. It was a letter. The first one in Jerry's name, apparently. He owned a pet who knew how to write. At first Harchi thought Jerry was pretending, like Chad when he was a hatchling. 'Look at me, Harchi-pa, I can write, like a big scaler!' And there'd be nothing but claw-scribble on screen. But Jerry had made the same shape again and again.

He could count too. Amazing! (And strange that Jerry had bungled the counting trick the other day . . .) Jerry told Harchi he was making number marks next to every J so all he had to do was follow them in descending order, once he left the dwelling, until he reached the chute. Which was a very clever idea, for a pet.

Harchi gave a skip of anticipation. For the first time ever there'd be no end-of-journey disappointment tonight – Jerry would definitely be there to meet him.

An idea began to bubble up. What if they toured the Quadrants, performing writing and counting tricks to audiences waiting to watch Jarbo tournaments? Jerry would be a big asset afterwards, helping Harchi get commissions for Weather Portraits.

It was a terrific idea, but Harchi couldn't develop it now. He had to direct all his energies towards rolling out his Best

Idea Ever: the Jannan Random Rain Scheme. Picking up his pace, Harchi wished he hadn't left so early because no one else was about yet and he wanted to bellow at commuters: 'Stand aside! Stand aside, you hallway-hoggers – Harchi Jannan is on his way to make Weather Enhancement History!'

*

Morton looked round her dwelling and felt like roaring her ridges off. What a night. Depressing, utterly exhausting and unbelievably pointless. She'd have to get some Duty Fossics to clean up, then waste yet more time adjusting their memory and time logs.

It was three orange, one ochre. Still early. The split screen view on her Infoscope showed Chad and Jerry sleeping, but Rashila heading for the wallow room. Another reason to roar. Now Morton wouldn't be able to get her dwelling cleaned until tonight. She'd have to get into the lab before Rashila arrived, though at least that would get her away from the smell.

It must be longer than Morton realised since she'd last handled a molecular scrambler. Not that she'd had any difficulty using it. She'd waited until the clock scrolled indigo, taken the scrambler to ground level in her private chute, opened the hidden exit portal and fired into the night sky. It was no more than Kaye said he'd done.

Given the result, Morton regretted not having run a more precise calculation. Except the need had been so urgent, and the portal of opportunity so narrow, she hadn't the time. It was far more likely that an ignorant creature like Kaye had damaged the scrambler than a scientist of her supreme grandeur had made an error.

A flash of white light had cracked the night-black and something landed, unconscious, at her feet. An area on the back of its neck was singed and smoking slightly, possibly a friction burn from speed of entry. Was it dead? No, Morton could see its body moving as it breathed. It was nothing like a Jerry-pet – much smaller, with swirls of knobbly white fur covering its entire body.

Putting the scrambler aside Morton cradled the creature up, surprised to find four spindly legs tucked under its body and its fur coarse and springy to the touch. Didn't weigh much either. Shifting her grip to hold it one-armed against her chest, Morton grabbed the scrambler and returned to the privacy of her dwelling.

Almost as she put the creature down in her living area it came round, wobbled to its feet – all four of them, so it obviously wasn't an upright – and stared at her. The only part of its body not covered by off-white fur was its black nose and the inside of its ears, which were pale pink. It had a short, stubby tail, too. Still staring. Was it waiting for her to speak?

'Greetings, and welcome to Pastinare,' said Morton with a gracious smile. Then, to let it know it was in the presence of greatness, added: 'I am Director Morton of the Bureau of Fossic Affairs.'

The creature twitched its ears, then from beneath its tail sent a flurry of what looked like nibrim pellets skittering over her floor. Morton was wondering whether the arrangement of pellets spelled out a greeting, when the creature spoke. It sounded like 'baa', but however Morton adjusted the Universal Translator on her Infoscope, it failed to provide a meaning.

By the time Morton had keyed in the pellet pattern to see if the Infoscope could decode the message, the creature had wandered off down the living area, depositing several nibrim-style flurries as it went. The quantity of pellets was creating a rather dank smell.

Then Morton noticed a puddle of pale yellow liquid beside one of the flurries. She gave a low growl as she realised the alien messages were actually expellations. On hearing the growl the creature started behaving as if the floor was too hot for its feet, making 'baa' sounds as it jiggered round the room, squishing pellets and bumping into furniture.

That's when Morton summoned Kaye. He deserved to be woken in the middle of the night for damaging the scrambler and forcing Morton to suffer a fouled dwelling, when she should have been talking to a new Jerry-pet.

'What are you giving it to me for?' asked Kaye, as he entered the lab and Morton shoved the creature into his arms. 'And couldn't it have waited till morning?'

'I thought you were an animal lover,' Morton told him.

'I love them more in daytime,' he crabbed back.

Morton put his rudeness down to sleep loss. 'You're not the only one whose sleep's been disturbed, Kaye. The Duty Fossic looped through to alert me the Baa was agitated. I thought it cruel to keep it in the lab when your facilities are so superior.' The flattery worked.

'I run the best pet shop in the Quadrant,' he boasted. 'Although I've never seen a Baa before – where d'you get it? And what happened to its neck?' asked Kaye, sniffing at the scorch mark as the animal struggled to be put down.

'That's classified. But as I know I can trust you, I'll tell you this – the Baa was part of a BFA experiment which failed,' said Morton, ushering Kaye towards the portal.

'So what am I supposed to do with it?' Kaye asked, feeding it a zambon leaf which seemed to calm it down.

'I don't want to teach you your trade, but shouldn't you sell it? You'll get a good price; it's unique.'

'I have your permission?'

'As long as you trade it outside the Quadrant. You'll understand – I have to protect the BFA's reputation.'

'Of course.'

'And as a gesture of goodwill, I assign you the BFA's share of any profit which, given the prices you charge Kaye, will be substantial.'

From the look on the despicable creature's face as he left, Morton had more than made up for Kaye's broken sleep.

Now, taking care to avoid the puddles and flurries as she picked her way to the wallow room, Morton reflected on her remarkable generosity. At least Kaye would make money from the Baa, whereas all she'd gained from the encounter was a soiled and stinking dwelling.

As she stepped on to the shower pad, Morton consoled herself with the thought that she may not have a fresh Jerry-pet, but she still had her competitive education scheme. Until another thought hit her as shockingly as the blast of icy water she'd programmed to jolt her into action after her sleepless night . . .

If she set up a system whereby one Fossic taught a group of Podders, what would all the other Fossics do? Morton's mood turned sourer than a puddle of Baa-water.

*

Gale was in the kitchen, preparing Chad's breakfast. She was doing a dish for JerryPatterson too (even though it was wasteful feeding a pet who was about to be terminated) because she'd calculated he would be more docile with a full gut.

Since booting up, Gale had been running a termination-scenario programme, to determine the most effective method of disposal. One which ran no risk of Chad suffering further emotional trauma through witnessing his pet's passing. And took place in a location with minimum disruptability, which ruled out the wallow pool due to the inconvenience of draining and refilling it.

Gale had never self-run such a complex programme. If ever she had a pride chip added to her motherboard, she assessed it would be operating at maximum if she ran anything like this again. She posted a prompt. In the event of a pride chip being inserted, it should run an automatic historical burst to mark this event.

She altered that to two bursts. The first to commemorate her first termination scenario programme, the second to commemorate programming which could log an action prompt against a future Upgrade. Or should that be three? One, to acknowledge arrival of pride chip; two, to commemorate term.scen.prog; three, to celebrate sophis. of prog. that delivered 'one' and 'two'. Or was three covered by two?

Gale felt something thud against her casing and looked down. She'd hovered against the chiller unit. Leaving two future pride bursts logged, she deleted the process strand and continued preparing breakfast.

*

Jerry lay in bed exhausted, Sneb asleep on his chest spread like a raggedy blanket. His nocturnal hidden camera hunt had produced two more echo spots – one in the wallow room, one in the kitchen. He'd double-checked the living area, but still only picked up the two he knew about either end of the room. Although when Jerry stood under the one by the Infoscope he could have sworn he heard 'baa' echoing back at him, not 'lah'.

Could he have confused the two after sliding his way round walls all night saying it? No – there was a difference between calling 'la, la, lah' and a lamb's bleat. And Jerry had been so freaked by it he'd tested again and again, but it kept coming back the same. Definite shades of sheep. But Sneb sounded like a cat, so who knew what the creature on the other end of the baa looked like? At one point, Jerry thought he'd heard Morton echoing behind one of the 'baas', but it only happened once so he thought he must be so tired he'd started hearing things and had crept back to bed.

Now Jerry lay there, scratching Sneb's back, wondering where the echoes were coming from. Yesterday afternoon he'd heard Rashila, who must have been at work at the time. Last night he'd heard an animal. And possibly Morton. Think, Jerry, *think*! Morton and Rashila worked in a lab. Animals and labs, animals and . . . hang on! Labs experimented on animals. Pets were animals. They thought Jerry was a . . . *ohmycompleteanduttergod*!!!

Sneb flew backwards as Jerry jerked upright, clammy with cold sweat. The hidden cameras were for spying on him! Why? What were they planning? Were they going to lock him in a cage and force him to smoke? Cross-breed him with sheep aliens? Chain him to a post and poke him with sticks till he danced? No wonder Rashila flat-out refused to talk about sending him home!

'Are you all right, Jerry?' Chad called across.

'What? Oh . . . oh, yeah, I'm . . . fine.' Jerry mopped his face with the front of his top. 'Bad dream, that's all.'

Calm down, moron, they're watching you! What do they know? They know you hear voices! Waves of sweat surfed down Jerry's face as he went into stress overdrive, thinking that if they thought he was a head case they'd have him put down.

Chad had lowered his bed and stepped out of it. 'You're leaking, Jerry!' he sounded alarmed as he padded over.

'No I'm not, Chad.' Jerry hoiked a grin from somewhere as he leapt up. 'It's kind of like a . . . self-cleaning thing we have, you know.' He swiped fresh sweat away. 'Reminder, so I don't forget to wash my face.'

'That's clever. I was worried you were hearing voices again.'

'Voices? Me? That was *so* yesterday, Chad. All gone now. Probably a touch of intergalactic jetlag or something.'

Should he tell Chad about the cameras? No! He'd think he'd gone barking Tonto and there was one in here anyway, so he . . . woah . . . Chad! Rashila's weak spot. And Jerry had the lashed legs to prove it. He'd play the Chad card to win her round. It's not like he had anything else to go on.

'How you doing today, Chad? D'you sleep OK?' asked Jerry, realising that Chad had been staring at him rather carefully. Please, please, don't say he'd been muttering to himself just now!

'Not great, Jerry,' sighed Chad mournfully. 'I kept seeing bad images all night. Mostly with Gilpin in them.'

'I'm sorry about the football, Chad.' Are you listening out there? 'We should never have played. But your mother's so clever, I'm sure she's right when she told you Gilpin will have forgotten all about it by now.'

'I'm just not convinced.' Chad plumped into his chair, looking glum.

'I know you wanted to play, but it was me who told you about the game,' said Jerry. 'So I'm going to make sure this comes right for you. Are you seeing Gilpin today?'

Chad nodded. 'Social Session's at hers, this afternoon.'

'Right. By the end of Social Session everything's going to be back to normal.'

'Really Jerry? How?'

For the first time since Chad's defeat, Jerry saw hope in his eyes. How was Jerry going to pull this off? Good question. So . . . what d'you do when you want to stop someone thinking badly of you? For some reason, a picture of a mini Woolfie, a bald Barbie and an empty wallet popped into Jerry's head.

'Here's how, my friend. You are going to buy Gilpin a present.'

'Why?'

''Cos it'll stop her feeling disappointed.'

'How does that work?'

'Um . . . not sure. But it does. Trust me.'

'I do trust you, Jerry. What sort of present should it be?'

'She's your girlfriend. What do you normally buy her when you buy her something?'

'I don't normally buy her anything.'

'What – you guys don't have birthdays?'

'Hatchdays, yes.'

'So, what did you buy her on her last hatchday?'

'It was so long ago, I'd have to ask Gale.'

'Oookay.'

'You don't look happy, Jerry. Does that mean this isn't going to work?'

'Course it's gonna work! This isn't my unhappy face, Chad; it's my thinking face. And I'm thinking it's much better if you hardly ever buy Gilpin presents, 'cos that means she'll be even more pleased when you do.'

'Really?'

'Definitely.'

'Has buying presents worked for you?'

'Many, many, times.'

'Jerry! Does that mean people have often been disappointed by you?'

'No! Well, sometimes. Not that often. And it's not always my fault – like it wasn't yours yesterday, right? It's just . . . stuff . . . happens. Let's call them misunderstandings. Believe me, it's easily done. 'Specially if you had to live with Andy and Woolfie.'

'Are they your parents?'

'My brother and sister.'

Chad's brow-scales dipped into a frown. 'Sorry, Jerry, that didn't translate. Is 'brotherandsister' a type of Bonded Partner?

Jerry's jaw dropped. 'You don't have brothers and sisters?'

Chad shook his head. 'What are they?'

'A pain, mostly.'

'Can you get it treated?'

'Not that kind of pain,' said Jerry. 'My mother has more than one child. There's another boy, my brother Andy, and a girl, my sister, Woolfie. Her real name's Sarah, but everyone calls her Woolfie, 'cos she used to lug this stuffed toy wolf everywhere and . . .'

'Jerry!' Chad exclaimed, eyes wide with surprise and washing-line-eared. 'There were *three* hatchlings in your pod?'

'Um, doesn't work quite like that. At least, it can . . . but it didn't – hey let's not go there. Andy was . . . hatched . . . first, then a couple of years later I came along, then after a while, Mum had, I mean, hatched, Woolfie.'

'Unbelievable! And how does your mother know which one's which?'

'Because we all look completely different.'

'No!!!'

*

Morton took some long, deep breaths to slow the thud of her beating hearts. Multiple Podders! The potential for increased

211

Fossic usage was beyond measure. Assuming she could devise a way to do it. Ridiculous thought. She was Morton.

'Is something wrong, Director?' Rashila called from her desk.

'Nothing,' Morton looked away from the screen. 'Just sighing with relief because Chad seems happier this morning. Jerry's just suggested buying Gilpin Carney a present to help her get over the football disappointment.'

'But it's not a Hatchday Year!' Rashila lost no time appearing at Morton's elbow.

'It must be an alien custom. I can't see that it would do any harm.'

'How do I explain to Gilpin's parents why Chad has given their daughter an unplanned gift before they were fully Bonded?'

Morton felt her ears tilting. You offered them a claw and they wanted your tail. Rashila wisely noted the tilt and altered her tone.

'But if you feel it's appropriate, Director, I'm sure it will be acceptable.'

'Thank you, Rashila.'

They watched Jerry tell Chad they had to buy the present this morning.

'We can't,' said Chad. 'I've got Lesson Sessions.'

'We must!' Jerry insisted. 'The whole present-giving thing only works, if you do it the first time you see the person after you've done the bad thing – not that you did a bad thing – I mean, the first time after the bad thing happened. You've gotta ask Gale if the two of us can go shopping.'

Mother and son gasped in unison as both realised Jerry meant they should go shopping on their own. It surprised Morton too, but she refused to dilute her seniority by showing it.

'He's a very independent creature, isn't he?' was all she said.

Rashila gave a snort of contempt. 'He's obviously been allowed to roam wild.'

Chad said Gale would never agree to cancel any more Lesson Sessions, and it was unthinkable she'd let Chad out alone. Jerry seemed amazed by this, but said Chad would never know if he didn't ask – unless he didn't want to repair the damaged relationship. As the two of them left Chad's quarters to find Gale, Morton decided she had to make the most of Jerry before his mental health got any worse.

'Rashila, quick! Message Gale and tell her to cancel this morning's Lessons Sessions.'

'Director! Surely you're not suggesting I . . . we . . . allow Chad to go shopping alone?'

'Don't be absurd! Tell Gale to take him. And Jerry.'

'But cancelling Lessons Sessions two days running, will—'

'—heal the conflict between your son and Gilpin

Carney?' Morton applied the logic that had just worked for Jerry. 'Unless you'd rather it continued?'

'I'll send the message.'

*

As Chad and his pet approached across the living area, Gale lifted their dishes and heard the alert sound which signalled the generation of the termination scenario programme results log, followed, almost immediately, by an Inbox alert. The message, from Rashila Jannan (sentence structure match confirmed) instructed her to cancel this morning's Lessons Sessions and take Chad and Jerry shopping. Only if Chad asked.

Chad had taken his breakfast and was now asking. While she conversed with her Podder and, to his evident surprise, agreed to take him shopping, Gale scanned the results log. The scenario it recommended was well within her capabilities.

Podder insisted pet was essential to the expedition. Rashila Jannan must consider the expedition vital or she would not have instructed Gale to disrupt Chad's routine for the second day running. So Gale logged a prompt for their return:

Proceed with JerryPatterson's disposal at the first opportunity.

CHAPTER NINETEEN

Harchi bit into his cissbury ring, waited until the acidy filling had oozed over his tongue and assaulted his taste buds, then chewed. It was the only way to eat cissbury, otherwise you lost that eye-watering kick of bitterness in amongst the chewed fruit.

He'd seen his new friend Tsooris eat his by clawing the tubular circle apart round its outer edge, licking each half clean of filling, then eating the fruit. For Harchi, this made what should be a uniquely bittersweet experience into two quite separate events. Bitter, followed by sweet.

Not that Harchi thought any the less of Tsooris for his chosen method. He was only a Quality of Plantation Rain team Trainee and had barely de-Fossicked; he probably wouldn't appreciate the other way until he'd matured. And Harchi didn't want to be unkind about his cissbury style because Tsooris had been so helpful today.

Spotting Harchi padding past his door this morning, he'd called out (between mouthfuls of cissbury, which was excusable because they rotted almost the moment you broke into them) that if he was heading for Gornish's office he'd better hurry, because another big meeting was about to start.

Tsooris's advice had been good. And Harchi wished he'd followed it. When he'd first arrived at the Unit he'd tried to see Gornish, only to find his office still locked. It was when he'd been on his way there for the second time that he'd run into Tsooris.

Harchi finished his cissbury ring, thinking that if he hadn't stopped to find out from Tsooris that the meeting was to discuss another unidentified energy surge over the Metropolis last night, then gone to buy a cissbury ring to satisfy the craving from watching Tsooris eat his, he'd probably have seen Gornish. But there was no guarantee of that. And the cissbury ring had been delicious.

Harchi brought the weather portrait of Rashila up on screen, admiring it while he licked cissbury stickiness from his claws. He refused to panic. There were still several bandwidths before Harchi was due to meet Jerry at the chute. He was sure to find a bar of opportunity in there somewhere to demonstrate his Random Rain Scheme to Gornish.

*

Morton was taking the first cautious steps towards determining how to turn her visionary idea of Multiple Podder Parenting into a reality when a call looped through. With a

216

low growl, she changed screens and barked her name. It was the Senior Duty Fossic to inform her that Bluhm was in the workshop with Conway.

How was she supposed to concentrate on scientific breakthroughs when everyone from the Chair of the Ministry Committee down kept interrupting? Halfway through gouging the underside of her desk to release some anger, Morton had a directorial brainwave. She'd send Rashila. Bluhm would admire Morton for concentrating on the Upgrades; she'd have the lab to herself; and Rashila would be in Morton's debt for letting her deal with such an important dignitary.

Even in the midst of devising the most tradition-shattering Upgrades of her career, and on the verge of shedding her tail tip from exhaustion, Morton could still come up with outstanding managerial solutions. She really was magnificent.

*

Jerry was on sensation overload as he tried to make sense of the sights, sounds and smells which bombarded him as he followed Chad and Gale off the chute at the outdoor market. He was vaguely aware of the throng of Pastinaceans, Fossics and Podders pushing past, smiling and nudging each other as they saw the stunned look on his face and heard Chad boasting: 'He's mine! A Ridgeless Pink. It's his first time at market.'

There were hundreds of stalls scattered about across the

baked clay ground. Each with a purple oval canopy, presumably to protect stallholders from the trio of suns shining down on them. The rule seemed to be one type of produce per stallholder, but no one was short of customers, and most had small Fossic-type assistants helping them do brisk business in what Jerry guessed were fruit and vegetables.

The smell was really hard to pin down. As soon as Jerry thought he'd caught a familiar whiff, another one shoved it aside . . . curry, lemons, runny French cheese, vinegar, freshly cut grass, carrots, swimming pools . . . so many, he gave up in the end.

'Did I cancel Chad's Lessons Sessions for you to stare at a market all morning?' beeped Gale loudly in Jerry's ear. He wasn't sure if she'd done it to snap him out of his tourist trance or be heard over the grunts, rasps, snorts, beeps and whirrs of the crowd.

'Who died and made you Headmistress?' Jerry bristled, sick of the way she kept getting on his case.

'That is an inexplicable response,' whirred Gale, but she did hover off slightly.

Chad clearly hadn't got it either, but he'd picked up the vibe. 'How does this work?' he asked Jerry, inserting himself between pet and Fossic. 'Do we just walk round until you see something you think might be suitable for Gilpin?'

Jerry nodded. 'Except I don't know what any of this is so you'll have to explain.'

'OK. And if we haven't found anything by the time we get to the other side of the market, there's some shops over there.' Chad waved a claw at the horizon.

'Cool. And is it all fruit and veg?' queried Jerry, thinking that half a kilo of zambon leaves probably wouldn't cut it as a let's-forget-you-disappointed-me gift.

'No,' said Chad as they moved off. 'It's just that the chute comes out at the fresh produce section. There's all types of goods for sale here.'

'That's not really balancing on thin air, is it?' said Jerry, eyes on stalks as they walked past a stall filled with floating pyramids of immaculately stacked perrin roots.

Chad laughed as he shook his head. 'There's an ice-filled shelf to keep the food fresh, but it's invisible because of the neuromagtric force generated by the solar-powered canopies and . . .'

Chad seemed to be enjoying himself so Jerry let him bunny on, nodding if there was a pause, thinking how Woolfie would howl with laughter when he told her he'd been shopping. Usually he'd rather have his teeth pulled without anaesthetic, but how many times in his life would he get to shop in an alien market? Hopefully, just this once.

Jerry decided to see if he could blag Chad into springing for some going-home prezzies for Mum and the others. (Maybe even a little something for Rachel Davis?) Because whatever else happened today Jerry was absolutely determined, one way or another, that he was going to get one step closer to delivering them.

*

Harchi hadn't wasted his morning. In between checking Gornish's availability (no change) he'd worked up some ideas for outfits he and Jerry might wear when they toured the Quadrants performing writing and counting tricks and selling Weather Portraits. Current favourite: matching shorts – maroon or green, and tunics – orange or yellow. (Either to go with either.) With their names on the front. And for fun, 'Owner' and 'Pet' on the back.

Looping through to Gornish, Harchi was frustrated to get voicemail. Again. And bored. The outfits were finished – what was he supposed to do for the rest of the day; sit here and loop through to voicemail, bar after bar? He felt like marching up there and forcing Gornish to watch the pilot, then he'd . . . Tails up! Was that the answer?

Unlike yesterday's low-key pilot pilot, it would be impossible to miss the full strength version. Gornish was guaranteed to race outside to see what was happening. Where he'd be met by Harchi, with a detailed explanation and a back broad enough to receive the many congratulatory pats that would doubtless follow.

A tempting solution. Harchi saved the outfit notes and colour charts he'd made, to show Jerry and opened the Jannan Random Rain Scheme file. In a blink, Rashila's weather portrait stared out from his screen. Harchi stared back. Should he run the pilot? Or shouldn't he?

*

Rashila bent into the crook of Conway's dismantled arm, held steady by one Duty Fossic at wrist, the other pre-shoulder, wiring a new elbow joint into its housing. She was the acknowledged Jolty Elbow Expert and it was an honour to have been given this opportunity to demonstrate her skill for Bluhm.

Rashila sneaked a glance at the Chair of the Ministry Committee, who sat sipping sour tea beside her temporarily one-armed Fossic. Rashila hoped she'd look that elegant when she was Bluhm's age. Her scales had faded slightly and lay looser on her throat, but Bluhm's hair clump was an immaculate cluster of thick, perfectly sculpted, night-black peaks. Her finger-claws were painted to match while her toe-claws were sparkly silver, echoing the trim on her designer tunic and shorts.

Bluhm caught Rashila's eye and smiled. A warm, open smile, unlike the cold-eyed grimaces Morton flung out. Rashila smiled back then quickly returned to her work. She'd hate Bluhm to think she was being impertinent by staring.

Why had Morton given her this honour? She'd looked exhausted when Rashila had arrived for work today. And there was an odd smell down her end of the lab, though Morton denied it. Was she getting too long in the claw to cope with Upgrade stress? Except however stressed she was, Morton would usually still drop everything for Bluhm.

What was so important she'd risk offending the Chair? And why didn't Rashila know about it? Or was that the point? Was Morton working on something so extreme, she wanted Rashila out of the lab?

Rashila's tail tingled with apprehension. So far, Morton had been so casual about the impact of the research on Chad that Rashila dreaded to think how he might suffer from whatever outrage she was planning now.

Should she talk to Bluhm about her concerns? Rashila didn't want to behave improperly. And she'd be taking a monumental risk. Morton would never forgive Rashila if Bluhm started an investigation – and she'd dismiss Rashila's fears as the anxieties of a neurotic mother.

Clipping the last illmington on to its ebrington rod, Rashila sealed the hinge with her solder-stick and straightened up. 'Double-check the connections, oil and run a test, then re-attach the arm,' she instructed the Senior Duty Fossic.

'Affirmative,' he whirred, beeping orders to his under-Fossic as they took the limb across to Conway to finish off.

'All done?' asked Blum, walking over.

'Yes.' Rashila smiled. 'Conway should be jolt-free now. At least on the left. I'm sure you're aware, it's a Phase 9 weakness. I'd be happy to replace the other elbow joint while you're here if you like?'

'That's very thoughtful,' said Bluhm, 'but I've taken up quite enough of your time.'

'Chair Bluhm! My time is your time. I'd be honoured to—'

Blum held up a claw. 'Conway is only a stand-by Fossic. And I'm sure you have an immense amount of work waiting in the lab. How are the Upgrades coming along?'

Was Bluhm being polite? Or did she really want to know? Rashila was in an agony of indecision. Should she risk it? Would she find another job at this level if Morton found out? What if . . .

Rashila realised Bluhm was waiting for an answer. 'They're coming along nicely, thank you Chair.' Rashila decided to dip a claw in the pool. 'I think you'll find this year's Upgrades . . .' She left a deliberate pause. '. . . rather interesting.'

Had she been too subtle? No. The yellow of Bluhm's eyes glowed deeper and Rashila caught the smallest upward twitch in her ears and tail. Though Bluhm's only comment was: 'My Committee and I look forward to the results.'

*

Morton wasn't sure what made her activate Conway's I-Cam to check on Rashila when she did. But she was glad she had. Because the camera came on just in time for Morton to see Bluhm key a number into her two-faced assistant's hand-held then hand it back with a smile, telling her to call if there was ever *anything* she wished to discuss.

*

223

Jerry was explaining to Chad why a metal broom for brushing your scales wasn't an ideal present for Gilpin, when a low rumble rolled out overhead.

'What was that?' Chad asked Gale nervously.

'Scanning for data now, but early indications—'

'It's thunder,' said Jerry. 'At least, it sounded like it.' Go Harchi! He must have finally got hold of Gornish and was running his Random Rain Scheme demo.

'What's thunder?' asked Chad, surprised to find his pet able to supply information where his Fossic had none.

'Um . . .' Jerry scrabbled through his weather knowledge, came up empty-handed and decided to busk it. '. . . It's trapped air escaping from clouds as the wind crashes them into each other.'

Chad and Gale looked up. At a cloudless sky. Without a hint of wind. Ooookay. 'Mum always says it's God moving his tables and chairs.'

'How can someone moving furniture make a noise in the sky?' frowned Chad.

Jerry was about to do a spot of improv on heaven, with a small riff on hell, when he was silenced (spooky, or what?) by a monstrous huge thunderclap. He flinched, even though he loved a good storm. Judging by the reaction in the market, Jerry would be on his own with that today. From way over by the chute dock to right up to where Jerry, Chad and Gale stood near the far edge, the area fell thickly silent. And nobody moved. Not even a tail twitched.

As if waiting for quiet before making an entrance, a colossal whip-crack of electric-blue lightning stabbed through the purple sky – immediately followed by torrential rain, which poured down with the force of a shattered celestial water main.

Jerry turned to tell Chad it was only Harchi testing some weather, to see him being dragged away by Gale. He was about to follow, when another thunderclap detonated, setting off a stampede of noisy panic.

'It's all right! It's only a storm! There's nothing to worry about!' yelled Jerry as creatures pounded past. His voice was buried behind a near-solid wall of rain, patterned by flash after flash of blue forked lightning reaching down into the market place like the veins on the back of a granny's hand.

Every single being was running to escape the storm, but numbers were so high it was impossible to clear the area fast enough. Soon they were pushing and shoving into the backs of other shoppers, snarling at them to get out of the way.

Carried along by the momentum Jerry began to panic, terrified he'd be knocked over and trampled in the rush. He ducked under a stall, thinking it'd be safer to shelter there until the storm passed, and was congratulating himself on his quick thinking when the canopy was struck by lightning, shocking it over and sending the goods shooting to the ground.

Forcing his way back into the jungle of legs charging past, Jerry saw stall after stall hit by flickers of lightning, which sent them crashing over and their once superbly displayed stock was instantly crushed underfoot.

Deafened by the petrified grunts and roars Jerry stumbled along, all kicks and elbows as he fought for space, desperately trying to stay upright. As yet another thunderclap exploded the crowd redoubled their efforts to leave, and Jerry was lifted off the ground by the surge of frantic activity, pedalling air as he screamed at the baying, snarling creatures not to crush him.

Disorientated and gasping for breath Jerry scrabbled his way up through the bodies, pulling on waistbands, necklines, ridges – anything, until he was climbing over shoulders, backs and heads to get out from under the crowd. There was a frenzy of snapping and slashing, but compared to a Pastinacean Jerry was a featherweight, and he managed to dodge and duck most of the attacks as he surfed his way across the top of the mob.

Spotting some shops not too far away, Jerry knew it would be safer to shelter in one until the storm passed rather than risk his life in the crowd. He surfed a bit further before forcing himself back into the pack and managed to slither down until he felt the ground beneath his feet.

Jerry felt sick – he'd slithered too early; the shops were on the other side of a walkway. He had to get across it to safety. There was no choice but to battle his way through the tide of creatures charging along the walkway: a task made more dangerous by the rain which had turned the clay path into a slippery-as-wet-glass slide.

Another thunderclap bammed overhead, sending the throng into even higher levels of hysteria. Jerry, halfway across the walkway, kept getting knocked to the ground. Each time he got to his knees a creature would hurtle past, bashing him over in a shower of orange mud. Then he'd desperately struggle up only to be flattened again.

Choking back his fear Jerry summoned one last scrap of energy, staggered to his feet and lunged for the nearest shop. He'd almost made it off the walkway when a huge Pastinacean smashed into him sideways which sent Jerry slamming into other bodies like a pinball in an arcade until a tiny space opened up, which he promptly crumpled into.

The wet clay was silky cool against his cheek. Jerry felt it tickling its way into his nose and ears and decided to lie there and let the rhythm of the noise from the crowd lull him to sleep. Just a nap. A snatched moment of quiet amongst the chaos. He'd get up in a minute. He wouldn't be late for school. Woolfie was in the shower, no point hurrying . . .

A sharp pain on his wrist forced him into consciousness. Someone was dragging on his arm. Get off, Andy! I'm sleeping! Ow! All right, stop pinching, I'm up – look I'm up! Jeez! Jerry's vision was cloudy, but half-stumbling, half-dragged, he felt himself heaved off the walkway by two strong claws which swung him round, then abruptly dumped him, backside first, against the front of a shop.

Jerry smeared mud from his eyes and found himself peering into a pair of bright yellow orbs, topped off by a pea-green hair clump.

'Clacket Layne!' Jerry gulped air.

'Saved your life,' came the reply, with no trace of a smile. 'You belong to me now.'

Jerry would have cracked back with a witty one-liner. If he hadn't blacked out.

CHAPTER TWENTY

Morton was ignoring the fact that someone had repeatedly been trying to loop through to Rashila, shutting out the sound by submerging herself in chromosome manipulation theory. But when the caller looped through for the umpteenth time her patience finally snapped. Charging over to her assistant's desk, Morton activated the screen and roared: 'She's not here! *Whatdoyouwant!*'

Whatever had happened, it was bad. Harchi didn't even flinch at seeing Morton's livid face come up on his wife's screen.

'There's a batch of Rogue Weather.' Harchi's eyes were wild, his voice urgent. 'You need to put out an All Fossic Alert. Now!'

This was not the moment for Morton to quibble about the protocol of a weather technician issuing orders to the Director of the BFA. 'Are you sure? There's been no interference on our equipment.'

'It's isolated over the Market Sector. I'm doing everything I can to control it, but the rainfall's way past

Plantation maximum and I'm worried about Fossic malfunction!'

'I'll launch an Alert. What's caused it?'

'Um . . . I'm not sure . . . it could be linked to the unidentified energy surges Gornish is investigating.'

'Why isn't he dealing with this?'

'He's in a calls-barred meeting with the rest of the Department. I wanted to make sure the BFA were issuing an AFA, before I went up to get him.'

'Good work, Harchi Jannan.'

As she cut the loop, Morton caught the flicker of surprise in his eyes.

*

Barrelling along corridors and hurtling round bends, Harchi tried to work out what had gone wrong. He'd re-programmed the pilot to run over the Business Sector where the Unit stood, but the instant Harchi pressed 'enter' the screen showed it had shifted to the Marketplace. Worse, the meteorological elements had quadrupled in power from the playful levels he'd programmed.

Harchi tried to cancel the pilot but the system refused to accept his command. Then he'd noticed a cissbury-scented sticky patch coating his 'cancel' key, so he'd licked and licked until he was certain he'd got it all off, but by then the keyboard was drenched in saliva so 'cancel' still wouldn't work. Nor would any of the other keys.

With a potential disaster on his claws, Harchi knew he

should be doing something more effective than trying to blow his keyboard dry. That's when he'd looped through to Rashila. Again and again. Becoming increasingly desperate, until salvation arrived in the unlikely shape of Morton.

Hysteria rising at the prospect of being sacked if he was identified as the cause of the problem, Harchi gave his keyboard one last try before going to get Gornish. Almost shedding his tail tip with anxiety, Harchi claw-tipped 'cancel'. Silence. Silence. Ping! He nearly sobbed with relief as the command was accepted.

Harchi's claws were a blur over the keyboard as he disappeared every shred of evidence that his beloved Random Rain Scheme had ever existed. So long, statue. Farewell, plinth. No time to mourn them now – he had to get Gornish. He was already out of his chair when Harchi noticed that despite having deleted everything, the elements continued to run at maximum. With a whimper of panic, he dashed out.

Skidding to a halt outside the meeting room, Harchi barged in without knocking. Twenty pairs of Departmental ears stood up and twenty pairs of eyes widened in surprise as Harchi panted at Gornish: 'There's Rogue Weather over the Marketplace. The BFA's issuing an All Fossic Alert. I need help!'

*

Jerry drifted back to consciousness, trying to figure out where he was. He was lying on something hard, so it wasn't

231

his bed. And he recognised the smell. He was fairly sure it wasn't Morton's lab, but definitely familiar. Warily opening his eyes, Jerry was horrified to see his view on all sides crisscrossed by wires.

'Kaye-pa,' a small voice snortled near his head, 'Jerry-pet's wakey!'

Jerry sat up, banging his head on the top of the cage. *Ohmygodhewasinacage!* He was distracted from a full on, bells-and-whistles panic by a toddler-sized Pastinacean who danced into vision, pointing and giggling at him. She was dressed in a wincingly bright, multi-coloured tunic and shorts set with an acid pink ribbon round her turquoise hair. Jerry reckoned he should be the one pointing and laughing.

'Hello, Jerry-pet!' She waved a claw. 'Me Yash. Can oo say hello?'

'I would, only being shut in a cage doesn't exactly make me feel sociable.'

'What's he chatting, Kaye-pa?' she called over her shoulder.

Jerry had to pretend he was coughing to cover his gulp of surprise, as a plump-bellied Pastinacean waddled over in an outfit identical to his daughter. Minus the ribbon. But surprise turned to fear as Jerry heard a muffled chorus of grunty, snuffly, barky type noises coming from the area Plump Belly had just left. These two were wearing clown outfits. And the place was full of animals. Had Clacket Layne sold him to a circus?

232

'How you feeling?' asked his host, banishing Jerry's jelly legs by taking the side off his cage. 'I'm Kaye, by the way.'

'I'm feeling. . .' Jerry crawled out of the cage into the bare room expecting every single bone to ache after the battering he'd taken, then realised as he stood up that he felt surprisingly well. '. . . great, thanks. Kaye.'

'Amazing! You really can talk!' said Kaye, with washing-line ears. 'I thought that was just a piece of Clacket Layne wackiness.'

'Nope. I'm fully functional in the vocal department.' Jerry stretched to loosen up. 'I can't believe I got away without a scratch.'

'You didn't. I had Yash's Fossic go over you with her medicinal claw, then stuck you in the isolation cage in case you were going to die.' This guy was all heart. 'Not good for business, keeping sick animals in the shop.' Kaye swooped his daughter up and shook her in the air. 'Is it, Yashi? Is it?'

No wonder the smell was familiar – this must be the pet shop where Harchi bought him! 'Thanks for looking after me,' Jerry shouted, to be heard over the shrieks and giggles.

'Never had a pet thank me before!' Kaye snorted, putting Yash down. 'All part of the service.' He grinned, revealing a long tooth studded with tiny coloured jewels which put the finishing touch to his outfit. 'Wouldn't want Harchi giving me a hard time – the Jannans are good customers. Although I wish I'd known you could talk, I would have really hiked the price up.'

233

'Win some, lose some eh?' said Jerry, wondering if Kaye had been a second-hand car salesman before he bought the shop. 'Listen, I need to talk to you about how I got here.'

'Clacket Layne brought you in.'

'No . . . I meant . . . how I got to Pastinare.'

'Naughty, naughty!' smirked Kaye, tapping the side of his snout with a claw. 'If I told you that, you'd be out there undercutting me faster than I could shout: alien!'

'I wouldn't, I promise, it's just I have to know how—'

'No,' Kaye kept the smirk, but his voice was steel. 'You really don't.'

'But . . .' Jerry's protest was interrupted by a loud 'baa' from somewhere behind him. 'What's that?' he asked Kaye, fighting to keep it casual.

'It's a Baa!' shrieked Yash, jumping up and down. 'Come see!'

Jerry looked across at Kaye, to check if that was going to be a problem.

'It's out the back,' said Kaye, saving his charm for someone who mattered. 'It came in this morning – haven't had time to process it yet.' He swung his belly in the opposite direction. 'Better get back to the shop.' And he was gone.

'Come on Jerry-pet!' Yash tugged his hand. 'Clacket Layne there, too.'

Jerry let Yash pull him down a dingy hallway. His clothes were stiff with dried mud, which meant he'd probably been unconscious for a while. Then Jerry realised the storm had stopped. Either Harchi had cancelled the pilot or it had run its course, but why had he programmed such a belter?

The hallway led into a covered area, cram-stacked with boxes of stock and equipment. And Clacket Layne, crouching by a cage, tickling a lamb through the wire. It had to be the animal he'd heard last night. But where did Morton fit into all this?

'Look! Me got a Jerry-pet!' shrilled Yash, hurling herself on to Clacket Layne's back and flinging her arms around her neck.

'Look! Me got a Baa!' yelled Clacket Layne, scratching the lamb's ear with one claw and reaching behind her to tickle Yash with the other.

Jerry went closer to check it really was a lamb. Never lambier. Except this one had a ruff of scorched fur around its neck.

'I know you belong to me now, but I don't want you any more,' said Clacket Layne, looking up at him. 'I want this.' She nodded at the lamb.

'Yeah, I'm feeling much better, thanks.'

'And that's the reason why,' said Clacket Layne, standing up with Yash clinging to her back like a multi-coloured rucksack.

'Why what?'

'Why I don't want you. Because every time I say something, you say something back.'

'Hey, don't knock it – I gather it's one of my selling points.'

'There you are – you've done it again. Buy me the Baa.'

'Pets don't have money.'

'Jannans do. Get Harchi to buy it. As a thank-you for saving your life, which is only polite. And to help me get over my Big Disappointment.' She turned her head and nuzzled Yash's small snout with her own. 'I'm not Bonded, you know.'

'Yashi Bonded. Sad Clacket Layne. Sad.' Yash released her grip, slithered down Clacket Layne and ran off, screeching, 'Kaye-pa! Kaye-pa! They going to buy the Baa!'

'Are we, Jerry?' Clacket Layne started frantically scratching her tail tip. 'Tell me it's true! Tell me! Before I scratch myself skinny!'

'You really want it that bad?'

The scratching went up a gear. 'Can you see? Can you see how bad I want it?'

'But you live in a flat! You can't house-train a lamb, you know.'

Clacket Layne looked puzzled, and with perfect timing the lamb provided a graphic demonstration.

'It's a Baa. I'll make it special shorts.'

'It's a lamb. Your parents will kill you.'

'Won't. Saved your life.' She took a deep breath, narrowed her eyes and jabbed her tail tip in the lamb's direction. 'Want. It.'

There was no question in Jerry's mind, Clacket Layne

had saved his life. Why shouldn't she have the lamb? What was the worst she could do – love it to death? Anything was better than leaving it here. 'OK. I'll get it for you.'

'Jerry Patterson, just Jerry, that's kind, so very kind, that if I didn't have the Baa, I'd go back to having you, really I would, but it's more furry and cuddly and cuter than you and it won't take up so much room, eat as much, or answer back.'

'Thanks for the ego work-out.'

Kaye's belly turned a corner, bringing Yash and the rest of Kaye with it.

'Has Yash got it right – you want to buy the Baa?' Kaye asked Clacket Layne, doubtfully. 'I haven't had time to price it, but lemme tell you it's going to be waaaay out of your league. Have a snebbit instead?'

Clacket Layne took a deep breath, but Jerry jumped in before she could go off on one. 'I'm getting the Baa for her, Kaye. As a thank-you for saving my life.'

'You?' came the snorted retort. 'I don't sell pets to pets! Even if I did, where would you get the money for something as exotic as a Baa?'

'I don't need money. Because *you* are going to give it to me.'

Kaye's ears and tail raced Clacket Layne's to the ceiling, but their grunts of amazement were a definite tie.

'I. Am going to give it. To you?' sneered Kaye. 'I don't think

237

so. Alien.' The word was iced with contempt. Yash backed in behind her father and peeped out from behind his legs.

'Oh I'm an alien, all right,' smiled Jerry coolly. 'And that gives me the advantage here. 'Cos I've seen Baas before. So many of them, I even know what breed this is. See that mark round its neck?' Jerry tried out Barkow's best pay-attention-class tone. 'We call that a ruff. Which makes this a Ruffhead Baa. I know something else about it too. That there's a well dodgy story about how it came to be here.'

'You're bluffing,' spat Kaye.

'Am I? Send me out of here Baa-less, then and see what I do. You'll be fine if I am bluffing. And if I'm not. . .' Jerry winced and sucked air. 'Now, you looked after me today Kaye, so I'm gonna give you a break. I'm not bluffing. So why don't you hand the Baa over to my very good friend, Clacket Layne. And we'll be on our way.'

There was a long, yellow to blue eyeball moment until, with an angry growl, Kaye dropped his gaze, walked his belly to the cage and sprang the lamb.

*

Chad sat at the table, staring at the dish of walsh-pods Gilpin had split for him, fighting to control the fear that welled up in him. He felt a claw on his arm and looked up.

'Cheer up, Chaddy,' said Gilpin, reaching to scratch his ridges. 'Harchi's not going to be mad at you for losing Jerry.'

'But I've only had him three days! How could I be so

careless? I should have put him on a lead.' Chad gave a huge sigh which sent some walsh-pods rolling across the table.

'What's done is done,' said Gilpin, 'Harchi'll buy you another pet. Hopefully something smaller this time.' She gave his arm a comforting squeeze.

There was a silence, while Gilpin speared the scattered walsh-pods on a claw, then slid them into her mouth against the point of a tooth. And Chad considered how fitting it was, given the reason for their trip to the Market in the first place, that the last act his pet might have done before . . . Chad couldn't finish the 'before' . . . was to bring him and Gilpin together again.

'What were you doing at the Market during Lessons Session anyway?'

'Oh, um, Jerry wanted to go,' said Chad, not wishing to remind Gilpin of yesterday's Great Disappointment.

'And what Jerry wants, Jerry gets?'

'It wasn't quite like that, Gilpin.'

'There you go, defending him again!'

'I'm not. Well, I am, but—'

'Chad! Stop blaming yourself for something Jerry wanted to do and paid the price for. I'm sorry you've lost your pet, but I'm not sorry everything's going to get back to normal again.'

The portal swished open.

'Hi guys!' grinned Jerry, strolling in with a casual wave.

239

'Jerry!' beamed Chad, leaping up.

Gilpin growled softly as Chad charged over to his pet, ignored the fact that he was caked in mud for some reason, and flung his arms around Jerry's waist to jig about with him, while Jerry laughed and struggled to get his feet back on the floor.

They were quickly joined by Sneb who shot out of Rashila's quarters, dashed up the wall and across the ceiling to perform a precision flip and drop on to Jerry's head, where he draped himself across the top like a pink, purry hat.

Chad felt a tap on his shoulder. Gilpin was staring at something behind him. He put Jerry down and turned to see what it was. Clacket Layne had walked in with the strangest four-legged creature frisking about on the end of a lead, belted into thickly padded shorts. It made an odd, tremblyvoiced noise. Sneb yowled, and Jerry grabbed him so he couldn't attack.

'What is that?' Gilpin asked Jerry. He opened his mouth to answer, but Clacket Layne gave a far from subtle cough so he waved her on.

'This,' said Clacket Layne, with the satisfaction of someone who's waited a lifetime for something to boast about, 'is my Baa. She's called Ruffhead. Jerry got her for me for saving his life. She's quite unique. And unbelievably valuable.'

*

240

'Jerry's back!' Rashila announced, forgetting she'd been trying not to disturb Morton. She'd returned from repairing Conway to an extremely hostile reception, possibly because Morton regretted not having dealt with Bluhm herself. Probably because she'd had to launch an All Fossic Alert and deal with owners looping through to report malfunctions caused by Rogue Weather water damage.

Rashila had taken over from Morton, setting two Duty Fossics to answer the barrage of calls while she scheduled repairs. Gornish had issued the All Clear shortly after that, so Rashila cancelled the AFA, and as the calls gradually stopped she'd sent the Duty Fossics back to the workshop.

All Morton had told her was there'd been Rogue Weather over the Marketplace – and that Harchi had raised the alarm. She clearly wasn't in the mood for questions and Rashila daren't make a personal call to Harchi to find out more. Instead, Rashila had worked her way through the repair bookings, checking them against workshop stock to make sure they had all the right parts, and ordering fresh supplies of equipment where necessary.

Having finished that, Rashila went back to the screen to check on Chad just as Jerry arrived back at their dwelling. By then the smell down that end of the lab was utterly snoutish, but there was no point mentioning it again. Her boss was already in such a temper, and for some strange reason seemed determined to ignore it.

'Clacket Layne saved Jerry's life apparently,' said Rashila, as she heard Morton padding over. 'And somehow he's got hold of an exotic pet to say thank you. I think it's called a Baa. I've never seen one before. Have you?'

'No,' came the barked reply. Rashila was amazed – it was extremely unusual for Morton not to show an interest in something so rare.

'Wouldn't your time be better spent staring at the screen instead of me?' Morton snarled, before marching back to her desk.

Rashila spun round, her mind racing. Why hadn't Morton been curious about the Baa? And Kaye's was the only shop which sold such exotic animals, so how had Jerry, a pet with no money, persuaded a profit-obsessed trader like him to part with it?

While Rashila watched Gale usher Clacket Layne out, she listened to Jerry telling Chad and Gilpin about Baas that lived on his planet. If the creature had come from there, and Jerry sounded like he was telling the truth, then how had Kaye got hold of it? And why couldn't Rashila shake off the uneasy feeling that Morton had seen the Baa before?

CHAPTER TWENTY-ONE

Jerry put the chibbert tin away, thinking how great it had been having the place to himself while Chad and Gale were at Gilpin's. The silence was bliss after all the fuss and excitement when he'd first got back: the only sound now, the crunch and purr of Sneb scoffing the chibberts Jerry had scattered, so he'd be able to leave to meet Harchi.

Jerry had told Chad he was going so he wouldn't panic if he came back and found him missing. And Chad told Jerry what colours to look for on the clock so he could leave in time to be there before Harchi's chute docked.

Jerry was about to activate the front door when he half-thought he might need what Mum called a 'just-in-case' pee. Rats! He'd have to go now he'd thought about it. He'd learnt through painful experience that if you didn't go once the doubt was planted, you'd spend the entire journey wishing you had.

Checking the clock, Jerry saw the seventh bar of purple hadn't completely appeared over the single bar of yellow. He still had time. Cursing his mother for drumming dumb habits into him, Jerry hurried off for a quick leak in the plumbing suite.

Standing astride his loo-box, Jerry heard the door swish open behind him. Sneb! 'Forget it furbucket, no more chibberts!' he called, bracing himself for the impact of Sneb whamming against his back to scrabble on to his shoulder. Nothing. Turning his head, Jerry was poleaxed to see Gale hover into his eyeline.

'Turn off your hose!' she beeped loudly. 'And step away from the litter tray!'

It was lucky Jerry had finished, because there was no mistaking the tone of Gale's voice.

'You could have knocked!' said Jerry, zipping up and facing her. 'What d'you want? And keep it short – I'm off to meet Harchi.'

'Negative.'

'Affirmative. I asked Chad; he said it was OK.'

'I am countermanding that consent.'

'And I'm countermanding your countermand.'

Jerry moved towards the door. Gale shot round him and blocked his way.

'You will not meet Harchi.'

'Why?'

'Because I have come to terminate your existence.'

244

'WHAT?'

'BECAUSE I HAVE COME TO TERMI—'

'I heard you!'

'I warned you when you first arrived of the problems associated with imprecise use of language. If you mean 'why' you should say—'

'Could we save the English lesson for another time?'

'There will not be another time. Your existence is about to be terminated.'

'WHY?'

'Correct. Because you are disrupting Chad Jannan's life. With potentially disastrous consequences. My Prime Directive is to protect my Podder. Therefore, you must die.'

'Hey! I never asked to come here!'

'This is not about you. It's about Chad.'

'Going to have to quibble with you over that one, Gale.'

'This discussion is over.'

'We had a discussion?'

Gale was edging closer so Jerry backed away, his brain working overtime as he tried to figure out what to do next. Even if he could make it to the door, he'd never outrun her. Whatever he came up with was going to have to be verbal.

'You're making a big mistake!'

'Impossible.' Gale's claw snatched air as she grabbed for Jerry's arm and he swerve-dodged around the corner of the tank. 'I ran a complex Termination Scenario Programme.

You are to die by drowning. Step into the tank; I wish to begin.'

'I'm not talking about the method!' Jerry kept backing away, twisting and ducking to avoid Gale's snapping claws. 'Killing me goes against your Prime Directive!' he yelled, holding on to the tank to stop himself falling over as he ran backwards, not daring to turn around in case she swooshed up and jumped him. 'Chad's very sensitive – if I die he'll never get over it. And it'll be your fault!'

Sweat was dripping into Jerry's eyes. He swiped it away. Gale seemed to be slowing down slightly, so he matched her pace and lowered his voice. 'You want to get rid of me? Believe me, I'm *really* keen to go. Let's make it happen, without hurting Chad. That way, we both get what we want.'

'I have no interest in providing what you want.'

'I'm trying to stop you ruining Chad's life here. If you don't want that as much as I do, Gale, then you're not interested in protecting him, your Prime Directive's meaningless and you should cancel the killing.'

'I am drowning you to protect Chad.'

'It won't work. Me being here is a unique situation – you can't possibly know how it's going to play out. But I can.'

Jerry heard Gale's circuits whirring as she hovered on the spot. Beads of sweat raced each other down his face, but Jerry forced himself to keep his voice steady.

'I look different from Chad, but inside we're the same. We both have brains. We both think. We both feel. So I know, with absolute certainty, how he's going to feel about me dying. You don't. Because you can't think. All you can do is process. And you definitely can't predict.'

'I shall run a calculation through my probability chip, to assess the likelihood of your statement being accurate.'

'You can run calculations till your circuits burn out; the answer's going to be the same. A probability. Mine's fact. And unless you believe me, the only way you're going to find out I'm right is by killing me and watching Chad suffer. For the rest of his life. Does that tie in with your precious Prime Directive, Gale? Does it?'

There was a pause. Then Gale startled Jerry by hovering into the side of the water tank. Again and again, before juddering to a stop.

For the second time that day, Jerry found himself challenged to a bout of eyeball chicken. Only now the stakes were way, way higher. He played enough computer games to know what the odds were of beating one. So checking there was a safe distance between them, Jerry locked on to Gale's eye-lights as if his life depended on it.

*

Harchi sat in the chute, hugging his briefcase, barely able to keep his ears up he was so exhausted. What a day! As

247

he yawned, his tongue brushed against something wedged between two back teeth. Reaching in, Harchi recovered a crushed walsh-pod. He flicked it off his claw and the sight of the falling fragment was enough to encourage guilt to invite anxiety out on a tour of Harchi's mental state.

Tsooris had rounded up some Technicians and they'd piled into his office to present Harchi with a congratulatory walsh-pod platter with cissbury ring centrepiece. It had been utterly luscious. (Harchi had covered up his keyboard before they all tucked in.) Tsooris even made a speech – about how lucky they were to work with such an industrious colleague as Senior Technician Jannan, who'd averted a mass Fossic-malfunction through his quick thinking.

Gornish appeared as Tsooris was wrapping up his speech, and Harchi nearly choked on his cissbury thinking he'd come to fire him, but he patted Harchi on the back before leaving again with a wave and a 'Well done, Harchi.' In all the years Harchi had worked at the Unit, Gornish had only ever visited his office to roar at him.

As everyone started leaving, sucking their claws clean, a Depth of Warmth Assessor from the Sun Ray Section paused to tell Harchi she thought he was a hero. He was overcome. And nearly asked her to loop through and repeat it to Rashila, then changed his mind in case it looked boasty.

Collecting empty pod sections, Harchi began to feel uncomfortable about all the fuss. Was he a hero? Had he deserved a walsh-pod platter and a speech? Licking cissbury stick from his desk before uncovering his keyboard, Harchi decided he was. And he had. Who'd raised the alarm? Harchi-the-Hero Jannan, that's who. But would it have needed raising if he hadn't run his Random Rain Scheme pilot?

It hadn't taken Gornish long to stop the elements. He knew more clever electronical things than Harchi that you could do to force power levels down. Nor had he said anything about it being Harchi's fault. Although he had appointed an Investigation Group to investigate. But that was standard procedure.

As the chute slowed to a halt Harchi thought that if, as a result of the investigations, he lost his job, he and Jerry could still tour the Quadrants doing writing and counting tricks. He hugged his briefcase tighter – it contained the outfit notes and colour swatches, just in case Gornish looped through tonight and told him not to come in any more.

Harchi unclicked his chute-belt and stood up, cheered by the thought that Jerry would be waiting for him. It'd be good to talk to him about the Rogue Weather. Even though he was only a pet, Jerry had a way of seeing things that somehow always made Harchi feel better.

The chute flipped open and Harchi stepped off, holding

his briefcase out for Jerry to carry home for him. The hallway was empty. What a mischievous creature – Jerry was obviously trying to make Harchi laugh by pretending he wasn't here! Harchi crept to the end of the hallway, then jumped round the bend roaring: 'I know you're there!' scaring the elderly couple who often arrived to take the chute he came home in. He grunted an apology as the husband hurried his wife away.

Trudging down the hallway, gloom clung to Harchi like a second set of scales. Jerry must have heard about the Rogue Weather, blamed Harchi for spoiling his lovely thunder and lightning ideas and didn't want to be his pet any more.

Rounding the bend into another depressingly Jerry-less hallway, a more appealing reason came to Harchi. Morton had probably told Rashila he'd raised the alarm. What if she'd told Chad his father was a hero – and he and Jerry were preparing a surprise party? Gale was probably carving a fruity tribute even now. (Please let it not be cissbury-based.)

Harchi's spirits soared. Except . . . could he cope with another round of congratulations with the inevitable guilt chaser? Plummeted again. Suddenly giddy from the speed of the day's emotional highs and lows, Harchi headed for the roof to get some air – where he'd decide whether to roar his ridges off that he was a hero. Or sob quietly in a corner.

*

Jerry crouch-ran all the way to the chute, checking doorposts as he went to make sure he was running in the right direction. He reached the dock just as the inner door started closing, but there was no sign of Harchi. Hardly surprising – it had taken about a gazillion, buttock-clenched years of staring to get Gale to back off.

Breathless from the run Jerry slumped against the wall, hands on his knees to recover, and spotted an elderly couple inside the chute. Bending lower and lower, his back and thigh muscles screaming for mercy after all the crouching, Jerry yelled through the ever-decreasing gap to ask if they'd seen Harchi.

The female gave a whimpered snort, then covered her face with her claws as the male shot from his seat to stand in front of her, his arms out protectively. 'Only asking after a friend; I wasn't going to mug you!' Jerry felt like shouting, standing up again as the chute's outer screen slid down.

Jerry figured Harchi must have gone to the roof. He felt bad for disappointing him a second time, but what could he do? When it came to unavoidable demands on your time, a robot trying to kill you is going to beat a stroll to the chute, no contest.

Jerry blocked Gale from his mind. It was going to totally do his head in if he started going over that now. Harchi. That's why he'd come out. Both times Jerry had found his way to the roof he'd done it by accident. So deliberately not thinking about the route, he took off again and before long was turning into the familiar dead end.

Waving his foot at the base, the door swished open and Jerry hurtled in, pulling up short at the sight of Harchi standing at the safety rail, arms raised to the sky, head back, roaring: 'I'm a hero! I'm a hero!' Jerry grinned and marched over, punching air in time to his harmony line: 'Weatherman hero! Weatherman hero!'

The delight on Harchi's face as he spun round, and the bear hug that followed, made Jerry feel totally safe for the first time since the horror of his near-miss with Gale.

'Sorry I'm late, Harch-a-Darch!' said Jerry, disentangling himself. 'Gale wouldn't let me out until she'd had a word about Chad.' He'd already decided to save the Gale story for Rashila in case his second going-home-persuasion routine needed a boost tonight.

'That's all right – you're here now!' laughed Harchi, picking up his case. He turned to look at Jerry, suddenly serious. 'D'you really think I'm a hero?' he asked, anxiously.

'You're a hero to me, Harchi,' joked Jerry, taking his case. 'Why? What d'you do?'

As the two of them set off for home, Harchi recounted the saga of how his playful pilot had inexplicably turned into a terrifying batch of Rogue Weather. By the time he'd finished, Harchi had worked himself up into such a state Jerry didn't dare tell him he'd nearly died in the storm. So he just made a throwaway remark about shopping and the visit to Kaye's, then switched the chat back to what appeared to be Harchi's main concern. Was he a fraud for letting his workmates treat him like a hero?

'They thought you were a hero because you rang Morton to launch the All Fossic Alert, then raised the alarm at the Unit about the Rogue Weather, right?'

'Right.'

'Did you ring Morton?

'Yes.' There was a pause. 'Well, I'd been trying to loop through to Rashila actually, but Morton answered.'

'Same difference. And did you go and get Gornish?'

'Yes! And I ran all the way, Jerry!'

'Then you did everything everyone thinks you did. So you *are* the hero everyone thinks you are.'

'Am I?' Harchi grabbed his tail and gave the tip a nervous scratch. 'Am I really?'

'Yes!' Jerry tugged Harchi's tail free. 'Congratulations, my fine heroic friend!'

Jerry shook Harchi warmly by the claw and they laughed and laughed (although Harchi's was tinged with hysteria) then carried on walking, Jerry swinging the briefcase, enjoying the pressure of Harchi's hand on his shoulder.

'Shame about the Random Rain Scheme,' Harchi finally broke the companionable silence. 'It was such a good idea.'

'I should have told you about something more low key,' said Jerry. 'If we'd kicked off with a Random Snow Scheme it wouldn't have caused so much damage. Not that I'm saying it was down to you!' added Jerry hastily, as Harchi's ears and tail flopped.

Harchi didn't look convinced, so Jerry distracted him by setting off on a trail about snow, covering everything from avalanches to snowmen. As Harchi's ears and tail started repeaking, Jerry went for a full-peak finish, swooping aeroplane-armed around Harchi, squeak-singing, 'We're walking in the air,' refusing to stop until Harchi joined in.

Harchi's snowman impression suddenly melted under fire from a cissbury acid hiccough attack, whatever that was, which turned out to be such a scale-shaker, the two of them ended up snorting with helpless laughter against the nearest wall.

As the laughter died down, Harchi looked serious again. Going into anxious spy mode, he checked the hallways were clear, before bending down to whisper in Jerry's ear: 'Are you good at keeping secrets?'

'Very,' Jerry nodded, wondering what was coming next.

'Good,' Harchi stood up again. 'I'm not. But I'm getting better – I've kept one about you for nearly three days now!'

'Really?'

Harchi nodded. He was so proud of his achievement, Jerry could hardly bring himself to do it, but he had to.

'What's it about?' he asked, keeping his voice so casual it was practically in pyjamas.

'I'm not allowed to say. But I'm going to ask you to keep a secret for me. So that's one secret each which makes it fair.'

'It won't be fair, Harchi.'

'No.' Harchi looked stricken. 'Why?'

'Because both of us will know your secret. But you're the only one who knows mine.'

'I'm not. Rashila knows it, too. And Chad. Oh yes, and Gilpin.'

Jerry sighed and looked disappointed. 'That's even more unfair, then,' he said, walking away, to express quite how disappointed he was.

Harchi scratched his ridges and thought hard. 'I know!' He hurried to catch Jerry up. 'I'll tell you my secret. And if you don't think it's big enough to make it fair again, then I'll tell you yours. Which would make two each. And you mustn't tell anyone I told you, which means you'd actually have three.'

'That'd really make up for everyone else knowing mine.'

'That's what I thought. *If* you don't think mine's big enough.'

'*If.* Thanks, Harchi. Hope you don't think I'm being greedy or anything?'

'Of course not, Jerry-pet.'

There was a lot more corridor-checking and waiting for creatures to pass before Harchi told Jerry that no one must ever find out about the Random Rain Scheme. Even though Harchi knew with absolute certainty that he hadn't programmed such violent weather, he couldn't be certain his pilot hadn't somehow brought the Rogue Weather on.

So far, so obvious. Jerry did a lot of imaginary beard-stroking, before sadly informing Harchi that he still felt rather hard done by and maybe he did need to be told the other secret after all.

Harchi seemed relieved to unburden himself of the information he'd managed to hang on to for three long days. If Jerry had possessed poseable ears they'd have won flagpole awards as Harchi informed him that he hadn't arrived on Pastinare by molecular scrambler. He'd been found stowing away in the cargo hold of an inter-planetary trade ship. And couldn't remember, because of hyperdrive trauma.

*

Morton was slumped at her desk, waiting for the Duty Fossics to arrive and blitz her dwelling clean. Her brain buzzed with furious thoughts but after being up all night, then having to cope with an All Fossic Alert and two shockingly unprovoked acts of betrayal she was so tail-droopingly exhausted, Morton couldn't even summon the energy for an under-desk gouge.

The air was thick with the stench of Baa expellant, which had gathered strength from the warmth of the day and now hung draped over the lab like an invisible cape. Morton deliberately snorted up a huge snoutful, hoping to force herself into action with an extra hit of anger. It didn't work. The most she could manage was an ear-flip.

Why had Kaye let Clacket Layne have the Baa? After Morton had specifically instructed him the creature could only be sold outside the Quadrant. How dare he repay her unbelievable generosity so maliciously! She was a claw-tip's width from looping through to the pet-shop owner and roaring his ridges off to find out.

Except Morton had a strong sense that it would be wiser to wait for the answer to come to her than charging off to find it. Particularly in her present state.

She glowered at her disloyal assistant's empty chair. Morton wouldn't be a bit surprised if Rashila was mixed up in this somewhere. She'd pushed herself forward shamelessly to look after Bluhm today, and now the two of them were in league. Had they enlisted Kaye's help to try to trap her?

No. That was her tiredness talking. And anyway, what would they be trying to trap Morton into revealing? That she was striving to provide the best life-start for every single Podder on Pastinare? Let them trap her for that and put her on trial. She'd be proud to be found guilty.

The portal swished open and the sight of a cluster of Duty Fossics hovering in lifted Morton's mood. Standing to greet them, rivers of renewed energy coursed under her scales.

She might be exhausted, but it was from protecting the future of the planet. She was the Director of the Bureau of Fossic Affairs. She was all powerful. She was Morton.

*

'Excuse me?'

Rashila swivelled her seat away from her Infoscope to find Chad's pet standing inside her archway. How dare he enter her quarters *again*! Insult to injury: Sneb was perched on his shoulder. As if reading her thoughts Jerry reached up and placed Sneb in his nest, then turned to approach her.

'Stay!' she barked. 'I thought I made it clear last night; you're not allowed in here.'

Jerry stood where he was. 'I need to talk to you.'

'Need?' Rashila's irritation at Jerry's insolence was stoked by Sneb scuttling across the ceiling to drop on to his back and drape himself across Jerry's shoulders. 'I cannot think of a single topic about which you and I would ever 'need' to talk.'

Actually Rashila was keen to talk to Jerry about the Baa, but wouldn't encourage him by doing so.

'How 'bout hidden cameras?'

Rashila felt her ears peak in surprise and scowled at Jerry for causing it. There was no conceivable way he could have discovered the cameras. Unless he'd been awake the night she'd installed them? Except she knew he hadn't been because he was in such a deep sleep when Sneb attacked him. However he knew, she refused to enter into a discussion with a pet.

'If you do not leave I will call my husband,' she growled.

'He won't hear you – he's in the wallow room with Chad and Gale. That's why I came in now so we could talk in private.' He gave it a beat. 'In the one room that doesn't have a hidden camera in it.'

How did he know that? *How?* 'Speak.'

'I want to go home.'

'Impossible.'

Jerry shook his head. 'You don't know that for sure.'

'I do.'

'I didn't stow away on an inter-planetary trade ship.'

Rashila's tail followed her ears.

'Gale told me.'

'Harchi told you.'

'I didn't stow away because where I come from, there's no such thing as inter-planetary travel.'

Rashila's brain started racing. Kaye must have lied to Morton, so there had to be something devious about the way he'd acquired Jerry.

'I think the hidden cameras are linked to your lab. So you'll have seen the lamb.'

'Lamb?' There was no point denying the cameras.

'The Baa. It's from my planet. And I reckon Morton's mixed up in why it's here.'

'Preposterous! You got it at Kaye's.'

'This afternoon. He said it came in this morning. But I

heard it last night. And I'm certain I heard Morton's voice too.'

'What do you mean, "you heard it"?' Rashila was so amazed, she jumped up from her desk and marched over to Jerry, glaring down at him. 'How? Where?'

He flinched, but stood his ground. 'I don't understand how it happens.'

'Continue.' Rashila barked, backing away and pacing as she listened.

'If I stand near where a camera's hidden and say something I get this odd kind of echoey feedback. And if someone's talking in the lab I can sometimes hear that too. Last night, when you were all asleep, I was checking for echoes to find all the cameras and I heard the Baa. And Morton.'

Rashila stopped pacing. 'Have you told anyone else?'

Jerry gave a faint smile. 'Who'd believe me?'

'Are you telling the truth?'

'Kaye gave me the Baa 'cos I told him I knew there was something dodgy about how it got here. He didn't strike me as someone who'd give anything away if he could help it.'

'You are correct.' Jerry had been brave, confronting Kaye. And coming to her with this information not knowing how she'd react. Brave or desperate. 'Even if I can get to the bottom of all this, it doesn't mean I'll be able to find a way to send you home again.'

'But you could try. Please, Rashila, *please*! You're my only hope. I'm scared to stay here now. Gale tried to kill me this afternoon.'

'You go too far!'

'It's true!' Jerry's anguish seemed genuine. 'She was going to drown me in the plumbing suite and make it look like an accident. Said she was complying with her Prime Directive to protect Chad, because I'm such a disruptive influence on his life. She'd run a . . . what did she call it? . . . Termination Scenario Programme and everything!'

Extraordinary. Again he had to be telling the truth. 'And you managed to stop her!'

'I'm here, aren't I? I persuaded her it would be better for Chad if I didn't die.'

'Thank you. You did the right thing.'

'I certainly think so.'

Rashila suddenly realised how harsh her last remark must have sounded. 'I . . . apologise.' The words stuck in her throat. 'A mother's response.'

'And because you're a mother, I'm asking you to imagine how bad mine will be feeling now I've been missing for three days.'

'Unless you *were* transported here by a molecular scrambler with a time-fold overlay pump.' Rashila was beginning to suspect Morton had lied, though she couldn't think why. 'In which case she won't have noticed.'

'Whether she's noticed or not, is only a part of it! I know you think I'm nothing but a low-life, disposable pet, but on my planet I'm a Chad. I miss my mum – and the rest of my family. And I want to go home. Please. Help me?'

Staring at the vulnerable scrap of a creature standing in front of her, Rashila suddenly had a flash of how devastated she'd feel if she lost Chad. And it was hard to resist the opportunity to be the first scientist on Pastinare to attempt to return livestock to its home planet. Rashila nodded at Jerry and watched his face flood with hope.

CHAPTER TWENTY-TWO

Kaye was in the wallow room, bouncing about on all fours pretending to be the Baa to make Yash laugh so her Fossic could scrub her teeth without a fuss. The portal swished open and his wife hurried in to say someone was sounding the shop's entry alert.

Abandoning his entertainment duties Kaye padded downstairs, leaving a trail of muddy footprints and apprehension in his wake. Morton. He'd been expecting her to make contact ever since that jumped-up, mouthy alien had blackmailed him out of the Baa.

Walking through the stockroom at the back of the shop activating lights as he went, Kaye wondered whether he'd be able to get the BFA to stump up for his loss of profits. Why should he be out of pocket because he'd had to give the animal away to protect Morton?

The entry alert was getting another good going over. 'All right, all right, I'm coming! Keep your claws on!' Kaye roared, hurrying into the shop and putting the lights on which woke the animals, who let loose a chorus of noise to get his attention in case there were after-hours snacks to be had.

Kaye ignored them as he headed for the portal, composing his features into a respectful mask in what he knew would be a wasted attempt to deflect Morton's fury. Clawing the entry code into the night security keypad, the respect turned to surprise as the portal swished sideways to reveal Rashila Jannan.

Ever adaptable, Kaye began to rearrange his face to friendly shopkeeper who's puzzled to see an evening customer, when he recalled his wife snortling on once about how Morton never set foot outside the BFA. He left his face on respectful – a couple of smarms down from a Morton – who'd obviously despatched her assistant to give him the hard time instead.

'Rashila Jannan.' Kaye inclined his head, to invite her in.

'Kaye,' she stated. She entered and the portal swished shut. 'I think you know why I'm here.'

'I can guess.'

There was a pause as they eyed each other up. Kaye, wary and defensive. Rashila, cool. 'Well?' she asked.

Kaye took a deep breath, which sent his belly up before bouncing it down again. 'The *only* reason I let your pet have the Baa,' he stabbed air with a claw to emphasise his sincerity, 'was to protect your boss! You have to make her understand that.'

Rashila mentally ticked boxes to make sure she was following the bluffing instructions Jerry had drilled into her before agreeing she was ready to chute down here on her own.

Maintain eye contact. Tick. Keep ears and tail relaxed – no giveaway peaks. Tick. (Although they were already starting to ache from the effort, given Kaye's first revelation.) Say as little as possible as casually as you can.

'Go on.' Tick. Tick.

'Jerry said he'd seen them on his own planet. He even knew the breed! He wanted it for that cracked scaler, Clacket Layne, for saving his life. I know I was supposed to sell it outside the Quadrant, but what could I do – say no and let him walk out of here, telling everyone where the Baa came from?'

'I see.' Rashila was trying to work out how to get Kaye to tell her more, when Jerry's 'say as little as possible' bore fruit as he took her silence for disapproval.

'You should both be grateful to me. Maybe even compensate me or something,' said Kaye, carried away by the injustice. 'Morton told me I could keep the BFA's share of whatever I got for the Baa, if I took it. I mean, what kind of benefit's that now I've been forced to give it away? To protect *her*,' he added, in case Rashila hadn't got the point yet.

Morton gave Kaye the Baa? Rashila was so surprised, her ears flicked up, and although she forced them down immediately, Kaye spotted it.

'You didn't know that?' Kaye was outraged.

Rashila decided to drop the pretence and deal with the consequences later. 'No, but I—'

'So, I bail your boss out and she does the dirty on me.' Kaye marched up and down, fuming. 'She told you *I* got the Baa, didn't she? Well, I didn't. She said it was part of a BFA experiment gone wrong. But that can't be true because you'd have known about it.' Kaye stopped marching and swung his belly at Rashila. 'How'd she say I got it here? I've a right to know.'

'With an unlicensed molecular scrambler,' guessed Rashila, throwing in the last connection and seeing if the system fired up. She wasn't disappointed.

Kaye threw his ridges back and let out a roar that unleashed a terrified answerback volley from his stock. When he looked at Rashila, he was narrowed-eyed and flip-eared with fury.

'I got nothing against you, Rashila Jannan, but I won't be played for a fool,' growled Kaye, his voice edged with menace. 'If Morton starts putting it about I used that scrambler again to get the Baa, I'll squeal louder than a squashed snebbit that it was her! You clear about that?'

'Very.' Rashila's ears and tail were cramping from the strain of keeping them steady after Kaye's 'used that scrambler again'. 'I'll try and get your message across.'

'You'll want to do better than try,' rasped Kaye, 'because

I've got proof she told me to cover up how I got Jerry. And she said it was to protect your Podder.'

'She said what?' Rashila's ears and tail flew up.

'Don't play the innocent,' Kaye sneered, until he noticed the peaked state of her extremities. 'OK, maybe you didn't know – Morton gave me phoney documentation about Jerry's arrival. So if I go down for illegal scrambler use, I'm taking both of you with me!'

'I don't like being threatened, Kaye.'

'Neither do I. Which is why I'm doing the threatening.'

Rashila had one final question for which she was already certain she had the answer.

'I presume you no longer have the scrambler?'

'Morton took it. Said she'd destroy it. She must have meant *after* she got the Baa.'

Rashila left the shop, then paused further down the walkway once she heard the portal swish shut. Reaching into her shorts for her hand-held, she debated whether to make the call. The risk was enormous. But so was the situation and Rashila wasn't sure how to cope with it on her own. She clawed in the name search and pressed 'loop', her hearts thumping quadruple time as the screen lit up with the open, friendly face of Chair Bluhm.

'Rashila. How may I help?'

*

Chad's arms were trembling: they ached so much from holding the cushion jammed against the wall above his

267

head, but he tried to ignore the pain. Even if he wanted to complain, he couldn't because Rashila-ma had insisted on silence until she'd taken the hidden cameras off line.

She'd shown him and Jerry where to jam the cushions to blind the cameras, and they were both standing on chairs at either end of the room with their arms up, but Jerry's must hurt worse because they were so skin-and-bony compared to his.

Chad turned his head until he could just see the empty Infoscope-housing and his mother and Gale moving in and out of his eye-line as they worked furiously fast on the exposed Infoscope circuitry. Their access was made easier by Harchi-pa, who'd rested the bottom of the screen on the floor and was holding the top against his front so the back sloped towards them.

Turning his head the other way to ease his aching neck, Chad's stomach protested as he saw the table laid for supper. He could eat a Plantation. When he and Harchi-pa emerged from wallowing, Rashila-ma had disappeared but left instructions with Gale for them to wait for her to get back before dining.

When she'd re-appeared a couple of bars later she'd beckoned Chad into her quarters and told him things he wished he didn't have to hear, then told Harchi-pa, who from the sound of his anguished roar hadn't liked the revelations any better than Chad.

Rashila-ma was going to try to send Jerry home even though everyone knew he might never get there. And if

268

Jerry died, and Jerry was his pet, didn't that make Chad responsible? Though surely the duty of care ran out once a pet left their owner's orbit? Cooling his forehead against the wall Chad wished he could talk it all over with Gale, but he didn't dare. Something about his behaviour had obviously prompted her to try to kill his pet, and he didn't want anyone blaming him if she tried to do it again.

The snap of the Infoscope going back into its housing told Chad his arm-aches (if not his brain-aches) were over – confirmed by Rashila-ma's voice announcing, 'Right every-one, let's eat.'

Chad jumped from the chair, letting the cushion fall to the floor as he massaged some blood back into his aching arms. He could see Jerry doing the same up the other end of the room, and Gale was already hovering over with dishes of food.

'You all right, son?' asked Harchi-pa, as he took the chair to the table and sat down.

'Yes thank you, Father,' replied Chad, stretching his neck from side to side to loosen up the shoulder scales.

Going to sit next to his mother, Chad saw Jerry heading for his quarters with Sneb and a dish of food and realised this might be their last evening together.

'Rashila-ma, can Jerry . . . ?'

A frown played across his mother's face, though her voice wasn't angry. 'Sorry Chad, we don't feed . . . where are you going, Harchi?'

269

'To eat with my pet,' stated Harchi, scrambling from the table. Chad moved to follow.

'All right, you two,' Rashila sighed. 'Jerry?' she called. 'Would you care to join us?'

Harchi and Chad grinned at each other and sat down again, as Jerry turned and walked over to the table. 'Thanks, Rashila,' he smiled. 'I'd like that very much.'

*

Morton wondered how long the live feed had been down. It was working while the Duty Fossics were cleaning her dwelling because she'd glanced at the screen every now and then as she'd supervised them. Don't say it was another batch of Rogue Weather! She was tip-sheddingly tired again and hadn't the energy for another All Fossic Alert. The screen wasn't crackling with static though.

Looping through to the Jannans' to see if the fault was at their end, Morton was irritated to get vision off/voicemail. Switching to Rashila's hand-held, her irritation deepened to be met by the same response. How typical of her assistant to fail to be available when there was a vital equipment fault!

Hacking in to the Weather Enhancement Unit at Classified level, Morton discovered that all weather was currently operating according to Ministry Approved Standards. So . . . no weather glitches. Morton's tail twitched.

Clawing Gale's I-Cam number into the control panel delivered an instant view of Rashila sitting at an Infoscope in what Morton presumed were her quarters, since it was a room she'd never seen before. From the sound of it, she and Gale were calculating a spatial displacement of quite staggering proportions. But why? And to where?

The answers were dancing about in the shadows at the back of Morton's brain. If she hadn't been numb with exhaustion she'd have spotted them in a tail-flick. She was about to give up and step to bed, when a call looped through and on-screen vision replaced Treacherous Assistant Jannan with Architect of Betrayal Bluhm.

'Director Morton,' barked Bluhm. 'You are summoned to appear before the Better Homes, Better Planet Ministry Committee at five orange, three ochre in the morning.'

Morton growled as the loop was cut before she'd had a chance to speak. Bluhm had never addressed her with such disgraceful rudeness, so she must have found out about the unlicensed scrambler in Morton's possession. And the Baa.

The spatial displacement was suddenly spotlit, too. Rashila was clearly on a glory quest to be the first Pastinacean to export livestock off-planet even if it killed Jerry. Which it probably would.

*

Jerry was heading for bed when he heard a monster sigh as he passed Harchi's room. He'd been so sad all evening; it had been a real choker. 'G'night, Harch-a-Darch!' Jerry called through the archway, beauty-contestant cheerful.

271

'Good night, Jerry-pet!' called Harchi, aiming for cheery, and nearly hitting it until 'pet', when a crack appeared.

Jerry stepped quietly into the room and saw Harchi wilting at his desk, staring at his Infoscope.

'What you looking at?' asked Jerry, going to peer over Harchi's shoulder.

'Nothing!' he said, shooting upright and changing the screen as if Jerry had caught him doing something mucky, but from what he'd seen all he'd been staring at were some little kid's drawings of disgustingly bright tunics and shorts.

Harchi ejected a disc from his Infoscope and shoved it in his briefcase. His ears were floppy and his tail drooped, giving away the lie of the smile he forced on to his face as he caught Jerry watching him.

'Sorry, didn't mean to snap at you.' Harchi nodded at his case. 'Just a bit of confidential Weather stuff, that's all.'

'Sure. No problem. I did creep up on you a bit. Sorry, too.'

There was an awkward pause. Harchi took a deep breath.

'Look . . . I know I was . . . a bit . . . down . . . at dinner. I hope I didn't spoil your last night?'

'Course not. Anyway, it may not be my last night.'

'D'you mean . . .' Harchi's eyes lit up.

Jerry shook his head. Dimmed again. 'Sorry, no. I meant, it depends on what the Committee says tomorrow.'

Harchi tangled his hair clump. Another deep breath. 'Jerry, are you sure you want to do this? You could die!'

272

Jerry shrugged. 'If I'm dead, I won't know about it. I have to take the risk, Harchi – that's how badly I want to go home.' Harchi flinched. 'Oh, Harchi! I'm sorry! It's not that I haven't enjoyed myself here. 'Cos I have – honest. 'Specially our walks from the chute.'

'Really?' Harchi didn't sound convinced.

'Cross my heart and hope to . . . never mind. Yes, really.' Jerry put a hand on Harchi's shoulder, looked him straight in the eye. 'You're the best owner a pet could ever have. And if I was a proper pet, I'd want to stay with you, *always*. But I'm desperate to see my family again so I have to take this chance. Can you understand that?'

Harchi looked away, but he nodded. The movement dislodged a big fat tear, which trundled over his face-scales, dripped off his jaw and spattered on to his shorts. Jerry squeezed Harchi's shoulder then turned and left the room, knowing if he stayed a second longer he'd be in danger of matching Harchi in the spattering stakes.

CHAPTER TWENTY-THREE

Gale adjusted the wallow room to Chad's preferred morning temperature, then swept mud from the walkway to prevent him slipping when he came in, re-checking the spatial displacement calculations as she swept. If she and Rashila Jannan became the first Pastinaceans to scramble livestock off-planet today, Gale intended to open an Acceptable Firsts file; the pet's export to be her first entry. She'd already drafted a message to her entire address list, revealing herself as the Phase 12deluxe2 whose data had made the export possible.

She'd also logged a prompt to archive her Unacceptable Firsts file. With Chad's life on the brink of returning to pre-pet normality, there was a high probability it would require no further entries. And if Rashila Jannan's export attempt failed, Gale assessed that with minor refinements her Termination Scenario Programme would prove highly effective as an alternative method of dispatch.

*

Jerry shifted in his seat to ease his aching backside. If this Committee bunch were such big smells on the Pastinacean cheeseboard, why didn't they fork out for decent chairs, instead of numb-bumming visitors on hollowed-out boulders? They'd kept their hands in their pockets with the decorating too.

After seriously talking up the Committee all the way down here, Rashila had led Jerry to expect shedloads of swank, but this place was about as swanky as the inside of Andy's laundry basket and only slightly less murky. Rashila kept referring to it as a Chamber, but it was more like a giant, pod-shaped cave, finished in the same rough flower-pot look as every other building Jerry had seen.

A massive, oval, metal table took up most of the room, so Jerry guessed it must be a huge Committee, although there weren't any seats so it was hard to know for sure. And that was it – apart from a few pedestals around the edge of the room which, according to Rashila, displayed Committee Member pod fragments. Whatever they were. The place was Yawnsville Arizona on the eye.

The door swished open and Jerry looked round expecting to see the Committee troop in, but it was Morton, who'd ditched the nutty professor look for an aubergine tunic-and-shorts set to match her hair. Not as posh as Rashila who'd togged up like she was about to meet the Queen.

Morton was lugging a long bag stuffed with something bulky. Could it be Jerry's scrambler home? A guard offered to carry it but Morton declined, and with a nod at Rashila and a smile for Jerry, walked to a boulder at the far end of the room, then carefully placed the bag on the table before sitting down. If Morton was deep in the dog house, as Chad had told him last night, then somebody had forgotten to tell her.

A low warning tone sounded and Rashila stood up, smoothing her tunic with one hand, clawing Jerry out of his seat with the other. The gloom vanished as a galaxy of pinprick spotlights lit up in the walls and ceiling, drenching the Chamber in golden-yellow light, dotted with rich blues and greens.

There was a soft hissing from the far side of the room and a set of ridges appeared at table level and kept rising, bringing a black-haired Pastinacean with it. When her shoulders had cleared the table, two other sets of ridges rose into view on either side. As all five creatures continued to elevate Jerry saw they were seated on boulders, the central one being the largest. From Rashila's description, its occupant had to be Chair Bluhm.

As the boulders hissed to a halt, long strips of black fabric dropped from slots in the ceiling behind them with a treble-width one behind Chair Bluhm. Each strip was decorated with gold and silver symbols, identically shaped to those the Committee had on their tunics, except theirs were studded with jewels which winked as they caught the light.

Bluhm motioned to Jerry, Morton and Rashila to sit. If

this was what these guys did for openers the meeting itself should be the kipper's knickers! As Mum liked to say. And with a bit of luck Jerry would be able to hear her say it soon.

Bluhm started talking, but Jerry couldn't understand her. He fiddled with the Universal Translator, but it didn't help. Bluhm seemed to be addressing a question to Rashila, but when she stood and replied he couldn't understand her either.

Having said her bit, which must have had something to do with him since a few gestures were thrown his way, Rashila sat down again. Jerry felt himself go pink as all five Committee members stared at him, his blush setting off a low raspy murmur along their length.

Luckily they turned away when Bluhm started talking again, directing her remarks at Morton this time. Whatever she was saying went on till the end of all time. Jerry could have eaten his boulder, he was so bored. Then Morton stood up to reply. Jerry's heart sank as she looked set to go on even longer than Bluhm, who was chipping in from time to time.

Jerry was just nodding off when a unison of gasps sucked away the drowse. He might not be able to understand, but Jerry knew surprise when he saw it. Whatever Morton had just told them had made five pairs of Committee ears flip up like a row of metal ducks at a funfair shotgun sideshow.

*

If Morton ever got to be Chair – and why shouldn't she, Bluhm wouldn't last for ever – the first act she'd pass would be to banish the ridiculously antiquated language the Committee insisted upon using in their meetings. So they didn't want guards or visitors to understand their inner workings? Then make them wait outside the Chamber while official matters were discussed.

It was high time this Committee looked to the future instead of clawing back at the past. Fresh ideas, that's what kept a planet spinning. And Morton had just proposed something fresh enough to make it spin right off its axis. If Bluhm and her fellow members were imaginative enough to adopt it.

She smiled as she recalled their gasps when she'd announced her Multiple Podder Parenting Scheme. It had been many years since she'd high-peaked a set of Committee ears. She'd give her right claw to be a snebbit on the wall of their Boulder Room right now as they debated her revolutionary proposal.

At first Morton thought the five of them would vote against anything she said, they'd seemed so disapproving of the unlicensed scrambler. But she'd ignored their stony stares and wooed them with the truth.

'Yes, Kaye broke the law and should be punished,' said Morton, 'but I implore you – deal with him leniently. If he hadn't illegally imported that exotic pet,' she'd gestured towards Jerry, 'I might never have devised Multiple Podder

Parenting, for he was the unlikely inspiration. Which would have deprived the Ministry Committee of . . .' Morton had made meaningful eye contact with Bluhm, '. . . *substantial* increased revenue opportunities.

'And yes, I admit disguising the details of JerryPatterson's arrival. Foolishly, but with the purest of motives.' Here, she'd smiled fondly at Rashila. 'I did it to protect my assistant's Podder, who'd grown so attached to his pet.' Morton replaced the smile with earnest sincerity. 'Although allow me to stress, your most revered Honours, that Rashila Jannan remained entirely ignorant throughout.

'I feel ashamed,' said Morton, flopping her ears, 'that the Committee discovered the unlicensed scrambler, as I was about to hand it in. I was literally leaving the lab to deliver it to Chair Bluhm, when I had reason to suspect the pet's mental health was failing. Desperate at the prospect of losing my only research resource with multiple podding capabilities, I used the scrambler to try to obtain a replacement.'

'The Rogue Weather in the stratosphere affected the scrambler, which delivered a Baa instead of a biped. Always thinking of Podders, I gave the Baa to an unBonded female to provide the poor scaler with a morsel of comfort through the barren loneliness of her adult years.'

'Chair Bluhm, Committee Honourables, I see now that my actions were ill-advised, but due to the extreme sensitivity of my work, I felt it selfish to involve anyone else at

279

the time. I can only beg you to accept my humblest apologies.'

Morton thought back to how she'd worked a tremble into her voice for the apology, before plumping into her seat, as if overcome. Who could fail to be persuaded by her passion? Her commitment to the Podder cause.

It would be interesting to see whether Bluhm granted Rashila's request to use the scrambler to export Jerry off-planet. Morton couldn't believe a pet would miss his family so much he'd risk his life to return to them. Far more likely, her selfish assistant was so frantic to be rid of him she simply hadn't told him. Let them both get on with it; Jannan family life was no concern of hers.

The Boulder Rise alert sounded and the Committee rose into the Chamber. Bluhm waited for everyone to settle again before speaking.

'We have considered the evidence put before us today,' she said, looking sternly at Morton, 'and our conclusions are as follows . . .' Bluhm paused to give emphasis to the importance of their findings. 'The Better Homes, Better Planet Ministry Committee will permit the Multiple Podder Parenting Scheme to proceed,' she said.

Rashila couldn't stop a gasp of surprise escaping. Morton's chest puffed with pride.

'To be carried out by a separate Multiple Podder Unit,' Bluhm continued, 'operating under the patronage of the Bureau of Podder Production.'

Morton sat straighter, ready to graciously accept the additional title and responsibilities.

'The Committee hereby appoints Rashila Jannan, Director of Research and Development.'

It was Morton's turn to gasp. 'It was my idea!' she cried, unable to stop herself.

'But it wasn't a new one.' Bluhm's tone was glacial. 'The Committee scanned the archives for assistance in reaching a decision on so far-reaching an issue. Records revealed that there has been Multiple Podding on Pastinare, but the right was withdrawn during the Diaquordial Period. However, a census scan proved its reintroduction would no longer be harmful to our eco-system.'

Bluhm looked at Morton, who inclined her head to acknowledge the bitterly disappointing information.

'Moving on to the question of the unlicensed molecular scrambler,' Bluhm continued, announcing matter of factly: 'It is to be destroyed.'

Bluhm nodded to one of the guards, who walked over to Morton's end of the table and took the bag. Rashila looked shocked and glanced at Jerry, forgetting he couldn't understand what Bluhm had said. He caught the look and was on his feet in an instant.

'What? What's happening?' Jerry shouted, while Rashila tried to claw him back into his seat, by grabbing the back of his top. He swiped her away. 'Get off! I have a right to know!'

Rashila jumped up and went snout-to-nose with Jerry. 'If you do not return to your seat *immediately*, I shall have you removed!' she growled.

'NO!' Jerry dodged round Rashila and ran to the centre of the table to address the creature towering over him from her boulder, who could cancel his future with a click of her claw. 'Please, Chair Bluhm, *please*! What did you say?'

Chair Bluhm held up a hand to stop Rashila and the guards advancing on Jerry. 'I will address the visitor,' she told them in Pastinacean he could understand, before peering down at him. 'And I shall forgive this breach of protocol because of your youth and alienacity.'

Rashila's ears flopped in shame at having caused such a mortifying situation.

'The unlicensed scrambler is to be destroyed.'

'You can't!' yelled Jerry. 'I have to get home!'

'I cannot permit you to risk your life in this way.'

'It's my life, I'll risk it how I want!'

Rashila growled at Jerry to show her outrage at his unbelievable rudeness.

'It's all right, Rashila, his display of ignorance only goes to serve my point,' Bluhm said firmly. 'JerryPatterson,' she barked, 'you are unable to understand the consequences, therefore I must protect you from them. You are a pet. Pets are separated from families. You will get used to it.'

'Never!'

Rashila knew Jerry's anguished wail would lodge in her memory like a mental splinter, as it echoed round the chamber, while his face drained of colour and he collapsed to the floor.

CHAPTER TWENTY-FOUR

'How is he?' asked Harchi, hurrying into Chad's quarters, still carrying his briefcase.

'Shshshsh. The same,' whispered Chad, going to hug his father.

'He hasn't moved since the Chamber Guard left him there three bandwidths ago,' said Rashila quietly.

The Jannans stood in a group staring at Jerry, who was curled up on his bed, facing the wall, Sneb a protective blanket along his side. He gave a low warning yowl as Harchi crouched to get a better look.

'Jerry? It's Harchi. Can you hear me?' he called softly.

'He won't answer you,' Rashila told him.

'He touched his eyelids together!' said Harchi hopefully.

'He often does that,' countered Chad.

'There's a crumbled-up sweet stick here, would you like some?' Harchi held a chunk up to Jerry's lips. Nothing. Just a blank, dead-eyed stare.

'He won't touch it, Harchi-pa, I've tried,' said Chad. 'He won't drink anything either.'

Harchi gave a sigh and stood up.

'Thanks for coming, Husband. Did Gornish mind?'

'No. I told him it was an emergency.'

'And he'd know it was true,' said Chad. 'Rashila-ma's never looped through and asked you to come home before.'

'Er . . . yes,' said Harchi, flustered by the innocent bluntness. 'And um . . . what did the vet say?' he asked his son, feeling too shy to look at his wife.

'We haven't looped through.'

'I don't think Jerry's ill, Harchi,' said Rashila. 'I think he's in shock.'

'Then all we can do is wait until he snaps out of it,' said Harchi with another deep sigh.

'He will snap out of it, won't he, Harchi-pa?' asked Chad anxiously, staring at his pet.

'Of course he will, son,' said Harchi, raising his brow-scales questioningly at his wife, who gave a doubtful shrug.

*

Sometimes Jerry thought he heard voices, but wasn't sure if they were talking to him. And he was too tired to find out. More than tired. Unable-to-function exhausted, his limbs as heavy as lead. He couldn't move at all. What was wrong with him? Or had Andy superglued his pyjamas to the bed again?

Jerry went to call Mum, but couldn't get his mouth

open. Even Andy wouldn't glue his lips together. Jerry felt a flutter of panic, in case he'd somehow woken up in the middle of an operation and couldn't let the doctors know. Oh, so what? He couldn't feel anything. The numbness felt good.

He thought he saw Woolfie beckoning in the distance, and started walking towards her. But however fast he walked, Jerry couldn't close the gap between them and it was hard to see now with the fog coming down. He could hear her calling to him, but her voice sounded strange. And she wasn't making sense.

'What if he dies in the night? I don't want to wake up with a dead pet in my room!'

Was Barclay ill? Why hadn't Mum told him? But Barclay was a 'she' not a 'he'. He'd think about it later. Too tired. Too foggy. He couldn't see Woolfie any more. But the fog was nice. Soft. Supported his weight. Jerry leant in, rolled it around him and drifted off in it . . . down, deeper, deeper and down, wrapped in the welcome embrace of an oblivion cocoon that someone had so thoughtfully laid on for him.

*

Harchi closed the bed seal around Jerry and stood up. 'See, Chad?' he whispered. 'He's sleeping now, he'll be fine by the morning.'

'Thanks, Harchi-pa. Sorry to wake you, but I caught a fright when he started making strange noises.'

'That's all right, son. He's better off inside the bed, anyway.'

'He's pining for home, isn't he?'

Harchi nodded, sadly.

'I don't want to be cruel, keeping him here against his will.'

'We don't have a choice now, Chad. There's no way to send him back.'

'I wish there was.'

'I know. But we'll love him and look after him and he'll soon get used to it.'

Harchi ruffled Chad's hair clump and helped him step back to bed. 'Sleep well.'

'You too, Father.'

Harchi went to the kitchen to mix some sour tea, knowing he was too upset about Jerry to sleep well tonight. He heard claw-clicks on the floor and turned to see Rashila heading towards him.

'What are you doing up?' he whispered, offering her his mug.

'Couldn't sleep,' she whispered back, accepting his tea and taking a sip.

'Too excited about your new promotion?' asked Harchi, proudly.

'I was thinking about Jerry,' said Rashila.

'Me too. I've just sealed him in his bed,' said Harchi, mixing another sour tea. 'Chad came to get me because he was making noises.'

'Any change?'

'No. Although he's sleeping now.'

'I can't stop going over what Jerry said, about him not being a pet, but being a Chad. What if that's true, Harchi? We'd be distraught if someone took our son away.'

'I know Rashila, but what can we do about it?'

'Look . . . I don't really know how to say this, but . . . what if we went to see Kaye?'

'Please don't ask him to take Jerry back!' begged Harchi.

'Is that what you think of me, Husband?' Rashila's voice quavered and a tear rolled down her scales.

Harchi spilt sour tea in his rush to hug Rashila. 'I'm sorry, Wife. Forgive me! What was I thinking? More to the point, what were *you* thinking?'

Rashila dried her eyes and gave her husband a long look. 'The only possibility Jerry has for going home is by molecular scrambler.'

Harchi's eyes were the size of cissbury rings. 'You don't mean . . .'

'He got one before, he could get one again.'

'But if anyone found out . . . with your new position . . . I mean, shouldn't we try applying for a licence first?'

'Bluhm would never grant one.'

'You know where the scramblers are kept. Why don't we just go in . . . and . . . borrow one?'

'Missing scrambler, missing pet? It wouldn't take them long to get to me.'

'I'll go and see Kaye, Rashila. It's too dangerous for you.'

'No, Harchi. I couldn't let you do that for me. I'll go.'

'We'll both go. And what are we going to say, when Jerry disappears?'

'That he's run away,' said Chad.

Harchi and Rashila whirled round to find their son standing behind them.

'Do you understand why we're doing this, Chaddy?' asked Rashila.

'Yes, Rashila-ma. And it's the right thing to do,' he said, giving her a hug.

'You won't ever be able to tell Gilpin,' she said, feeling terrible about asking her son to keep a secret from his Bonded Partner.

'I know,' Chad sighed. 'But that's how it has to be.'

'Right, you stay here with Jerry, we'll be back soon,' said Rashila.

'We're going now?' spluttered Harchi, checking the clock. Nobody left their dwelling during indigo.

'We have to,' Rashila insisted. 'We can't risk anyone seeing us.'

*

'We want to send Jerry back,' said Rashila, trying to avoid watching Kaye's belly make a very successful bid for freedom from the waistband restraint of his sleep shorts.

The pet-shop owner stared at the Jannans through the

gloom of the unlit shop. Surely they hadn't come here in the middle of the night to ask for their money back? Although that was worth being woken up for – Kaye could teach that talking pet a lesson for cheating him out of the Baa *and* sell him for a proper price this time.

'All right.' Kaye nodded. 'But he's second hand, so it won't be a full refund.'

'We're not asking for a refund, Kaye,' said Harchi.

'Are you trying to palm him off on me? If he's injured, I'll hit you for the vet's fees.'

Rashila, took a deep breath and jumped in. 'We want to send him home. We need to borrow a molecular scrambler.'

'With a time-fold overlay pump,' added Harchi.

'Is this some kind of sick test?' rasped Kaye. 'Didn't you think one Committee fine was enough to teach me a lesson?'

'I'm not testing you, Kaye, we're serious,' said Rashila.

'We think Jerry should be with his own kind,' Harchi told him.

'Even if getting there kills him?' Kaye couldn't believe his ears. Harchi Jannan was dumb enough to suggest it, but Rashila knew the risks involved better than anyone. It was such a waste of valuable stock.

'It's what he wants,' said Rashila. 'And we want to help him.'

'So can you help us, or not?' asked Harchi.

'Won't be cheap,' snorted Kaye, running some figures through his head and loving the way they crossed the total line together.

'Go on,' said Harchi.

Kaye named his price. It was so utterly inflated Harchi thought his ears would ping off, they peaked so far and fast.

'You can't be serious,' said Rashila, trying to keep the loathing from her voice.

Kaye shrugged. 'Gotta find something to make a dent in that Committee fine. Take it or leave it, it's no scales off my snout.'

'We're leaving it. Come on, Harchi,' said Rashila, turning to the door.

Harchi was about to follow, when a small bundle hurtled from the back of the shop and threw itself around Kaye's legs.

'Yashi couldn't sleep, Kaye-pa! Couldn't find oo!'

Kaye's tough business act crumbled as he bent to scoop his daughter from the floor and cradle her in his arms. 'It's all right, Yash-Yash, I got you now. Let me see these customers out and we'll step you back to bed.'

'You obviously love your daughter as much as Jerry's mother must love him,' observed Rashila.

'All parents love their offspring. Animals get over the separation, so that sentimental tosh won't work on me.' Kaye's words were harsh, but he delivered them softly to avoid disturbing Yash who'd curled up in the crook of his arm, closed her eyes and was sucking her tail tip.

'Did you hear about my wife's promotion, Kaye?' asked Harchi.

'No. But d'you mind if we by-pass the small talk? Only you may not have noticed, but it's kinda late,' said Kaye, moving them towards the exit portal.

'Director of Research and Development of the Multiple Podder Unit,' announced Harchi, smiling at Rashila's frowned enquiry. Don't worry, Wife – Harchi Ideas Factory Jannan just started a night shift.

'There's no such thing!' scoffed Kaye, but Rashila just stared at him, so he wasn't getting any help there.

'What a shame,' said Harchi cheerfully. 'Because if there was, Rashila would have *really* been in a great position to help you.'

Harchi saw Rashila had suddenly clawed on to where he was going. He raised his eye-scales and she gave him a tiny nod of encouragement.

'What are you talking about?' asked Kaye, surly, but curious.

'You could have been the first Pastinacean on the planet to have a second Podder.'

Kaye flicked his gaze from Harchi to Rashila. 'You're even more desperate to trick me than I'd realised!'

'Suit yourself,' she told him. 'Don't believe Harchi. It's no scales off my snout.'

'Isn't it odd, Rashila,' said Harchi, as they headed for the exit portal. 'You'd think a successful trader like Kaye would have spotted the potential.'

'I know,' she agreed. 'Who'd have thought he'd turn down all those opportunities for free publicity for the shop.'

'Wait!' Kaye called to their backs. 'I may be able to help you, after all.'

CHAPTER TWENTY-FIVE

Jerry woke to find three pairs of eyes staring down at him. Personal space, guys! What were they staring at anyway? He checked his watch, it was 08:34. What? Why had Mum let him sleep in and miss the bus? It wasn't Saturday, was it? Nah – no way Andy'd be up this early, or Woolfie and . . . oooooh . . . Jerry forced himself to re-check the eyes. Still yellow. In green scaly faces. Oh.

'It's all right, Jerry, don't be sad,' said Harchi, patting his arm. 'You're going home.'

Jerry sat up and threw his arms around Harchi's neck, hugging him so tight, Sneb yowled a protest at being squished while on guard duty around his fellow pet's neck.

*

Morton was at her desk, re-reading the recruitment ad she'd posted Infoscope-wide, for a new assistant. There'd be no shortage of applicants. And this time, she'd conduct thorough background investigations and only appoint one with a proven history of loyalty and honesty, rather than allowing herself to be blinded by mere academic brilliance.

Morton felt no ill-will towards her ex-assistant once she'd realised what Bluhm was doing. Yes, Rashila was intelligent and hard-working enough, but totally devoid of flair or vision. The Committee was obviously using her to claw the Multiple Podder Unit together and get all the dull, administrative work out of the way before handing it over to Morton's inspirational care.

Before that day came, she intended to keep a very close eye indeed on her ex-assistant. It was Morton's duty to protect Bluhm and the Committee, not to mention the citizens under their control, from the countless mistakes such an inexperienced appointee was bound to make.

Morton almost pitied Rashila for the difficult time that lay ahead, building up her Unit only to have it snatched away. Yet how could Morton pity someone to whom she'd given every opportunity to shine, who'd shown her gratitude by clawing her boss in the back? In future, if Morton wished to avoid the disappointment caused by creatures like Rashila and Kaye taking such shameless advantage of her, she realised she'd have to learn to be much less of a soft touch.

*

If Harchi arrived by the time Jerry counted to ten, he'd get home alive. If he didn't . . .

One. Jerry hated goodbyes. 'Specially when he didn't

295

know if he'd make it to the next hello. But he dreaded the thought of leaving without saying goodbye to Harchi. They'd been eating a late dinner, waiting for night so they could use the scrambler which had mysteriously appeared in the flat, though no one would tell him how, when Harchi jumped up, shouting he had to go to the Unit, then charged out. Maybe he'd been too upset to see him off? **Two.**

The day had passed in a blur. Chad had helped Jerry pack his rucksack, stuffing it with sweet sticks, socks and replicated trainers. He'd even found a chunk of glittery rock for Jerry to give Rachel. If he was brave enough. (Who was he kidding? If he got home alive, he'd be brave enough to do anything!) **Three.** The hardest part of his whole day had been when Chad went to Gilpin's and there'd been no one around to stop Jerry's imagination torturing him about the impossible journey he'd insisted upon taking.

And it was as if Sneb knew he was leaving. As they'd started packing, Sneb had stuck to Jerry like bubblegum, and nothing would shift him. Now he was wrapped around Jerry's neck like a sticky pink scarf, and they'd probably have to get Gale to wrench him off. **Four.**

It was dark on the roof, but Jerry could still see Rashila, holding the molecular scrambler while Gale removed what looked like a memory stick from it, which slicked back into a housing on her front. **Five.** As Rashila walked towards him, Jerry could tell the scrambler was heavy although it didn't look it. Weird that he might be killed by something that looked like the monster pump-action water pistol he and Andy used for ambushing Woolfie. **Six.** Until Mum confiscated it.

'The spatial displacement programme has finished loading, Jerry, so we're going to have to . . .' Rashila clearly wasn't sure of the right form of words. Who would be? '. . . export you . . . quite soon.'

'What about Harchi?' Jerry had trouble keeping his voice steady. **Seven.** He was starting to feel sick. Get over it, Patterson. What's the big deal about saying goodbye to someone you've known for less than a week?

Rashila shook her head. 'Sorry.'

Jerry nodded. No point putting it off. 'Chad, would you mind?' He gestured at Sneb.

'Of course.' Chad went to unpeel one of Sneb's suckers, and received a slash and yowl for his troubles.

'Don't chance it, Chad,' said Rashila. 'Gale?' **Eight.**

Chad patted Jerry on the back and gave him a small smile. Jerry moved his lips, but couldn't work a smile, trying to decide if he was going to throw up before he fainted, or afterwards. **Nine.** Gale hovered over and prised Sneb from Jerry's neck in a flurry of fur, claws, teeth and unsuckerings.

Jerry picked up his rucksack and put it on his back. It weighed an elephant. Shouldn't have made Chad replicate trainers for Andy, Woolfie and AJ. Rashila gestured for Chad to move away from Jerry. **Nine and one tenth.** Sneb was a bundle of furious yowls as Gale held him between her

297

claws in a vice-like grip. 'I shall return the snebbit to our dwelling, Rashila Jannan,' she beeped, moving towards the door.

'Don't!' shouted Jerry. 'I want Sneb here, when I . . .' He couldn't finish the sentence. **Nine and two tenths**. Rashila nodded at Gale, who hovered over to Chad, holding the writhing, spitting bundle of knitting at arm's length.

Taking a huge breath, Jerry stood with his back to the wall. He could feel the safety rail against his head. Facing the scrambler as it fired would be the hardest thing he'd ever had to do. Not facing it, a physical impossibility. **Nine and three tenths**. Please, Harchi, *please*. Please come and say goodbye. Jerry pinched himself hard for being such a total plank. Six days. That's all. Big bloke with scales. No biggie. **Nine and four tenths**. *Please*.

Rashila was raising the scrambler. Oh God, she was getting ready to fire. Jerry gagged. He was going to puke. He absolutely couldn't puke. He wouldn't. If he puked and she fired, it might follow him through space. **Nine and five tenths**.

'Ready?'

Of course I'm not bloody ready. Who'd be ready to leave anywhere, looking down the barrel of a gun? **Nine and six tenths**. But I want to go home, so bad.

'Yes.' Sneb's cries were breaking Jerry's heart. **Nine and seven tenths**.

Rashila supported the scrambler against her chest with one arm and moved her free claw to curl around a lever poking up on top. **Nine and eight tenths.** Jerry flinched. Her finger's on the trigger. No sign of Harchi. I'm going to die. **Nine and nine tenths.** There was a swishing sound over Sneb's yowling and Harchi's agonised 'Waaaaaait!' before his body appeared, ducking under the door as it slid up.

Ten. I'm going make it home! Jerry held out his arms and Harchi hurtled over and scooped him up in a breath-whooshing hug.

'Thought I'd have to go without saying goodbye, Harch-a-Darch!'

'Sorry, Weather-pet!' said Harchi, putting Jerry down and rearranging his rucksack.

'Where've you been?' asked Rashila.

'I suddenly realised those energy surges happened on nights the molecular scrambler was used! I went to clear our air space of weather, so no one'll be able to trace this one.'

'Well done, Husband!' said Rashila.

'Thanks, you guys,' said Jerry, with a lump in his throat. 'I know what a huge deal this is for you.' Harchi squeezed his arm.

'Move away, Harchi. I have to do this now,' called Rashila. 'The scrambler's primed.'

'You have to wait a couple of claw-clicks!' said Harchi, looking up at the sky.

'What for?' she sounded nervous.

Jerry followed Harchi's gaze. A cluster of small white specks floated towards them.

'That!' said Harchi triumphantly, jabbing a claw in the air.

Everyone watched the clusters turn to flurries as it began to snow, but only over their roof.

'What is it, Father?' asked Chad.

'It's Flaked Snow, son,' Harchi told him proudly. 'If there's enough, you can walk in the air with it.'

Jerry shook his head in amazement. 'Go Harchi! You made snow!'

Harchi beamed as the flakes continued to fall, but faster now, so everyone on the roof looked as if they'd been dusted with icing sugar.

Chad caught one on his tongue. 'Ooh, nice and cold!'

'Yes,' said Jerry, copying him. 'And every single flake's a different shape!'

Chad examined his claw. 'No, they're not.'

Jerry held out his palm and watched it coat with a series of snowy Js. He looked at Harchi and some snow must have got into Jerry's eyes, because they were all watery.

'Harchi! That's the most totally brilliant goodbye present a pet ever had.'

Rashila's voice rang out. 'The dymock's nudging purple! If I don't fire now, the time-fold overlay pump will burn out!'

Harchi stroked Jerry's cheek with his claw, then backed away. Jerry burnt him into his memory, standing with his arm around Chad, grinning and crying at the same time. Jerry nodded at Rashila, who smiled goodbye as she clawed the trigger.

There was a blinding flash and shards of white light slashed through the night-black, illuminating the softly falling snow which filled the space where Jerry had been standing. The only sound to break the silence was Sneb's grief-stricken yowl.

*

Harchi was so miserable, he didn't even realise the chute had stopped until he heard Chad and Rashila calling him. Unclicking his chute belt, Harchi dragged himself upright and tramped out. What had he done that was so terrible, his wife had left work early and brought his son to come and tell him?

Either the Committee knew about the scrambler or Gornish had found out about the Random Rain Scheme and Rashila had come to tell him he was fired. But she was smiling. So was Chad. So it couldn't be bad news. Perhaps they were trying to cheer him up because he'd been so sad since Jerry left. Just thinking his pet's name made his ears droop.

'Gornish was trying to find you,' said Rashila, as Chad took his briefcase.

Harchi's stomach felt boulder-ish. 'Why?' he asked nervously.

'He wanted to talk to you about the Rogue Weather.'

Double boulder-ish. It had only been a question of time. Now Tsooris wouldn't want to be his friend any more.

'Tell him, Rashila-ma!' urged Chad.

Harchi stopped walking and prepared himself for the worst.

'Harchi!' exclaimed Rashila, all smiles. 'We're so proud of you! They're going to—'

'—put a statue of you outside the Unit,' finished Chad, unable to wait.

'In honour of the day you averted a mass Fossic malfunction,' said Rashila, then reached up to scratch his ridges. In public!

'It's going to have a plinth with your name on and everything.' Chad sighed.

Harchi split a huge grin as he, Rashila and Chad linked claws and walked home together. From the chute! He was the happiest Pastinacean on the planet. Well, a smidge under happiest. He didn't want to be ungrateful, but he'd have given his tail tip for Jerry to have been there to share the walk home.

*

Jerry drifted back to consciousness, trying to figure out where he was. He was lying on something hard so it wasn't his bed. And he recognised the smell. He was fairly sure it wasn't Morton's lab, but it was definitely familiar. There were hazy shapes above him, but he couldn't get his eyes to

302

focus properly. Jerry tried to sit up but his body was on strike, every last cell protesting. So he figured he must have just taken the mother of all inter-galactic poundings.

*

'Find anything?'

'No, his rucksack's full of twigs and socks and trainers!'

'Kid's obviously a weirdo.'

'Wait a minute, there's an exercise book under this lot. Oh, hello . . .?'

'What?'

'So *this* is the famous Jerry Patterson.'

'Who?'

'Our Rachel's always twittering on about him, giving it the long face, 'cos he never notices her.'

'Now's your chance to put in a good word.'

'Win me Brownie points all round, that would! Look, I'll go and ring the school to get hold of his mum. Can you stay and keep an eye on him?'

'Sure.'

*

Jerry heard the man walk away, then the click of a lighter, a long drag and even longer exhalation as the other man enjoyed a fag. Hang on . . . 'our Rachel'? Rachel Davis's Dad was a bus driver! No wonder the smell was familiar – Jerry was on the 183! Except it wasn't moving. He couldn't see any other passengers. And he was lying on the floor.

Never mind all that – he was alive *and* Rachel Davis

fancied him! If he'd been capable of movement, Jerry would have punched the air. What a coming-home present! Then he remembered his leaving present. And where he'd just left. There must have still been snow in Jerry's eyes, because they were all watery again. He swiped the excess away.

'You all right down there?'

Jerry looked up to see one of the drivers he recognised, crouching in the aisle by his head.

'Think so,' said Jerry, surprised at how weak his voice sounded.

'Reckon you must have passed out.'

Jerry nodded.

'You're in the bus garage at Harrow. Someone's gone to ring your mum. Feel well enough to sit up?'

Another nod. The man put an arm around Jerry's shoulders to support him and he was halfway up, when there was a blinding flash, a WHOOMPH and Jerry was thrown back to the floor by a stabbing pain on his front.

'What's happening?' shouted the driver in a panic.

'Don't know!' freaked Jerry, terrified he was having a post-scrambler heart attack. He grabbed his chest to ease the pain, only to clutch a handful of familiar scratchy knitting, and be almost deafened by the loudest welcoming 'buurrooop' he'd ever heard.

'Don't move, kid – I'll try and get it off you!' said the driver, trying to sound brave as he aimed a kick.

'Stop! He's my pet!' said Jerry, flinging his arms around Sneb.

'What?'

Jerry tuned out the driver's endless torrent of questions and lay on the floor, scratching Sneb's back, listening to him purr his paws off. Jerry was alive. Rachel Davis fancied him. And they'd sent Sneb. He was two galaxies beyond happy. Actually, it wasn't quite the full two galaxies. Jerry couldn't help feeling that he was always going to be a few stars short, without Harchi.

ACKNOWLEDGEMENTS

With thanks to Ben Barkow for being Chief Encourager and Christopher Pilkington for firing up my grey matter in the first place; David C. Hughes at the School of Biomedical and Natural Sciences at Nottingham Trent University for his help with matters biological and Dave Crawley at St Helen's School, Northwood for his help with matters electronical. Finally, I'd like to thank Caroline, Georgina, Sarah and Lizzie from the Pastinacean Tourist Board for all their support and Amy Brewer, for not bleating on too much about being forced to move to Pastinare for a year.